Totally Bound Publishing books by Nancy Adams:

Out of Time
No Matter When

The Soul Within
The Bannockburn Spell
Extinct

I0598551

EXTINCT

NANCY ADAMS

Extinct
ISBN # 978-1-78184-755-8
©Copyright Nancy Adams 2014
Cover Art by Posh Gosh ©Copyright February 2014
Interior text design by Claire Siemaszkiewicz
Totally Bound Publishing

Published in 2014 by Totally Bound Publishing, Newland House, The Point, Weaver Road, Lincoln, LN6 3QN, United Kingdom.

Totally Bound Publishing is an imprint of Total-E-Ntwined Limited.

EXTINCT

Dedication

For Mack,
For Ted, thanks for helping with the cop stuff,
and
For my editor Sue.

Prologue

My full name is Percival Theodore Grey. Yes, Percival, or Percy to my family and close friends. Thankfully, I have not been addressed by my full name since before the war. I must admit, I do prefer Theo.

I was born April the 15ᵗʰ, 1885 in London, England to Lord Theodore Grey and his first wife Anne, my mother, who died shortly after I was born. My father's second wife, Sybil, raised me in our town home in the affluent London district of Belgravia and at our large family estate near Dartford.

Because I was the oldest of five children and the only male, my father began to groom me to take over the family shipping business at an early age, and once my father passed, I would become Lord Percival Grey, the tenth Marquise of Dartford and would claim my seat in the House of Lords. My life was ideal, if maybe a bit dull. I had my own town home in Kensington, a beautiful fiancée, powerful friends, more money than I knew what to do with and a future that was secure and set in stone – until the war.

I enlisted in August 1914, my family and friends unaware of my intentions until I shared my decision with them.

Despite what they thought, I didn't join out of spite, or to rebel against the life I had been given. I joined because I wanted to experience more out of life than sitting behind a desk working with numbers, or debating with a group of old men who still wore silly wigs.

I envisaged myself as the soldier in the recruitment poster holding the gun. I wanted the thrill that going into battle would bring. I wanted to feel excitement and fear. I wanted to see the darker side of life. I wanted to be the type of man whom other men would follow into battle. I wanted medals covering my chest and I wanted everyone to see how brave I could be. I wanted glory.

I was stupid and naïve. World War One turned out to be the biggest mistake of my life. It changed me in ways I could never have imagined. It changed me from a man into something else entirely. It changed me into the beast I am today.

I'm speaking as though I am a single being, with only one spirit. To look at me you would never know otherwise. But as fate would have it, my body holds two souls – mine and that of the wolf.

I am both human, and Canis lupus columbianus, the British Columbian wolf, the last of an extinct species and the second human to carry the spirit of a wolf. I am, however, not a werewolf. This is not a fantasy storybook where a werewolf is half human, half wolf. I am either human or wolf – not once have I ever been both – with the exception of when I am in mid-conversion. But at the high rate of speed in which the conversion takes place, it is a state that I cannot maintain, nor do I wish to.

Even though the soul of the wolf is intertwined with my own, he understands that he dwells within my body and he respects that important fact. I am the alpha in this strange symbiotic relationship, the wolf only asserting itself when absolutely necessary.

Over the years, I have taught myself to swap at will, and unlike in books and movies, full moons are not necessary. We do not howl at the moon, it is dangerous for a lone wolf to give away his position. You see, we do not belong to a pack, there are no others who would answer our call should we have need, so howling would serve no purpose except drawing unwanted danger.

We have been shot many times, however bullets, silver or otherwise, cannot kill us. I'm not sure how, but the wounds we receive are quick to heal thanks to the wolf.

We do not prey on humans or use them as a form of food.

We do not kill humans. Unless there is a need, such as for self-defense or as a form of punishment for gruesome crimes we have witnessed.

We do not bite humans in the attempt to turn them into what we are. That is not how this works. Only the Nuu-Chah-Nulth people of western British Columbia are able to perform the wolf dance and only the wolf can choose the body its spirit will inhabit. Which is why I am alive today — the wolf chose me.

Chapter One

Kensington, London
20 January 1919

Theodore Grey sat at his handmade walnut desk and opened the first of three brand new journals. He didn't know how many he would need, because he didn't know how long he would live, so he had picked a number at random.

He flattened down the stiff spine and picked up his fountain pen with the intention of writing about his experiences while at war, but the sound of gunfire stilled his action. He held the pen for several minutes, the tip shaking as it hovered just above the first page. God, he hated this. He hated the memories that invaded his life and he was tired of fighting them, but he didn't know any other way. The driving need to see and locate the source of the shots tugged at the survivor in him, even though he knew his mind was playing tricks on him. He knew what he would see if he looked out of the window, knew it wasn't real, but despite the dread filling his stomach, he looked anyway.

Mud was everywhere. The rain had filled the trenches, pooled in shell creators and formed minuscule rivers in no-man's-land. Disfigured bodies hung limp from rusted barbwire and scattered about were the remains of once enormous trees.

The wolf, who up until this point had been sleeping soundly, woke when it felt Theo's anxiety. It pushed to its feet and after a yawn, forced a serene image into his head. Latching onto the image, Theo lowered his pen and, closing his eyes, took several deeps breaths. As usual, the animal's forced assistance helped to clear his mind.

When he looked out of the large window in his study a second time, Kensington Park sat across the street. Even on this cold day, the park was full of people enjoying the newly fallen snow. Children were squealing as they threw snowballs, and the adults laughed, enjoying the playful scene.

Theo exhaled slowly. He had purposely moved his desk closer to the window so he could see the park. The idea, of course, was to help with the memories, to witness the good instead of always remembering the bad. Some days it worked and other days—like today—help was required.

A knock at the door caught his attention. "Come in," Theo instructed.

James, his butler, entered. "Would you like some tea, sir?"

"No, thank you, James."

The man hovered in the doorway. Theo was getting used to the concerned frowns James would give him and like every other time, Theo gave him a reassuring smile.

"On second thought, tea would be nice and maybe some of Helen's shortbread."

"Very good, sir." James nodded, looking relieved and closed the door behind him.

Theo focused out the window, except this time he didn't see the snow or the sun reflecting off icicles. They were replaced with a dark forest covered in mud and blood. The people strolling through the park were suddenly the bodies of his dead men, their faces showing the gruesome details of their deaths. It was a horrific scene and one he had lived through, thanks to the wolf.

Picking up his pen once again, Theo started at the beginning...

The final moment of my life didn't arrive until well after dark, June 1915. I was resting silently in a Belgian forest against the base of a large chestnut tree. At the time, I remember being furious that most of my small reconnaissance team lay dead. Proud to have known such strong, honorable men, angry that I hadn't died as they had and jealous, because they were no longer suffering and I was.

As I lay in the dark listening to the sound of flares and random gunfire, I saw a shadow low to the ground, skulking through the forest. My body reacted before my mind and I gripped my pistol. I had no rounds left but I readied myself anyway. As the shadow drew closer, it slowed and I could make out the distinct outline of a very large dog. It looked to be an Alsatian Wolf Dog the Germans used on patrols, except larger...much larger. I tried to keep the dog in my sights — I had to be ready when he caught my scent — one whine and his handler would be all over me. I had no intention of suffering in the hands of the enemy. I wanted to die on my own terms, like any noble officer of the King's army.

I blinked quickly, trying to clear sweat and dust from my eyes. The dog, steadily approaching, dropped an inch from the ground, practically crawling. The Alsatian disappeared in the dark shadow of a tree and when I blinked for a third time, Private Jonathan Cook was standing in front of me. The man was covered in dirt, bleeding from a vicious wound to his right side and naked...completely naked.

Cook was considered the best scout on the Western Front and an even better tracker. I knew little about Private Cook, except for his skills on the battlefield. There was never enough time to learn about the man who stood before me. He had only joined my unit a month prior.

Cook staggered to the side then fell hard to his knees, holding his wound. His black eyes locked onto mine as he rested his hand on my shoulder, then very slowly he began speaking in a language that I had never heard before. His deep voice caused the words to vibrate low in his throat as he spoke, some seemingly closer to grunts than actual words. He then switched to English. "The wolf and I have waited many years for you," he began softly. "He caught your scent months ago when you visited the Canadian trenches looking for scouts. Once we had your scent, we tracked you, through forests and towns, no-man's-land and the German trenches. You have fought with many, killed many. The wolf, he smells the warrior in you."

I shook my head and hissed. The slight movement sent excruciating vibrations to the hole in my stomach. "What the bloody hell are you talking about, Cook?"

"I have spent three lifetimes in this world. Nina, the luuc I loved, died long ago. On that day I wanted to die too, to go with her, but I could not. The wolf kept me alive, for she was not our true mate."

"Wolf? Mate?" I shook my head again, trying to sort out the story he was telling me.

Cook shifted back onto his bottom, still holding his side. "The wolf is a survivor. He will do whatever is necessary in order to live. He has pulled me from death more times than I can count, so I made a pact with him. Pledged that I would find a man who would be worthy of him, yet strong enough to contain him, keep him to this world, so that I may join Nina. There has been none, until you. The wolf has chosen you and it is you he will have."

"Have me what – ?"

Cook raised his hand to quiet me. The snapping of branches could be heard echoing around us.

Without a single word he raised his face to the sky and inhaled a long, slow breath… Then he leaped into the air and landed in front of the German patrol as…Wolf.

I blinked, thinking my eyes were playing tricks on me. I was dying after all, the damage from the bayonet now extensive.

When I opened my eyes, the huge creature was still there. It leaped into the air a second time, its long muzzle locking onto the first startled soldier. It tore and ripped at his throat. The mangled body hadn't even hit the ground before the beast was launching itself at the other soldier. This one put up more of a fight, brought the barrel of his rifle up just in time to fire a round into the creature Cook had become. The bullet ripped straight through the hindquarters, but the animal didn't slow. It was too big, moving too fast. The man never stood a chance as the animal hit him square in the chest. Razor-sharp teeth bit deep into the side of his neck and shoulder muscle. The German fell back, air forced from his lungs by the weight of the wolf standing on his chest. The eerie silence that followed was filled with a low growl as human flesh was shredded and frayed.

Weak and unable to fight off the creature, I watched as it limped toward me. It stood for a minute, breathing heavily, studying me. I could see the puffs of steam coming from its nostrils in the cool night air, curling up around its black face, drifting past its dark eyes, and up to its fur-covered ears. I froze, wondering what it was going to do. Kill me?

Eat me? Leave? I didn't know and how could I guess at what a wild animal would do? How could I guess what Cook would do? He seemed just as wild as the beast he was a part of.

In a loud huff, it sat onto its hind legs and raised its head, rolling its shoulders back. What appeared to be a human head thrust from the chest of the beast as the black fur shed from its body and fell to the ground. The lean frame of the beast expanded, becoming a chest and shoulders. Front legs became arms covered in dark skin and its hind quarters became legs, one of which showed the result of the German bullet.

Private Cook now sat in the wolf's spot.

The man stared at me with eyes as black as the wolf's. Was he waiting for me to say something? What could I have said? And if I was able to babble out something worth remembering, what would it matter? I was dying and would be dead shortly, and everything I had just witnessed would follow me to my grave.

Cook gazed down at the gun I was holding and gave me an approving nod. "Even when death is standing beside you, you fight."

The edge of my vision was now rimmed with shadows. "I don't understand..." I mumbled. It wasn't a lie. I had no idea what had just happened and I had no idea what Cook really was.

Cook crawled next to me and gently removed my hand that was covering the hole in my stomach and placed it at my side. Slowly peeling away the bloodstained wool of my tunic, he spoke to me, "You are not Nuu-Chah-Nulth, but you are a warrior." He removed the pistol from my fist and allowed my other arm to drop to my side, then exposed the rest of my wound. "The wolf will accept no less than a warrior." His voice dropped with each word as he placed his hands over the gaping hole in my belly. Then he began to speak words I didn't understand, the same language he had *spoken before. The low vibrations of his words, mixed with the odd accent, proved to be quite soothing and I didn't fight the urge to close my eyes. I was so tired. I was ready to die. I wanted to leave the pain and confusion behind and be where I should be, with my men.*

I felt my body begin to slip to the side as Cook's palms began to heat up my wound. His words, though spoken with more force, slowly faded away with the last breath of my life.

Theo flinched when a silver tray was placed on the side of his desk.

"Beg your pardon, sir, but I did knock," James informed as he began pouring the tea.

"Of course, forgive me, James. I was…" He paused, not knowing what to say.

"Writing your…memoirs," James supplied.

No. What he was writing wasn't a life story, it was a nightmare.

He agreed, not wanting to explain, and accepted the cup and saucer. With a polite nod the butler left.

When I woke, it was dark. As I struggled to my knees I realized there was no visible moonlight peeking through the dense forest, but I could see everything. Trees, low bushes, leaves and chestnuts covered the ground. I caught sight of an animal darting into an opening and pausing — a rabbit. It was a good fifty feet or so away but I could see it so clearly, it was as though it was next to me. Inhaling a startled breath, I froze when the scent of fear filled my lungs. I could smell the rabbit, smell its fear. I could also smell dirt, leaves, sweat and blood.

Blood!

I could smell blood. My blood. I looked down at my red-stained tunic and pressed my palm against my gut, my body tightening, ready to take the pain my touch would cause. Nothing happened. My body didn't flinch or tremble like before. I tugged up my tunic and the shirt underneath. My mouth dropped open. The hole in my stomach was gone. I traced the area with my fingers and felt nothing but warm skin and muscle. Cook had healed me…somehow. Smiling, I searched the area for him, but there was only the dead surrounding me.

Low accented voices caught my attention and I swung to face the enemy, but there was no one there. I froze to the spot, listening. Again, there were the voices. They were closer this time, coming from the west, moving fast. There was a sudden shift under my skin, in my muscles, as though something was moving inside me. I shuddered as goose bumps covered my skin.

Kill.

It wasn't so much a word as it was an impression. I held my breath and shook my head against the idea. Attacking the enemy unarmed was a fast way to die and now that I was healed and feeling…alive, I didn't want to die. There was another shift, and a heavy sensation pushed against my insides, behind my ribs. I gripped my chest, struggling to breathe. My ribs expanded on their own, then settled back into place.

I had no idea what had just happened. I exhaled choppy puffs of air. Was it damage from the bayonet? No. It couldn't be – the knife had torn open my belly. Was it shell shock then?

A harsh German command sliced through my train of thought. I swirled around, looking for the threat but there was nothing. Again I could hear…movement. It sounded as though the men were only a few feet away from me, but I knew deep in my soul that they weren't. But by the sounds I was picking up, they were, headed in my direction and their pounding steps was indication that they were running, and closing the distance fast.

Danger. Kill.

My skin suddenly felt clammy and I began to shake as the impressions grew in strength. This time a commanding growl accompanied the thought.

I felt as though I was going crazy. First Cook changing into a wolf, then I woke from the dead and then I began to hear...feel voices in my head and something was moving inside my body...pulling at my bones and muscles.

The shifting became more urgent, more painful. The impression of claws scraping the inside of my body, trying to get free, filled my head. I bent over when I felt the odd sensation slash at my stomach. I clenched my eyes shut, breathing through the pain. When I felt it was safe to open my eyes, the sight of my dead men greeted me. I saw fathers and brothers, husbands and lovers. Those men had children and wives waiting for them, praying for their safe return, but they would never see these brave men again.

Anger rose swiftly at the unfairness of the situation. Those men, my men, deserved to go home to their loved ones, not lay dead in a Belgian forest... Forgotten.

A powerful growl rumbled in my throat and I was powerless to stop it.

The pounding of boots on the leaf-covered ground caught my attention, as well as the thing inside me.

Out. Kill.

The demand grew in intensity, and so did the shifting within me. My clothing became tight and constricting and I suddenly needed to rid myself of it. The second my chest and arms were free of the blood-soaked wool, a demand exploded in my head. Out!

It was a voice this time, not just an impression but an actual word. I froze, not knowing what to do. I was scared that the Germans would find me, but terrified at the voice I had just heard in my head.

Make free.

The voice whined in frustration. But it was the urgency mixed with a trace of fear that alarmed me. As though it knew something bad would happen, that I didn't.

Desperate for a calming breath, I raised my head but instead my lungs filled with the scent of six different men. They were men who were excited. Men who were high on the adrenaline pumping through their veins. Men who wanted to kill.

The thing inside me finally asserted its true strength and my body began to tingle as the whispered voices drew closer. I looked down at my arms and stared wide-eyed as soft black hair began to sprout out of each and every goose bump covering my skin. My arms began to reshape, the palms of my hands becoming thick with rough skin and nails pushing through the skin covering my knuckles. The last thing I remember was my head being snapped back and cringing as an uncomfortable pressure squeezed my chest, followed by a strong sense of satisfaction – that wasn't mine.

When I really try, I can pick out flashes of what happened the first time the wolf took over.

I remember the shocked expressions of the German soldiers. I remember men stumbling to get away and one even trying to run. I can see black claws digging into flesh, the sound of a gun firing, the taste of blood and the cries of pain.

Of course, when I woke, I was as naked as Private Cook had been the last time I had seen him. Blood seeped from my biceps where the result of what looked like a bullet had grazed it and I was covered in dirt and blood...most of which wasn't mine.

As I stumbled around searching for my clothes, I tried to ignore the lifeless bodies scattered on the forest floor. That simple task was impossible when the bodies were ripped apart, and that coppery taste of blood still filled my mouth, the different taste of each soldier swirling together as one.

Even their scents blended, the stench filling my sinuses. I tried to ignore that too, but I couldn't. The blurry memory of how I had changed into the creature responsible for the carnage littering the forest caused my stomach to turn.

Once dressed in my uniform, I bolted for the Allied line, praying that what had happened was a solitary occurrence, but I knew it wasn't. The beast – the wolf – knew those soldiers were the enemy. It could... I could smell their desire to kill anything that crossed their path. The wolf would take me over again and there wasn't a thing I could do about it.

I was right, of course, there were many more nights like the first before the treaty was signed and the war ended, and each time like the first, the wolf fought to be free so it could kill the enemy and protect me, and itself. Only when the wolf was satisfied that there was no lingering danger would it retreat inside so I could make my way to the safety of the Allied trenches.

It took only a few times before I began to block out the other soldiers' questioning looks or startled expressions when I returned, half or sometimes completely naked, and more often than not covered in blood.

It's funny, really. When I think about each of those times, and remember the way I ran back to friendly territory, it was as though I was trying to outrun the wolf.

But how can you outrun something that lives inside you?

By the time Theo was done, the sun was setting and his tea was cold. He sat alone in his study and stared out of the window. He was the only one of his kind. There was no one he could talk to about what he had become. He felt so lost at times that the need to run away was always with him. But where could he go?

A slow rolling beneath his skin reminded Theo of his constant companion.

"Home," the wolf suggested.

Then before his eyes, the scenery changed and Theo was looking at a forest with tall, lush trees, green ferns and other plants covering the ground. The ocean was in the distance, he could see the dark water topped with white foam caps of waves as they crashed onto the beach. The image was natural in its raw beauty and it took his breath away like it did every time the wolf showed it to him.

A sense of peace washed over him and he closed his eyes escaping into the vision.

Home.

Chapter Two

British Colombia, Canada
Present day

"Are you sure Angus is there?"

"There's a light on, he must be." Theo carefully lifted the wounded dog from his patrol truck and headed toward the front doors of the local vet. "Ben." He gestured to the doors.

"I'm on it." Ben jogged ahead of him and tugged on the glass door. When it didn't open, he pounded on it, rattling the glass.

Theo stepped up next to him as the interior light flicked on. Looking down at the blood-soaked fur, he noticed that the heavy panting was beginning to slow. This big girl wasn't doing good. "Ben, again."

Ben pounded on the glass a second time. "Angus!" he called.

As the exterior light flickered on, Ben asked, "Did Angus get a new dog?"

Theo peered over Ben's shoulder and saw a good-sized black dog staring at them. Slim fingers curled around the dog's head and a pretty blonde appeared. She approached the main door and paused, studying them, the dog standing protectively by her side. Her thin eyebrows knitted together in a frown as she looked from Ben to Theo to the patrol truck.

"BCPP, ma'am."

"What can I do for you?"

Ben stepped to the side and Theo was instantly taken by the woman on the other side of the glass door. "Can you help us out here?"

Her gaze widened and she quickly fumbled with the lock then flung the door open.

"Follow me." Then, in a quiet tone, she gave her dog a command, "Ruby, come."

Theo obeyed carrying the dog, with Ben trailing close behind.

Ruby flattened her ears against her head as she backed out of the way, her attention divided between sniffing at the wounded dog, growling at his partner Ben. The reactions were all perfectly normal. Theo had yet to meet a dog—or any other animal for that matter—that even liked Ben, so the growling wasn't a first. It also wasn't unusual for dogs to be wary of him. Theo knew the combination of his and the wolf's scents was confusing and he never pushed for friendship. The wolf was still a wild animal and just as wary of the dogs. Besides, he couldn't afford the wolf to take him over in front of other humans in an attempt to battle a new dog to establish a pecking order.

He carried the wounded dog into the only exam room the small clinic had, then gently placed her on the table. The scent of the dog's blood was strong and thick and it filled the room instantly.

"I'm Drew O'Bannion," the blonde said as she calmly pulled on a pair of rubber gloves. "What happened?" she asked, examining the wound.

"She got hit by a truck," Ben mumbled.

"Whose truck?" The blonde looked up.

"Ours." Ben sighed, running a hand though his hair. "Shit, she came out of nowhere. We weren't even going that fast."

Theo caught her surprised expression, and took notice of how her dark lashes brought her amber eyes to life. "Molly has a habit of escaping her yard". He felt the need to explain. "And wandering around town. She likes the nightlife."

He knew this because he had run across Molly many times at night, as human and wolf. On the nights when the wolf had run across Molly, he had been patient with her and after a little playtime, would lead her home where Theo would quickly swap and hook her to her dog chain.

Looking at Ben, Drew gave him an understanding smile. "It happens."

Ben nodded, "Haven't seen you around before."

"That's because I just moved here."

"When was that?"

"About six hours ago."

"No shit!" Ben blurted out.

"No shit," Drew smirked, holding a white dressing against the dog's wound. She nodded to Theo. "Could you hold this?" She indicated to the swab. "I need to shave around the wound so I can get a better look."

Theo placed his hand over hers, and pressed down and before she pulled away he felt a slight twinge. Almost like static electricity but there was a warm sensation that accompanied it.

Molly flinched and her confusion mixed with pain filled his nose. He gently petted her neck, hoping to ease her anxiety. Drew turned back to Molly, holding a syringe and, pinching the skin on the animal's neck, quickly delivered the shot.

"For the pain," she revealed. "It will help to calm her down too."

As Theo massaged his fingers into the thick fur covering Molly's neck, the woman bent her head close to Molly's face, smoothing down the black fur running along her muzzle. Theo's chest tightened and his arms flexed as he drew in a deep breath. Getting close to the face of an injured animal was not smart, but he couldn't sense any fear from the dog toward the woman.

"My goodness, you're a pretty girl." Drew soothed. "Don't worry, you'll be okay. We're going to help you." The dog seemed to understand and visibly relaxed. "That's a good girl."

Ben elbowed him and Theo shrugged at his questioning look. There was no question that this woman understood animals, yet there was something else. He drew in another long breath, this time pulling in Drew's scent. It was sweet, a mixture of vanilla and peppermint, and she had recently eaten something with chocolate and flour, salt and sugar. Probably a baked good of some kind. Yet there was something else he couldn't pinpoint, something else that caused his skin to tingle and every muscle to clench in anticipation...

"Mate..."

Theo froze as the word trailed off in his head.

The hairs on the back of his neck slowly stood up as the wolf shifted beneath his skin, the movement seeming restless.

"No," he rejected. The idea of a mate was absurd.

The wolf paced in his mind. Head low, ears perked, and with the help of Theo, his sharp eyes fixed on the woman as she tended to the dog. He studied Drew through Theo's eyes, pulling in her scent.

The beast raised its head and with a snort reinforced his previous statement. *"Mate."*

Theo frowned as his chest tightened again.

This was a first. It was odd that a human female would cause such a reaction in the wolf – he was normally dormant until well after dark. It was also a first time that the wolf had called anyone mate... *Ever.*

He breathed slowly, fighting the sudden agitation the wolf felt. It wasn't unusual for the wolf to recognize the scent of a woman that Theo found attractive. What was unusual was the fact that it was Theo who usually desired to 'mate'. The wolf would simply give a growl of irritation then curl up in a ball and wait for Theo to finish. The wolf knew better than to fight the urges of the human in which he dwelled. He'd learned very quickly that it wouldn't do much good. Theo was a human male and like every other male of his species, he had desires. Desires that were usually sated after an encounter or two. But for the wolf to call 'mate' at a woman that Theo found attractive was...disturbing.

He studied the blonde as she shaved the fur surrounding the wound. She was pretty. High cheekbones, slender nose, big eyes and her mouth... It was full and lush and the enchanting shade of pink lips made him wonder if she was wearing lipstick. She also had a confident air about her, which he always found attractive, and even though he considered himself a traditionalist, he liked how her hair was layered with different shades of blonde. Yeah, he could easily 'mate' with her. The problem was that Theo had no desire to lock himself to one woman. His life with the wolf was...complicated, and it didn't help that wolves by nature were the monogamous type, and he assumed his wolf would share these same traits.

He sighed inwardly, waiting to see what else the wolf would do. When it remained quiet, he relaxed and drew her scent into his lungs again. He liked that unexpected mixture—it was calming, yet fresh and lively. Would the woman be the same way?

As he watched Drew work on Molly, Ruby came up next to him and sniffed his pants. Both he and the wolf relaxed so the dog would know they were no threat to her owner. "Where's Angus tonight?"

"At home watching hockey would be my guess." She snapped off the clippers and set them aside, then concentrated on the open wound. "He mumbled something about not having watched a live game in ten years."

"Can we assume Angus has finally decided to retire?" Theo cringed when she tugged at the skin surrounding the wound to get a better look, then dipped her fingers inside. There was a small whimper from Molly that drew his, the wolf's and Ruby's attention. Ruby nudged his side as she stretched her neck to sniff at the dog on the table.

The vet addressed the dog, "She's okay, Ruby. Go sit down." Amazingly, the dog followed the command without any hesitation. She slowly circled the table and, as she passed Ben, a low growl filled the room.

"Ruby!" Drew scolded, then shaking her head she answered Theo, "Soon. He wants to make sure I'll fit in okay first."

"Why wouldn't you fit in?" Ben asked.

She shrugged. "Beats the hell out of me. I've been coming here since I was little."

The odor of blood had been strong in his nostrils since they'd hit Molly but the coppery scent grew in strength as she poked and prodded around inside the dog. Pausing, Drew frowned up at him. "What is tha... Ah got it!" And withdrew a bullet from the dog.

The three of them stared down at the blood-covered bullet. "Please tell me you didn't shoot her." Drew prayed.

Ben shook his head as Theo answered, "We didn't shoot her."

What the hell? He hadn't heard any shots tonight. Then again, Ben had driven him down to the station in Ucluelet late this afternoon and only picked him up about fifteen minutes ago and they had hit Molly just outside Tofino.

"Can you tell if this wound is fresh or a few hours old?"

"No. Not by the wound. But the blood on her coat is dry in some areas."

Theo nodded. If some of the blood had had enough time to dry on her coat, then Molly hadn't just been shot. "What would be your guess about the time she was shot?"

"I'm not sure. I've never dealt with bullet wounds before." She shrugged. "Maybe thirty minutes to an hour? But like I said this is a first for me."

That would explain why he hadn't heard the shot. An hour ago, he had been inside the Ucluelet Station and Molly had been over thirty kilometers away. His hearing had improved greatly since the wolf joined with him, but with the distance between towns, background noise and the sound proofing the forest offered, there was just no way for him to hear a single shot.

"Okay." She dropped the bullet onto a plastic tray and picked up the suturing needle sitting next to it. "Now for the obvious question, Officers...?"

"I'm Ben Barry and this is Theo Grey." Both men nodded their greeting.

"So, Officer Barry, Officer Grey..." She began stitching the dog's wound closed. "I always thought the draw to Tofino was fishing, surfing and whale watching, this is the first I've heard about dog hunting."

"Us too." Theo watched as Drew patiently pulled the inside of the wound together first, then moved to the outside.

Once finished, Drew straightened, then dropped the needle on the tray next to the bullet and began gently examining the dog for other wounds. Smiling, she patted the dog lightly.

"What's the verdict, Doc? Is she going to be okay?" Ben asked.

"I didn't notice anything major and I didn't feel anything broken. You couldn't have hit her that hard."

Ben's sigh was filled with guilt. "It was hard enough."

"I've dealt with dogs after they have been hit by cars and trucks and it is never a nice sight. Molly here isn't in too bad shape, considering she was shot. The bullet didn't even hit anything vital. If it makes you feel better, I'll X-ray her just to be on the safe side, but I have a feeling she'll be okay."

Theo nodded and looked to Ben. "You better go call Louise. Her boys should be in bed by now."

Ben left the room with a grim look on his face.

"Who's Louise? Molly's owner?"

"Yes. She's a single mom with three boys. She works over at Walter's Whale Hut."

"Oh." She frowned. Then bending over the dog, she nodded when she saw Molly's eyes close. "She's better now." She looked up again and asked, "Didn't that place used to be a burger joint?"

"Still is." Theo smiled. "Do me a favor?"

She smirked at him. "Maybe."

He couldn't help but widen his smile as he reached for one of his cards. "When Molly is ready to go home, call me and I'll take her."

"That's your idea of a favor?"

He chuckled this time, then looked her dead in the eye. "I want you to tell Louise this was on the house when she comes by."

"Pardon me?" she choked out. "Wow, when you ask a favor you go big."

"I'll pay for Molly's treatment."

"I'm sorry." She blinked wide-eyed. "What now?"

"Give me the bill. Ben and I will pay for it," he clarified. "Just tell Louise it was on the house." He gave Molly one last pat and left Drew to care for her.

"Hey, Dudley!" Drew called from the treatment room door.

Theo turned by the glass front door and smiled. "I get the feeling there's a joke in there somewhere."

Rosy lips. Full lips. Lips created specifically for sinful activities, parted in a smile that displayed her straight, white teeth. Theo couldn't help but stare at those lips. He liked the way they curled up to the side and he liked how the sexy lilt in her laugh matched her sexy smile. "Got that, did you?"

He nodded, still staring at her mouth.

"Why?" she asked, the smile dropping from her face. "Why are you helping this Louise? I'm not getting a romantic vibe here, so I'm a little confused."

"No. Nothing romantic." He chuckled "Louise is a great person, she just needs help every once and a while."

"So you are doing this out of kindness?" She leaned into the door frame looking down her cute, slightly upturned nose at him.

He wanted to laugh at her confusion and snobby attitude. "Yes."

"Oh Lord! I'm not sure I can be friends with a saint, it might tarnish my reputation."

Theo laughed outright this time and joked, "Do I need to be searching the criminal database for you?"

"No." She narrowed her eyes, looking to the side thoughtfully. "But if you do, I'm getting around to paying off those speeding tickets."

Laughing, he pushed open the door. "Don't forget to call me," he ordered over his shoulder.

"Oh, I'll call you all right." Her voice dropped low and he assumed she thought he wouldn't be able to hear her and if he had been a normal human he wouldn't have, but he was glad he heard that lusty twist to her remark. "Oh, Officer Grey, I have an emergency! I need you to spank me right here." A soft chuckle followed her cheeky comment.

Theo smiled. Having the wolf's acute hearing really paid off sometimes.

Chapter Three

Seven days. Drew had moved here seven days ago, and she hadn't emptied one box. She had known the first couple of days would be busy, what with moving to a new town and taking over Angus' practice, but she hadn't stopped since her first night when Officer Make Me Hot and Sweaty had brought in poor shot-up Molly. Then word had gotten out—thanks to Louise and Officer Grey—that there was a new vet in town, and that Angus was retiring. Everybody and their brother had suddenly dropped by to give their well wishes to Angus while she had struggled to remember everyone's name and each of their pets' ailments.

Angus had been great, explaining every bit of the practice he had built—literally—from the ground up. Then one morning he had walked into the clinic wearing a terrible Hawaiian shirt and with a cheerful grin, announced, "Well, young lady. Yer on yer own now."

"Oh yah, I'll fit in okay all of sudden?" Drew had joked.

"Oh aye! You'll be just fine." He had huffed. "Just being a bit overprotective." A slight blush had colored the skin not hidden by his gray whiskers. "Besides, me and the Missus went half wi'mah brother on a timeshare in Cancún. So…" He had rubbed his hands together and with a boyish grin informed, "I'm off tae Mexico today."

"Oh!" She had laughed at his giddy chuckle. "Okay then!"

He had stepped forward and wrapped her in his arms. The smell of aftershave and coffee had reminded her of her grandpa who had passed away the year before, when Angus had given her a hard squeeze. He had looked down at her with a warm smile. "I know I'm not yer granddad, but I'm just as proud as what I know Glenn would be. I gave mah practice tae the right person."

With those kind words having been said, he had kissed her head then shouted his goodbye over his shoulder.

That had been four days ago and this was the first calm moment she'd had since then. She leaned her head back on her beautiful cream-colored sofa – her beautiful sofa that was covered with old blankets to protect it from mud and fur – when she heard the soft clicking of nails down the wood stairs. A moment later, her Akita mix, Ruby, was sitting next to her. "Finally come down to see your old mum, eh! You ungrateful child." She scolded playfully, pulling the dog down onto her lap, then stroking her head.

After a few minutes of cuddle time, Drew got up and made them both dinner. She had a tuna salad and Ruby had lamb and rice kibble. Once finished, it took Drew only an hour to empty all four of her kitchen boxes and tidy up the mess from dinner.

She puttered around cleaning and organizing her new living room before calling it a night. She headed up to bed with her four-legged shadow trailing behind. She couldn't sleep though and kept thinking about what needed to be done the next day at the clinic. She needed to go through the business side of the practice and she wanted to see about getting a new billing system installed too. Angus had created a great business – it just needed a bit of updating and the settlement from her grandpa's will would help with that. Not only had he left her the house here at Cox Bay, but a comfortable sum of money to go with it, too. So, she could afford to buy a few things for the clinic to help her it run smoothly.

Sighing, Drew finally threw off her comforter and sat up. With her bare legs hanging over the side of her bed, she stared out of the window. If she angled her head to the right she could see the moon casting a silvery glow onto the top of the surrounding trees and easily sliced through the black wall of the forest. Actually, the moon was so bright she could make out the trail leading to the beach.

Looking over her shoulder, she smiled at Ruby. "Want to go for a run?"

The dog rolled onto her side with a loud sigh. "Suit yourself." Drew shrugged, leaving her great and powerful protector sleeping on the bed.

* * * *

The wolf raised its head and sniffed the air as it approached Drew's house.

"*Mate*," the wolf stated, as they both caught the sound of movement from inside.

"*No mate*," Theo stressed. "*Just Drew.*"

"*Just Drew, mate*," the wolf repeated.

Theo sighed from deep within the beast. "*No*," he began again. "*Drew is not our mate.*"

"*Mate,*" the stubborn wolf growled.

Since first meeting Drew, the wolf had demanded to be freed every night so he could come to her house. He would wander around sniffing the car, the front yard, boldly going up onto the porch that surrounded the house, searching for signs of another male. Theo didn't want to admit it, but he was just as relieved as the wolf was to find only her scent and that of her dog, and that there were no human male scents in the area. This meant that there were no males that he and the wolf would have to contend with. Which was good, because he didn't know what the wolf would do if that was the case—this was new territory for both of them.

He stopped focusing on the front of the house just as Drew opened the door. Theo watched through the wolf's eyes as she came to a stop at the top of the porch, zipped up her jacket and casually descended the steps. Stuffing her hands into her pockets, she followed the trail that led to Cox Beach.

From the cover of the forest, the wolf kept pace with her. She would look in his direction every once in a while but Theo knew the wolf wouldn't be seen. The trees and thick vegetation growing on the forest floor, plus the shadows, would serve as excellent cover.

The wolf sniffed the air again. Theo could feel the wolf's growing interest in Drew, or it could be the fact that she had recently eaten tuna. Even so, this was the first time since meeting her that the wolf had had a chance to get close to her and get used to her scent. Theo hoped by allowing the close contact, the wolf would finally realize that Drew could not be their mate.

As the trail reached the end of the forest, she stopped abruptly at the top of a small cliff, which the elements had carved out over time. He watched as Drew lifted her face to the wind and just looked out at the water. Theo could smell how calm she was, as though a sense of peace overtook her when she saw the water. He knew that feeling and so did the wolf. There was a soothing quality to the sound of the waves rushing onto the sands and the smell of the fresh sea air filling his lungs. Life was pure and simple while spent on the beach.

Stepping onto the old wooden stairs her grandpa had built, Drew slowly made her way down. She carefully crossed over the rocks the tide had dumped at the bottom of the steps and strolled out onto the sand, where she kicked off her shoes and rolled up the bottom of her pants.

Shoes in hand, she walked along the beach for a good ten minutes, the wolf silently following unseen, thanks to the trees that ran along the top of the cliff. She retraced her steps and ended back where she had started. She crossed to a rock that protruded from the sand and sat down on the top, facing the ocean.

Now that she was stationary, the wolf sniffed the air again, shifting anxiously from paw to paw. Curiosity was getting the better of the both of them. The wolf wanted to go closer to her but was waiting. Maybe Theo should just let him go. Then they could both get it out of their systems.

"*Go?*" the wolf whined.

Or… It could cause more problems. Theo sighed again and, giving in, gave the beast a mental nudge. In an instant, the wolf had launched itself off the low-lying cliff and landed without a sound on the beach below.

Drew pulled her feet up onto the rock and rested her elbows on her knees. Lord, this was peaceful. It seemed like a lifetime had passed since she had last been here. She smiled to herself. She had never been allowed down on the beach at night without her parents or grandpa. This was the first time she had been here alone. She jumped when she caught movement out of the corner of her eye and froze in place as her heart jumped into her throat. Okay, she was definitely *not* alone.

The largest, blackest wolf she had ever seen slowly stalked toward her. Blinking, she held her breath. *Oh God!* What the hell should she do? She had read a ton of books on wolves — she loved them, thought they were the most beautiful creatures on the planet — but holy hell, she didn't want to become a dinner for one!

Exhaling a shaky breath, she tried to think calmly of something that wouldn't get her ripped to shreds. If she ran, she was dead. If she looked it in the eye, it might take that as a sign of dominance and might want to prove he was boss. She'd read that climbing a tree was best, or, if necessary, fighting back with something solid, like a tree or rock face to protect from behind. Neither suggestion would work. She was on the freakin' beach and the only rock face she could see was now surrounded by water.

"Ha! Awesome!"

Drew shifted her eyes to the ocean, then paused. If she could make it to the water, she would probably be okay. Maybe.

Then again, maybe not. It was the end of June and the Pacific was still damn cold. "Great! So my options are become the Wednesday night special or prune up, turn blue and drown."

Jesus! This was highly unusual. Lone wolves didn't do this. They didn't normally stalk humans, they ran from humans. They only attacked when backed into a corner or caught in a trap and that was usually done in self-defense.

The black beast narrowed the distance and Drew noticed that it had slowed its pace. Studying its posture, she realized that it wasn't stalking her. No. It wasn't coming toward her, it was parallel to her and close, but not too close. Its head wasn't dropped low either, like the normal prelude to an attack. The animal's head was raised and its nose was twitching at the air. Its ears were up and its eyes sharp, but it wasn't stalking, not anymore. It seemed almost like it was...sauntering. An 'I'm the man' type of saunter. She had seen so many men try to pull that off and not one could do it as well as this creature.

It came to a stop about five or six feet away, a distance it could clear in the blink of an eye. Its head was still raised, nostrils twitching, eyes still fixed on her like she was a ham steak! *Shit!* She needed to calm down. It probably knew she was scared shitless.

Then in an instant the dark beast curled its lips, showing vivid white teeth and longer fangs that hung over its lower jaw. The tips reflected the moonlight and looked as though they had been honed to a fine point. Its ears flattened out as it lowered its head. Without realizing it, she had jumped up and was backing away when the creature swung around and faced the forest.

What the hell? Searching the shadows at the edge of the forest, Drew inhaled slowly. "Oh my God!" There at the top of the wooden steps was another wolf. Then off to the left another stalked out of the shadows, and a third appeared to the right of the steps. All of them were light gray with darker faces and muzzles and their eyes... They all had yellow eyes—yellow eyes that were focused on her.

"Okay. Make that a dinner for four."

The black brute standing in front of her stomped a large paw. The entire length of fur running along its body rose, right down to the tip of its tail. A growl, deep and full of rage, overpowered the sound of the waves. The wolf at the top of the steps slowly moved down to the beach, head low, eyes focused, as the other two waited on the cliff.

In a heartbeat, the black wolf charged and launched into the air, slamming into the large gray wolf. The distance the black wolf had cleared was astonishing and Drew felt her mouth drop open in surprise. The fight was brief, a tumbling of gray and black fur as sand was kicked into the air. Then her 'stalker' pinned the other wolf by the neck to the ground. Until that moment, Drew hadn't taken any notice of the size of the black wolf, but it was big. Really big—bigger than the new wolf, by a good thirty pounds or so. It was obviously stronger, because it exerted little effort as it held the other wolf down while it struggled to get free. A low, deadly growl rumbled from 'stalker', followed by a high-pitched whimper from the gray.

Then it was over. The black wolf released the now submissive animal and snapped its long muzzle in warning followed by a deep growl. The gray wolf, with its tail between its legs, bolted up the steps and into the forest. One of its companions followed, but the other, the smallest of the three, stopped and peered down at either her or the beast standing in front of her. Drew couldn't tell. The wolf relaxed a little and raised its head, sniffing the air, then blew out a snort. She heard a faint whimper and the smaller gray turned its head to the forest, then back toward the beach. It appeared as though it was undecided as to where to go. A loud bark echoed through the forest and the wolf followed the others, leaving Drew alone to face the beast.

The wolf swung around to face her. Drew couldn't help but step back again, but it followed, keeping a distance. Its eyes were full of interest as well as intelligence.

When she stopped, it stopped. "Oh, man! I wish I thought to bring my cell. I could call Hottie Cop Theo. He could come and rescue me. I bet he would love that." She stopped the high laugh before it escaped.

She studied the beast, then blurted out. "That was...fucking scary." She cringed. She was in the presence of a wolf. The volume of her voice might set him off. "You're fucking scary." She lowered her voice. "Beautiful, but scary." The wolf carefully sat and stared at her.

OMG. This beast had just saved her from the other wolves. She had never heard of anything like that before. *Yeah!* her inner voice chimed in. *He saved you so he doesn't have to share his meal.*

She frowned, then bit her bottom lip. "Holy shit, I can't believe you just did that." It cocked its head to the side as if it understood every word. "Holy shit, I can't believe I'm talking to a wolf."

They stared at each other as minutes passed. In that time she really had a good look at him and a feeling grew that she had seen this animal before. But not running wild — she had seen pictures of this brute, old black and white photos on the Internet and in books. Normally it would be a pain trying to examine a black animal at night, yet thanks to the moon she was able to see the same distinct traits as a—

"That can't be." She narrowed her eyes. "Oh my God! You're not just any wolf. You're a BC wolf." She took a slow, deep breath. "You're supposed to be extinct, my friend."

Theo and the wolf stiffened at the same time.

Run?

Drew knew what type of wolf he was. Not many people did. The wolf lowered his head. Her fear and confusion and sudden excitement filtered its way through the wolf to Theo. He fought the wolf's urge to bolt when he picked up the sudden nervous tension. *No.*

He needed a minute. He needed to figure out what that thing was between his wolf and the gray wolf. His wolf had become acutely aware of the smaller female, yet had kept his focus on protecting Drew. Theo wanted to know what that was all about, but he could feel the wolf's puzzlement.

Drew's sigh caught his attention. "And now you're looking at me like I'm your dinner. Ha! Great!" Theo smiled and commanded the wolf—and himself—to calm down.

Resting inside the wolf, Theo watched Drew. She wrapped her arms around her middle as she examined him. Then, giving him a slight smile, she asked, "How are you alive when the rest of your species was killed off?"

He could smell her nervousness, which was understandable, but she was curious now too.

"Don't worry," she spoke softly, moving toward the rock. "I don't expect you to answer." She sat down so slowly that Theo wanted to chuckle. He wouldn't hurt her or attack her, not even if she provoked him, and neither would the wolf.

He was still a little baffled over their collective reaction to the pack's intrusion. Normally he would have just walked away. Neither of them had wanted to get into a scrap with a pack of hungry wolves, yet when he had caught their interest in Drew, the wolf had almost taken over. It had been a long time since he'd had to struggle to maintain control of the wolf and it had been a long time since the wolf, through a red haze of rage, had demanded a kill.

Years had passed since the last time he had let the wolf free and allowed him to kill. He didn't tolerate any type of abuse toward women or children and the last time, he had come across a man about to kill a mother and her little boy. The bastard had even taken the time to dig holes in the forest, where he had brought them to.

The wolf had been quick and deadly in his attack, dragging the screaming man out of sight of the woman and her child while he finished ripping the man to pieces. To this very day he had never regretted his action, the kill was justified. He felt the same way just now — he would not tolerate any harm to come to their ma — to Drew.

Drew perched herself on the rock, angled slightly. Probably so she could see the wolf and the ocean. "I always loved it down here." The soft, sexy lilt to her voice caused the hair on his neck to twitch. *Shit*. Theo breathed as his body stirred inside the wolf.

"*Want mate. Want Drew,*" the wolf teased, with satisfaction.

Theo mentally shook his head. "*We can't have a mate, buddy. She is...*" He wanted to say beautiful, and sexy, and that he liked her sassy attitude, but he pushed his desire aside for the first time and simply pointed out the truth. "*She isn't like us. Drew does not have a spirit. She does not change into wolf.*"

The wolf growled aloud, and snapped inside his head, "*Just Drew is mate.*"

"No," Theo snapped back. It could never happen, even though he had many dreams about being in a relationship where he could be himself. But they were just fantasies...and stupid ones at that. The only difference now was that the woman in his fantasy had a face. Drew. He saw it as clearly as he saw at night. She made him second-guess his decision to remain alone, made him want to try...just one time? But doubt, forever present and relentless, reminded him of the danger.

"Okay," Drew slid off the rock and stepped away from him. "Guess that was my cue."

The wolf and Theo both heaved a sigh.

Without Theo's instruction, the wolf made an effort to not frighten Drew, and rising to all fours, moved away from her, giving her space.

"Well, as gorgeous as you are, I need to get to bed." She moved slowly around the rock and bent to slip her shoes on. She narrowed her eyes again and studied the wolf and Theo. "There's something different about you, wolf. I mean I'm good with animals, but no wild wolf is as tame as you."

She glanced at the wind-worn steps and asked, "You gonna attack me from behind or let me go?"

The wolf snorted then swung his head toward the stairs.

"Ahhh! Okay!" She frowned at the wolf. "I'm going to take that as you said I can go. So please, please don't attack me." And, turning her back, she then started for the stairs.

Normally, that would've been a deadly mistake but the wolf just stood there watching her walk away. She looked over her shoulder when she was halfway up the steps. "Best date I've had in a long time, thanks."

Drew had no idea that the wolf and Theo followed her back to her house. When they heard the deadbolt slide into place, Theo encouraged the wolf to make his way home. As the wolf trotted away from their hiding place, he suddenly stopped. The hair on the animal's neck rose and he held his breath, listening. Something wasn't right. Theo could feel it, too. He had that creepy feeling that something was watching them, but neither Theo nor the wolf could see or hear movement. The wolf sniffed the forest air but found nothing out of place.

"Let's go," Theo urged and the wolf took off at a dead run. The feeling remained until they were out of the area.

Chapter Four

"Morning, Drew, you're in early."

Drew looked up from her computer and smiled at Connie as she dropped her backpack on the front desk and called to Ruby. Never turning down a free bum rub, Ruby jumped up from her bed in the corner of Drew's office and trotted over to the young woman, expecting her reward.

Connie Ito had been Angus' newly hired receptionist-assistant and was now her receptionist-assistant. Angus had asked her to keep Connie on after he left. Why wouldn't she? Connie was a triple threat, a fully qualified veterinarian assistant as well as an accountant and receptionist. Plus, she was a great person with a fantastic work ethic, she practically ran the joint, and if Angus had trusted her, then she would too.

"Hey." Drew rested back in her chair and stretched. "I wanted to do some research before we opened up shop." She didn't need to look at the time to know that it was seven thirty. Connie was always in half an hour before the doors opened.

"How long have you been here?" Connie asked, peeling back her wet hood. Bright blue streaks ran through the black hair framing her face.

"About an hour or so." Drew pushed away from her desk and stood. She came around the desk and reached for her coat, hanging it on Angus' old coat stand. "Still raining, hey?"

"Mmm," Connie took a sip of the coffee she had brought with her. "And it's only supposed to get worse."

"Oh joy!"

Connie smiled. "What are you researching? Maybe I could help out."

"Just looking up stuff on the local wolf population. I had a run-in last night with a huge black wolf and three gray ones."

"What?" Connie coughed, choking on a mouthful of coffee. "Holy shit! Are you kidding?"

"No."

"And you survived to talk about it." Connie nodded approvingly. "That's badass."

"Yeah." Drew rolled her eyes. "That's me, Badass O'Bannion," she joked, pulling on her coat. "I'm heading over to Milk & Sugar—what am I going to need today, a latte, cappuccino, or espresso?"

"Well…" Connie looked at the appointment sheets. "The morning isn't so bad. Miss Evans is bringing in Mr Darcy, the cat, for his shots. Kevin Beauchamp booked a double appointment and—"

"Why a double? How many pets does he have?"

Connie laughed. "He doesn't have any pets as far as I know. Kev's the local Canada Parks Wildlife Officer, he wanted to come by and introduce himself." Connie wiggled her pierced eyebrows.

"What does that mean?"

"It means he's super hot." Connie wiggled her eyebrows again.

"Oh yeah."

"Yeah. Great body. He's a surfer. Blond hair, blue eyes, sexy bum chin."

Drew laughed. "A what now?"

"You know," Connie, pointed to her chin. "The little crease in the chin that looks like a little bum."

"Oh!" She laughed again. "Got it. What else?"

"Your afternoon is busy. It's the first Tuesday of the month."

"What does that mean?" Drew asked for a second time.

"This is the day Angus goes out to the Native Reservation on Opitsat." Connie frowned. "Didn't Angus tell you he travels around to the local Reservation?"

"Nope. He sure didn't." She sighed. She'd had no idea that Angus was a traveling vet. It was a great idea, and she liked something new to break up the humdrum of a normal day, she just wished he'd mentioned it. "Okay, so how am I supposed to get over there? I don't own a boat."

"Oh, don't worry about that. The BCPP will take you over. They do their police thing while you do your vet thing."

"Okay, where do I go to meet them, at the station? Do you know what time?"

"They'll call this morning and fill me in. So no rush just yet, you have plenty of time for a coffee run. I'll start putting together your travel bag."

"Thanks." She walked to the door and stopped. "So…?"

Connie wrinkled her nose in thought. "I'm gonna call… Cappuccino day."

That sounded good to Drew—a little excitement mixed with a dose of frothy goodness.

"Hey!" Drew called, stepping out of the door. "I like the blue. Looks good." She smiled as Connie tugged on her short black hair, a pink blush tinting her cheeks. "Thanks."

* * * *

"Nope, I don't want to put Mr Darcy on special food," Drew said, opening the door for Miss Evans. The fifteen-minute appointment with the eccentric Miss Evans had turned into thirty by the time she was done asking all about Drew's background and love life. During the interrogation, she had been able to give Mr Darcy his check-up and shots.

"As I said earlier," Miss Evans began again, "I'm on a fixed income and I can't afford that high-priced food Angus sells."

There was a snort from Connie sitting at the front desk.

"I understand completely." Drew reassured. "I don't want you to buy the pricey food, just cut down on the food you already feed him." She scribbled a basic daily feeding schedule for the older woman. "Just follow this and Mr Darcy will drop his extra weight."

"Okay, thank you." Miss Evans began to turn away when she stopped. "Don't forget about my grandson, now. He would love to meet a nice young lady like you."

"I won't forget." Drew noticed a man in khaki pants, a dark green rain coat and green baseball cap. Uneven strands of blond hair stuck out from the back and sides. She smiled politely as she addressed Miss

Evans, "Why don't you go on over to Connie, she'll help you out."

The man in green stood and smiled, drawing attention to the dimple in the center of his chin. "Doc O'Bannion?"

"Yes." She couldn't help but return his contagious smile and that chin dimple sure was cute. Not Officer Grey the smokin' hot cop cute, just plain old cute.

He extended his hand in offering. "I'm Kevin Beauchamp. I'm with Parks and Wildlife."

"Right. Nice to meet you, Kev—"

"Hello, Kevin," Miss Evans interrupted.

"Miss Evans," he greeted politely. "Mr Darcy." He scratched the cat's head.

"Now, Kevin…" The older woman took his arm. "Have you been able to catch those gray dogs I told you about? Poor Mr Darcy hasn't been in the garden in weeks."

"I'm working on it."

"That's a good boy. Bye-bye now, I'm off to get Mr Darcy a treat, he was such a good boy during his check-up. Weren't you, Mr Darcy?"

The calico gave a loud meow when she nuzzled his head.

Drew, Connie and Kevin all watched as Miss Evans took Mr Darcy for his treat. Drew sighed. "Guess I should have mentioned to her Mr Darcy doesn't need treats."

"Yeah, you should've! That is one fat cat," Connie called from behind her. "And just so you know that woman has more money than Fort Knox. She can afford to buy any food we have. Fixed income my ass."

Drew crossed to Connie and Kevin followed. "Really?"

"You didn't see what she pulled up in?" Kevin pointed his thumb over his shoulder toward the front doors.

"No." She shook her head. She couldn't care less what type of car a person drove.

"It's a nice ride," Connie confirmed Kevin's statement with a nod.

"Oh, and her grandson..." Connie began scratching Ruby behind the ear. "He's visited here a few times. Don't waste your time."

"Why?"

"Because he would be more interested in *me* than you." Kevin smirked.

She laughed. "Got it." She nodded, then faced Kevin and smiled. "Next!" She extended her arm toward her office. Kevin chuckled as he preceded her.

As Drew began to close the door to her office, Connie, who was still sitting at her desk, started fanning her face and mouthing the words, "*So. Freakin'. Hot.*"

Drew rolled her eyes and pushed the door closed.

After a brief description about what services Canada Parks and Wildlife performed in the area, Kevin mentioned how Angus had always offered to help with any injured animals that Kevin would come across, wild or otherwise.

Drew sighed to herself. Another important part of the job Angus had forgotten to mention.

"So how about it, Doc? You going to help me too?"

"Of course. I'll help in any way I can." *Angus*, she groaned in her head, *I hope you get your ass sunburnt.*

"That's great, really, thank you."

"No worries." Drew rested forward onto her desk, linking her fingers. "Can I ask you a question?"

Mimicking her movement, Kevin narrowed his blue eyes giving her a sexy smirk. "Yes, I will go out with you."

Drew snorted lightly and narrowed her own eyes. "That's not what I wanted to ask."

"Shitty, shitty, what a pity," he sang lightly, the smirk still present. "We can work on that later." He winked. "Then what *did* you want to ask?"

"I heard Miss Evans asking about gray dogs. Did she mean wolves?"

"Yes." He sighed, shaking his head. "I don't think she has any idea that wolves are looking to snack on Mr Darcy."

"And they *are* wolves and not dogs, like she thinks they are?"

He shook his head a second time. "There isn't a single gray dog in the area. There's a husky down in Ucluelet, but he's an old boy and has trouble moving around. And just recently, the BCPP passed along reports of sightings of gray wolves down on Long Beach."

"What about black wolves, any sightings reported?"

"No. I haven't heard anything. Why?" Kevin leaned forward again.

"I went down to Cox Beach last night and saw your gray dogs, which are absolutely wolves by the way. And I also saw...a black wolf. A huge black wolf. Huge."

"You went down to the beach at night, alone?"

"Yes." She did her best to hide her irritation. She had just said that.

"Angus didn't tell you not to go to the beach alone at night, did he?" Kevin guessed.

"No." She sighed out loud this time. "He didn't."

"Okay, well, now you know. How many gray wolves were there?"

"Three."

"And you're sure the other was a wolf? There may not be many gray dogs in the area but there are quite a few black ones. Are you sure it wasn't a black dog?"

"Yes." She kept her words crisp. "I'm sure."

"Okay, easy. It's just that the BCPP gets false reports of black wolves all the time, especially with Molly running around. I heard you met Molly."

"Yes." She had just seen Molly the other day. Her owner Louise had brought the dog by so Drew could take the stitches out.

She studied the picture of Molly in her head. She was a big girl, and she was mostly black, with only the smallest amount of white hair on her underbelly, but Molly had floppy ears, a shorter snout, and was female. The beast that had stood next to her at the beach was bigger, beefier, with pointed ears, a longer nose and was male. She was positive.

"How is Molly doing?"

"Sorry?" She shook her head.

"Molly. How is she doing?" Drew blinked when she saw the slightest amount of concern cross his tanned face and was unsure if it was forced or not.

"She's a little stiff but she's young so it shouldn't bother her for too long." She looked at him. "You know her?"

"Yup! I can't count how many times I've taken that mutt back home. She's my buddy. Plus, I know Louise and the boys."

She nodded. "So, what about these wolves?"

"You said you saw them on Cox Beach?"

"Mmm, and the black one too," she reminded him.

"Did you have any food with you?"

"Oh yah! A T-bone actually. I like having a midnight meat snack on the beach." She hoped he understood by her tone how foolish that question had been.

He held up his hands and chuckled. "Hey, I needed to ask. You'd be surprised how stupid people can be." He stared at her as if she was either full of shit or delusional, she couldn't tell. "All on Cox Beach... Last night?" he confirmed.

"Yes, I saw them all last night on Cox Beach. I know I'm not stuttering so what's the problem?"

He laughed at her. "Well, you see, most people that run across that many wolves at one time don't usually walk away without some kind of damage. And you..." He looked over the half of her that wasn't covered by the desk, his blue gaze lingering on the opening of her purple blouse. "Look pretty good to me."

She had to admit that the look he just gave her had heated her up somewhat, but the sensation was quick to dwindle.

"Okay so I was lucky then. But I did see those wolves," she stressed.

"All right." He pushed his chair back and stood. "I'll check out Cox Beach and let the BCPP know that there could possibly be a black wolf with the gray pack."

"They weren't together." She opened the office door for him. Ruby jumped to her feet and went to Kevin, giving him a good sniff.

"What do you mean?" Kevin petted her head, but for the first time ever, Ruby snubbed her nose up at a person who could supply a good scratch and walked into the outer office.

"I mean they weren't in a pack together. Well, I don't think so." She crossed her arms, thinking about the previous night and how the black wolf had saved her from the gray ones. Even when she thought about it the next day, the behavior of the black wolf seemed so at odds with that of a normal wolf. Then again, she was positive he wasn't a normal wolf.

"Why?" He stepped close, his chest almost touching her bent arms.

He smelled nice — she liked the spicy cologne he was wearing.

"What makes you say that?" he pressed gently.

She wasn't sure if she should tell him. It felt like she was giving away secrets that didn't belong to her. "I don't know, it just felt that way at the time." She placed her hand on her head, faking a bad memory. "I don't know, I could be wrong. Anyways, I did see that wolf." She pointed at him as he gave her another smirk. "Wolf. Not dog."

"Okay, okay." He brushed against her as he exited her office. It was a slow purposeful graze that was meant to warm her skin and spark a hunger. And it did but once again it was quick to fade. He grinned as he walked to the front glass door. "I'll pass the word around. Nice to meet you, Doc."

"Drew," she corrected.

He looked at her mouth as he nodded. "Nice to meet you, Drew. Later, Connie."

"Later, Kev," Connie called as the door drifted shut.

Connie swung in her chair to face her. "Well?"

"You're right. He sure is nice to look at."

"But not freakin' hot?" Connie gaped.

"I guess he is. I don't know." She liked Kevin and he was attractive. There just wasn't that sudden zing of awareness. She only got that when she saw Theo — it was strange and very unlike her.

"What about that bum chin, though?" Connie interrupted her thoughts.

"Okay." She smiled as she confessed remembering the way the little crevice accentuated Kevin's strong chin. "That is the cutest bum chin I've ever seen."

* * * *

"Have you tracked it down yet?" Hendrik Linde's heavily accented voice was as rough as ever.

"I've tracked it many times. I'm just waiting for it to sit still long enough so I can shoot it."

"Ken," Hendrik hissed into the phone. "You cunt. I pay you to track, not kill. If that wolf has one bullet hole in it before I get there, I'll be putting your head on my wall of extinct species next. Are we clear?" His South African accent gave an eccentric twist to his threat.

Ken felt his nostrils flare as he tried not to tell the old bastard to fuck off and find someone else. He was getting tired of dealing with the fucktard's shit. He looked up at the clouds while he took a deep breath. The only thing stopping him was that the prick paid so damn well. Walking away from that amount of money was flat out stupid and the old man knew it. "We're clear."

"Good. Now, I have business in the western United States in a three weeks' time. I will be able to join you once it's concluded. That should give you enough time to predict its normal routine. I'll call once I arrive in the US." There was a pause on Hendrik's end of the line. "You've given me a considerable amount of help over the past five years. I have some of the rarest animals in North America as part of my collection thanks to you. Don't think that your service to me hasn't gone unnoticed."

"Yes, sir." Ken rolled his eyes. Jesus, one minute Hendrik was threatening to mount his head on his wall and the next he was praising him. Great! The guy was bi-polar too.

"I will speak to you soon." The line went dead.

Ken stuffed his cell into his pocket, then crossed his arms and looked out at the ocean. This was the last job he would do for the infamous Hendrik Linde. The old bastard would have to find someone else to track his prey. He would do this last job and help Linde bag this wolf, then disappear into the fog. He'd have to be careful, though — the last two guys that had decided to call it quits with Mr Linde were never seen again. It was painfully obvious that Linde didn't take rejection well.

Good thing he had known what he was getting into with Linde and had given him a false name. *Shit!* Nobody in Tofino even knew his real name.

Chapter Five

Drew walked carefully down the rainswept dock, located behind the police station, her arms full with Angus' — now her — travel vet knapsack and a box stuffed with free treats for her patients. The rain and wind whipped up and once again blew her hood off, exposing her face and hair to the cold. "Shit!" She stopped and adjusted the box, balancing it with one arm, then she yanked her hood back into place.

"Need some help?" The words came from behind her as the box was plucked from her grasp.

She knew it was Theo. Knew that he was the one who would be taking her over to Opitsat, and just like when she had found out in the morning that Theo was her escort, her stomach did this freaky twist thing and her vision went a little blurry, or maybe she was lightheaded. If she was lucky, it was just a plain old fashioned seizure.

Those bizarre reactions were apparently becoming the norm where Theo was concerned. It happened whenever she saw him and distance didn't seem to affect it. He could be near or far, yet she still experienced the same childish buzz. It would happen when he drove past her on the street and nodded to her. Another time she'd seen him on the main road when she'd been driving home. He had pulled over what she'd guessed was a speeder. He'd been facing away from her but she'd still gotten all hot and bothered. Pathetic.

The sensation was even worse when he'd stopped by to pay Molly's bill and they'd been face to face. The second he had stepped into the clinic, that giddy, lightheaded feeling had taken over and she'd felt like she was back in high school, crushing on the head of the boys' soccer team. The meeting had been quick, and though she'd been focused on him, he'd seemed to have been distracted. She hadn't questioned it and had assumed it'd had to do with his work. As he'd been leaving, he'd stopped by the door and looked at her for what seemed like forever. His glare had become quite intense. When she'd asked if everything was okay, he'd given her a half-smile and nodded before leaving.

"Come on," he called, passing her on the narrow dock.

Following, Drew enjoyed watching him walk. His shoulders were back, his baseball hat-covered head was held high, his stride long and sure-footed as he marched toward the two boats tied off at the end. He didn't even shy away from the weather, he simply walked straight into it, taking the full force of the wrath Mother Nature was busy dealing out.

He hopped into the smaller of the two vessels, the added weight of her box of freebies not fazing him in the least. And once he had placed her box under the shelter of the cockpit canopy, then straightening he held out his hand.

She stopped short next to the black rigid inflatable and looked it over. "We're taking this?" She bent her knees, balancing herself when the waves hit the dock. The damn thing was so freakin' small, and the waves looked so freakin' big.

"Yes." He held out his other hand too as the inflatable rocked in the water. "Have you been on a boat before?"

"Yes, of course, just not in this type of weather." She pointed over her shoulder to the patrol boat sitting on the other side. "Why can't we take that one?"

"For a ten-minute trip? No way! Besides, the weather isn't that bad."

"It's bad enough," she mumbled, watching the rigid inflatable sway with the waves.

"The dock amplifies the waves. It'll be calmer once we hit open water."

With his hands still held out, he said her name. When she looked into his face, his gray eyes were intense but there was a boyish smirk curling one side of his mouth. "If there is anybody here that you should trust to keep you safe it's the BCPP—we're here to protect and serve." He gave her a teasing wink. "We'll be fine." He waved her forward. "Now hop on board." Even though he was making light of her fear, she fully believed that Theo wouldn't let any harm come to her. It was strange and a little disconcerting that she had faith in a man she barely knew.

She stepped forward at the same moment that Theo moved to the side of the inflatable, and in the space of a breath, Theo plucked her up and lifted her into the boat. He quickly reached for a lifejacket and forced her to pull it on. He pushed her fingers aside as she struggled with the wet zipper. "I can dress myself," she huffed as he tightened the side straps.

"I'm sure you can. But when you ride with me, I do it. That way..." That smirk tugged on his lips again. "I know it's done right."

Right then... Right at that moment, her vision went a little wonky. Her only explanation for her reaction to the close contact was a seizure, because she had never acted like this before, with anyone.

"Sit there and strap in." He pointed to the passenger seat. "Give me your bag." She handed him her vet bag and watched as he stowed it in a storage compartment with her box of goodies.

Another officer released the dock lines and waved. Theo zipped closed the protective canvas cover, then started the engine.

"So," Theo began as he steered the boat clear of the dock. "I heard Angus didn't tell you about the trip out to Opitsat?"

"No, he didn't. Then again Angus didn't tell me about a lot of other things either."

"That must mean he thinks you'll be able to handle whatever is thrown at you."

"Yeah!" She snorted. "Or maybe he was in a rush to get his ass on the beach."

He chuckled. "Could be."

They began slowly but once in the open water, they gradually picked up speed.

"See? Much calmer away from the dock."

She tightened her grip on the safety bar in front of her as a wave jarred her in the seat. "Ha! Not really."

He laughed, looking over at her. "That shouldn't count."

"It counts," she grumbled.

"Relax." Drew turned when she heard the deep silky tone to his word. "We're okay." The traces of silver in his eyes flickered in the lights glowing on the instrument board, giving him an all-knowing stare. Except this time, there was no boyish grin that accompanied his intense gaze, just a heavy dose of heat. Good heat, the type of heat that made your body ache in places where you had no business aching, especially while flying across the ocean in the middle of a storm.

"Stop looking at me and focus on what's in front of you." She mumbled the opposite of what she truly wanted.

He raised his dark eyebrows and did as she asked, even though she cried out in her head, begging him not to listen to her. She wanted him to look at her, she wanted to be the center of a man's attention. It had been so long since the last time.

"I didn't mean to make you feel uncomfortable. You're just easy to look at."

Drew gripped the bar as they ran headlong into a wave. "I'm not... I mean you didn't make me feel uncomfortable."

"Then why the blush?"

She placed a palm to her cheek and felt the heat. She groaned in her head as she answered, "I didn't realize I had."

His crooked smile caused small creases around his eyes. "Don't panic, it's cute."

Cute! Argh! That was the last thing she wanted to hear. Little girls with golden ringlets were cute, not grown women.

Theo casually directed the boat around a small island. She almost cried out when she noticed rocks protruding from the surface of the water but he easily avoided them. "Are you seeing anyone?"

"Huh? What?"

She looked over at him, puzzled by his questions. They had almost crashed into rocks!

"Are you seeing anyone? Here? Or back in Vancouver?"

"No. No, I'm not. Are we almost there?" God, her hands were starting to cramp up on her, she was gripping the safety bar so tight.

"Good and yes." He slowly lowered the throttle and the boat dropped in speed.

"Good and yes for which?"

He chuckled. "Good, I'm glad you're not seeing anyone and yes, we're here."

A small dock suddenly appeared in the distance and her heart sped up. It wasn't from the fact that she would be on solid ground soon. Well... Not entirely, but because he was glad. She knew why he was glad, she wasn't an idiot, but she had to ask anyway, "Why?"

"Because," he said, slowing the boat even more as they approached the dock, "I don't like the idea of having to deal with an angry boyfriend or husband. It might tarnish my saintly reputation."

"And why would you have to deal with angry...anything?"

"Well, if I was in a relationship and I walked in on my other half having sex with someone else, I'd be angry."

"We're having sex?" She knew her face heated this time, she didn't have to touch her face to confirm it.

"Not right now, we both have work to do," he teased. "But soon, I think." He was so casual about it, even waving to a man standing on the dock as he spoke.

"Ah… Okay. Got a date in mind? I'll pencil you in."

He gave a deep chuckle that sounded closer to a…growl? No. That couldn't be right. He stared down at her, heat in his silver eyes. "Soon."

Her belly flipped and her heart floated up as she blinked away her suddenly fuzzy vision. Then she watched as he stood over her, grinning like a typical arrogant male, satisfied that he was able to fluster her. Then, breaking her dreamy fog, he ordered, "Stay here while I get the boat tied up."

* * * *

Within ten minutes, Theo greeted Chief Tom Cook as they entered the front door of the community center, which doubled as a learning center, which in turn doubled as a meeting room for the tribe's council members, and, of course, on the first Tuesday of each month it became the vet clinic.

He clasped his friend's hand and gave him a genuine smile. "Tom. How are things?"

"Not bad, a few minor issues. Who's this?" Tom shifted to the side, smiling at Drew. She was standing behind him, holding the box of freebies she had refused to let him carry, patiently waiting to be introduced.

The wolf, who was calm while in Drew's presence, suddenly stirred, curling up its lips, exposing fangs and flexing his muscles as it fixed his attention on Tom.

Theo didn't like the look Tom was giving Drew any more than the wolf did, yet how could he get pissed off at his friend? Tom was Private Jonathan Cook's great-great-grandson. This man knew his secret, knew that he carried the soul of a wolf next to his own. Tom's grandfather had first helped Theo understand what he had inside him and how it had come to be. It was Tom's grandfather who had taught Theo how to dominate the wolf. It was Tom and his family, and other members of his tribe, who gave him unconditional friendship, had given him a piece of their land so that he could build a small cabin, where he and the wolf could be free from 'normal humans'.

So, no, he wouldn't allow the wolf to harm Tom in any way, even if he was looking at Drew like she was dessert.

Stop, he ordered in a low growl. *Tom is a friend.*

"Are we good?" Tom asked, catching his attention.

Tom had the uncanny ability to know when the wolf seemed to be acting up. Or maybe he just wasn't that good at hiding it.

Theo raised a single eyebrow confirming Tom's silent question, then made the introductions. "Tom..." Theo gestured to Drew to step forward. As she did so, he couldn't help but touch her lower back. Did he push for that or the wolf? "This is Drew O'Bannion, Angus' replacement."

Sudden enlightenment crossed Tom's face as he offered his hand in greeting. "Nice to meet you, Dr O'Bannion." Theo plucked the box from her arms as Tom shook her hand lightly. Then, as though he knew what the wolf wanted, Tom stepped away from her. The wolf gave a satisfied snort and calmed.

"I'm Chief here in these parts, so if you have any problems, you come find me."

"I will, and please, Drew is just fine. I'm not good with all the formal titles."

"You got it. Come on." Tom waved them on. "I'll show you where you can set up."

As Tom led them to the far end of the building, Drew leaned in close, her hand hovering over her mouth. "Do you have any breath mints?"

"No." Puzzled, he asked, "Why?"

"I forgot to brush my teeth after my lunch." She gave him a worried frown.

"So?"

"Didn't you see the way he backed away from me? There was onion in the pasta sauce I made."

Theo laughed. He laughed harder when she scowled back at him.

In a huff, she moved away from him. Still smiling, he tucked her box under his arm, then stopped her. He grabbed the side of her rain jacket, then pulled her close.

"What are you doing?" She pushed against his chest as her breathy words warmed his face. Even though he knew Tom had stepped away to appease the wolf, Theo still bent his head close to hers and drew in a deep breath. Ruby was the first odor he detected, followed by basil and parsley, thanks to their strong scents. The next all mixed together—tomatoes, celery, mushrooms, the slightest amount of onion—nothing to really worry about—and finally the pasta and…apples? Apple juice maybe? Then a new scent hit him. It was Drew. She was aroused by his close contact. He could smell her damp and honey-sweet fragrance. It was intoxicating. He clenched his teeth together, fighting the seductive pull.

"I don't smell any onion," he breathed. "You're good." *Better than good… You're heaven.*

"Thanks." She swallowed and slid away from him just as Tom stopped at the end of the hall.

"Here it is," Tom announced, marching inside the room. He pointed out a sturdy table that had been set up for her, as well as a small bathroom and a counter with a large stainless steel sink.

Drew crossed to the table and threw her bag on top, then began peeling off her rain jacket while Tom spoke to her. Theo followed and placed her box next to her bag.

Strands of blonde hair curled around her face thanks to the rain and her nose was a little pink, but not the lush pink that colored her lips. He struggled not to look at the way her purple blouse clung to the curves of her breasts and waist, or how her black dress pants hugged her hips lovingly. As he fought to keep his eyes on the acceptable parts of her body, the scent of another male hit him. The beast lurched to attention and gave a low growl in warning. Theo stilled. The scent was on Drew's jacket... No, it was on Drew. Another man had touched Drew. The muscles in his chest tightened as he inhaled the scent again. It was too hard to concentrate with the growling in his head and the conversation going on between Drew and Tom.

Quiet! He barked out the command in his head. The wolf rolled beneath his skin, now agitated by the scent and Theo's order.

He breathed again. He knew that scent, it was Kevin Beauchamp. She must have met Kevin recently. He had touched her or her clothes. The muscles in his neck and shoulders ached almost to the point of pain.

How in the hell had he missed that before? Better yet, why did he care so much?

"Okay, that's it." Tom studied him carefully over Drew's shoulder. "Theo and I have to go fight crime, but if you need anything, my receptionist Cheryl is just down the hall."

"Great, thanks for everything." Drew turned only seconds after Theo was able to control his emotions.

"I'll be back in a few hours." Theo saw Tom exit the room out of the corner of his eye. "You have everything you need?"

"Yeah! More than I was expecting. This is perfect." She smiled up at him, unzipping her vet bag.

Theo nodded and moved to the door, then stopped. He needed to know if she and Kevin... "How'd your meeting with Beauchamp go? Did he explain everything to you?"

She gave him a curious smile. "How did you know I met with Kevin?"

He shrugged. "I saw him heading toward your clinic. How was it?" He didn't like lying to her, but he couldn't afford to tell her the truth.

"Oh!" She nodded. "It went okay. He filled me in on how Parks and the BCPP work together with animal sightings and stuff and how Angus would help out when Parks needed it."

"Good." Both he and the wolf relaxed. "Kevin's a nice guy. He really works hard to keep the local wildlife safe."

"Yeah, he's okay." She stopped pulling items from her bag with a thoughtful expression. "Did he mention that I saw four wolves on Cox Beach last night?"

"No." Theo turned to face her fully and crossed his arms. Where was she going with this? "But he might not have stopped by the station yet." He studied her carefully. "You saw four?"

"Mmm. Three gray ones and one really big black one. I mentioned it to Kevin—that I don't think the greys and the black one were together. I mean... You know they weren't in a pack."

"Why do you say that?" He pulled in her confusion.

She paused with her mouth hanging open, as though she didn't know if she should continue.

"Drew," he used his best cop tone on her. "What happened?"

"I'm not sure." She sighed, her shoulders slumping a little. "I could have sworn I was going to be a dinner for four but I think... Well, it looked like..." She shook her head.

He stepped closer, Kevin's scent mixing with her uncertainty. "It's okay, you can tell me."

"You're probably just going to think I'm crazy."

"No I won't. Looked like what?" he pressed.

"I think..." She blinked. "I think the black wolf saved me from the other ones. He scared them away when they approached me."

Theo gave her a fake confused frown.

"I'm sorry, I know that sounds crazy, but that's what it looked like."

"Okay. Did you tell Kevin this?"

"No." She scowled this time. "I couldn't for some reason, it didn't feel right to tell him, and I don't know why."

"You told me," he pointed out.

"I know. And I don't know why." She exhaled. "Argh! Whatever. It's done. You know and he doesn't. No big deal."

But it was a big deal—she hadn't felt right telling Kevin important information like a wolf saving her from other wolves and it was a big deal to him, because she trusted him enough to tell her something she clearly didn't understand.

"Theo!" Tom called from the hall.

"I've got to go. Don't worry about the pack of wolves. We're keeping our eyes open for them. As for the black wolf, that was pretty cool. Sounds as though you have your own personal bodyguard. But do me a favor?"

"Another one?" She smirked.

He raised his eyebrows at her. "Keep off the beach at night. Didn't Angus tell you the animals hunt on the beaches at night?"

She blew out a long breath. "No," she huffed sarcastically. "Angus didn't tell me."

"Well, now you know." He walked toward the door. "See you in a bit."

Chapter Six

Closing the door to his office, Tom asked, "What is going on with you two?"

Theo relaxed on the worn couch Tom had added to his office. "Who two?"

"You and the wolf? You and Drew?" Tom poured coffee into a couple of cups and passed one to Theo. "Why do I get the feeling there is some weird love triangle thing going on here?"

Theo nodded his thanks for the coffee. He and Tom had just returned from doing a quick circuit of the Reservation. They'd interviewed a young mother and her son, who'd been bitten by a cat. The mother had wanted to press charges against the owner, until Theo had gotten it out of the kid that he had swung the cat around by its tail. A group of kids who'd broken a window playing then taken off had been rounded up and brought back to the scene of the crime and told to apologize. And finally, Theo had given a lecture to a young man who had been spotted driving an ATV under the influence the weekend before. But Theo hadn't actually witnessed the crime, so he hadn't been able to do more than give him a warning. For the most part Opitsat was quiet—coming over to the Reserve was one aspect of his job that Theo really enjoyed.

Theo took a sip of his coffee, then joked, "How can it be a triangle when the wolf and I are on the same side?"

"But you have different souls," Tom was quick to point out. "What's going on?"

Theo gripped the mug. "The wolf called mate."

"What?" Tom stilled. His jaw dropped slightly.

"The. Wolf. Called. Mate."

Tom slumped down on the edge of his desk. "I heard that part. That was me, in shock. Which, for the record, never happens."

"Yeah, well, you weren't the only one shocked."

They sat in silence until Tom opened his mouth, but Theo answered the question before Tom even asked. "Yeah." He nodded. "Drew. Happened the first time we met."

"And...?"

"And when we swap, he always goes to her house."

"And...?"

And I don't do a damn thing to stop him, Theo thought to himself. "That's it."

"Bullshit," Tom huffed. "Keep going."

"And we protected her when a pack of gray wolves wanted her as their midnight snack." And... He knew he couldn't afford to let anything happen with her. And... He wanted her more than anything. *And...* This was so far out of character for him that it was unnerving.

After placing his mug on the floor, Theo stood and began pacing around the office. "Did this happen to Jonathan? Did he ever call mate before?" He prayed silently, hoping this had happened at least once before. If so, that meant the wolf could be moved on…after.

"Don't think so." Tom stared off, deep in thought. "I only remember Grandfather talking about Jon's Nina. He married her a few years after the wolf joined with him and he was with her until she died of old age. He never mentioned any other women in Jon's life." Tom looked Theo in the eye. "If the wolf had called mate while its spirit still dwelled within Jon, I don't believe you would be standing here."

"Fuck, Tom. That is not what I want to hear." Theo yanked off his ball cap and slapped it against his thigh.

"You want her too," Tom pointed out.

"Well, can you blame me? Look at her." He swiped his hand down his face. Her scent still clung to his skin. "What man wouldn't want her? Jesus, Ben hasn't stopped talking about her, the guys at the station keep talking about her. Everybody is talking about her. Angus told me she was a looker, but I had no idea she would affect me or the wolf like this."

"Wow, you're really agitated."

"No, I'm annoyed."

"Annoyed because people are looking at her and talking about her?"

Theo rubbed the back of his neck. "No."

Tom placed his coffee down and sighed. "You're an idiot."

"Excuse me?"

"You know very well that wolves don't pick a mate based on beauty. There's a deeper connection, it's like a psychic link between the two. The wolf is picking up this link, and by your behavior, you are too, you just don't recognize it for what it truly is. You're thinking too much like a human."

"That's because I *am* human." Theo tugged his cap back on.

"You stopped being a normal human the moment the wolf joined with you. You are so much more."

Tom pushed away from the desk and stepped in front of him. "If the wolf claims Drew as your mate then maybe it would be worth looking into. Besides, with all the whispers and googly eyes, she wants you too."

Oh, he already knew that Drew wanted him, and it was more than the blushes and googly eyes—he could smell it on her. Her desire had flared the second he had looked at her standing on the dock. Sure, it had mixed with her unreasonable fear of traveling in the inflatable, but it had been there nonetheless, filling his head, making his muscles tight.

As much as he wanted Drew, there was no way in hell that it could go on for long. The longer he was 'with' her, the greater the risk became for him. His life, the wolf's life, could become endangered if she was to see what he really was. An image of Drew popped into his head and he cringed when he imagined her pretty face turning into a mask of horror when she saw him swap.

"*Drew no afraid on beach,*" the wolf reminded.

She had been, though, at first, thanks to the pack that had decided to show up. That fear had still lingered after but it hadn't been as strong and it had been overshadowed by her interest in the wolf instead. Still, it didn't matter because there was no way he would take the chance. He couldn't afford to risk himself or the wolf.

There was, however, a tiny little 'what if?' playing havoc with his desires. That desire to have someone of his own, that someone who would accept him for what he was. What if Drew was that someone? What if the connection the wolf had picked up was real?

Theo swore when Jonathan and his only love Nina suddenly came to mind. Could he do what Jonathan had done? He had already lost his parents and all of his younger sisters.

He posed the question aloud. "And if she...stays?" He crossed his arms. "Then what? I live with her until she dies of old age like Jonathan's Nina? That is *not* acceptable."

"If I'd lived as long as you have and alone for most of it, I would seriously consider it." Tom shrugged. "Then again, I haven't lived as long as you and I wasn't chosen by the wolf, so I really have no idea what it is you go through."

Tom had his wife Gwen and three kids. He had a family that would age as he aged. He would watch his children marry and have children of their own and when it came time, Tom would die and finally know peace. Theo would never have that.

"No, you don't," Theo bit out.

"I've been alone, though." Tom crossed his arms and gave him a serious look. "Long time before I met Gwen. I didn't like it."

Theo didn't like being alone either, it wasn't the best feeling knowing that everyone you either knew or loved was dead and all that was left were foggy memories, but at least he was used to it now. It was for that reason that he had chosen not to engage in a relationship for very long and it was for that reason that he couldn't stay in one place for too long either — although he did have a soft spot for Vancouver Island. He had come to this area repeatedly for short visits and this was the second time he had lived here as a permanent resident. There was no question that he was drawn to this place.

"Mate here. Just Drew here." Theo frowned at the choppy comment. Had the wolf known Drew would come here? Is that why he had been drawn back to this place time and again?

"Still annoyed, eh? Why don't you go see Drew? I bet she puts a smile on your face."

"Mmm," Theo agreed slowly.

"What's up now?"

Theo continued to frown. "Do you think the wolf knew Drew would come here?"

Tom frowned himself. "Maybe. He was able to enter the bodies of two humans, both from different times and continents. Sensing where his future mate could be found might be a bonus of his spiritual gifts or maybe it's just a natural instinct."

"What do you mean?"

"He's a British Colombian wolf. This area was the only place on earth that particular animal was found. The island is his home. It makes sense that he would return to find a mate. Wouldn't you like to go back to England and find yourself a pretty English girl?"

"No," Theo answered honestly. "I don't want to go back. I like it here." He forced his posh English accent to the surface as he spoke. "I lost my taste for home after the war. Being the only wolf in England and hunted because of it has a way of leaving a bad taste in one's mouth."

Tom laughed. "Man, it freaks me out when you talk like that. I like you better when you speak like a relatively normal Canadian."

Theo grinned. He did too and joked, "I'm going to go check on Drew, see if she's almost done, eh! Let me know if you need anything before I go."

After seeing three dogs due for their shots, a cat with a dislocated tail, a pet raccoon that would soon be a mummy and a dead goldfish—which was ceremonially flushed out to sea—Drew's afternoon had gone pretty well. The locals were friendly and easy-going. They came in an endless stream, asking questions about their pets or for the freebies, she couldn't tell. Not that it mattered—they kept her busy enough to keep her mind on her job and off Theo and their sex date, which would take place 'soon'.

Now that she was done for the day and alone, all she could think about was 'soon'—it got her all hot and bothered. But it kind of annoyed her, too. He was so certain that she would hop into bed with him. He was right, she totally would, it had been a year since Jamie and she was worried she might have a few cobwebs, but still there was a fine line between confidence and cocky. Confidence was a real turn-on. Cocky… Not so much.

Yet she didn't get the impression that Theo was the cocky sort—maybe when he had been younger, but not now. He had obviously paid attention to the lessons life taught, which was refreshing. So many men didn't, Jamie being one of them. Then again, that was what had attracted her to Jamie—she was drawn to the rebellious bad-boy, she had liked the thrill he could offer. Theo was a member of the British Colombia Provincial Police, the polar opposite of Jamie, or was he? He was a cop first and foremost, that was plain to see, but there was something else she couldn't quite get a feel for, yet instinctively knew that whatever that 'something else' was, it was aggressive in a dark sort of way. What that meant she had no idea. What she did know was that she couldn't wait to get to the 'soon'.

"Soon," she huffed. "And men say women tease."

Would he tease her? Or would he just flat out take what he wanted? And how would he take it? she wondered. Would it be slow and gentle or rough and hard? Both were great, but she could use a little rough and hard, she loved that frantic need that always accompanied it. The need to get at heated skin, the pulling and tearing of clothes, the nips and hard kisses and the feeling of a muscled body pinning her down. Oh yeah! She smiled to herself. She could use a little of that.

As she quietly packed up her belongings, her imagination sparked to life. She imagined Theo walking into the makeshift exam room in his dark cop pants and shirt, holding his jacket. His cap with BCPP stitched into the front was pulled low covering his dark hair, shading his gray eyes as he closed the door, but it didn't block the shadow of desire that crossed his face as he moved to her. It caused her stomach to swirl with anticipation and heated excitement pooled between her legs, making her limbs shaky and heavy. Once he reached her, he pulled her forward, his mouth coming down hard on hers. His hands slid from her waist to her behind, effectively sealing their bodies together. She liked that his lips were warm and that his whiskers were rough against her skin and man, did she ever like that he smelled of rain. But what she liked the best was when she opened her mouth for him and he groaned when their tongues met. That was hot.

The ringing of a phone unexpectedly pulled Drew out of her fantasy. Her eyes flew open at the sound and there was Theo standing over her, pulling away, licking his lips. Her breasts and stomach felt cool when he severed the close contact. He reached into his pocket and pulled out a cell phone.

"I've got to answer this," he explained, moving toward the window raising his cell. "Sergeant Grey."

Dumbfounded, all she could do was nod at his back. What the hell had happened? How could she have missed hearing him enter the room? How could she have gone from having a naughty daydream to actually kissing him? How could she not have realized he was real? "What the hell...?" she mumbled to herself.

Her confusion was interrupted when she heard the alarm in Theo's voice. "We're on our way." He flipped his phone closed as he addressed her. "There's an emergency in town, we've gotta move. Are you ready?"

"I..." She blinked, pointing to the door, then to him. "What—?"

He answered her question with a command, "We'll talk about that when we're on the move, but right now I need you to get your bag packed."

Nodding, she focused on throwing the remaining supplies into her knapsack and pulling on her coat. Theo grabbed her bag and moved to the door, opening it just as Tom appeared. "Ben called." Tom looked from her to Theo. "They need you back in town." Tom was trying to hide a smile as they moved down the hall, which meant he knew exactly what had gone on between them.

Well, that was just great! At least someone knew what had happened, because she sure as hell didn't.

As they reached the main doors, Tom thanked her for coming and quickly patted Theo on the back. "Remember what I said."

Theo glared at Tom over his shoulder and nodded. "Call if you need anything."

"Will do." Tom waved.

* * * *

Minutes later Drew was seated in the black BCPP rigid inflatable, gripping the handrail in front of her as they sped their way to Tofino.

"Can I ask what happened?" She squeezed the rail tight as Theo maneuvered the boat around the rocks.

"Another dog has been shot. They need you back to help him and I need to track down the shooter."

"That wasn't what I... Holy shit, another shooting!"

Theo quickly glanced at her before turning back to the water. "That wasn't what?"

"That wasn't what I meant." She looked at the front wind screen but not really focusing on anything. "I was wondering what happened between us. It all seemed..." She couldn't finish because she didn't know how to finish, she didn't know what had happened.

"We kissed," he confirmed.

"Yes, I was there. But I don't know how I..." She couldn't finish that either. She didn't want him to know she had thought she was having an erotic daydream about him and hadn't realized that it was real. How could that have happened?

"Don't know what?" He narrowed his eyes. "Are you okay? Too fast?"

"No," she blurted out. "Not too fast." Just too dreamy, too fantastic, too good to be true. "So... Do they know who is responsible for the shooting?"

Drew could feel Theo staring at her but she refused to face him and he finally turned his attention to the front of the boat. "When this calms down and things get sorted, we will talk this over. Okay?"

"Okay." God, she hated that her voice sounded so small. She cleared her throat and repeated her answer with more strength.

A smirk curled one side of his mouth but he didn't say anything else until they reached the dock.

Ben was there to meet them and help tie up the inflatable.

"What do you know?" Theo asked Ben as he helped Drew from the boat.

"It was Frankie." Ben gripped Theo's forearm and pulled him up onto the dock.

"Who's Frankie?" Drew asked, slinging her bag over her shoulder.

As the threesome walked up the dock to the waiting patrol truck, Theo explained, "Frankenstein is a very big Doberman Pincher. He likes to chase after cars and the occasional cat and he doesn't have the best of temperaments. He's charged at Ben a couple of times when we've tried to talk to George."

"George is the owner?" Drew guessed.

"Yeah, he owns a fishing boat and is gone a lot of the time. Frankie is his security and only family," Ben filled in.

"Who looks after Frankie when George isn't home?" Drew stopped by the truck.

"He has a roommate." Theo informed. "Randall looks after him when George goes out to sea. He's the one who called this in."

Theo opened the back door of the cab and instructed Drew, "Get in."

She hopped in with her bag and listened to the two men.

"What happened?" Theo asked, sliding into the passenger seat.

"He wasn't really clear. I think Randall has hit the sauce early today. So, I waited for you. You're the only one who he respects enough to talk civil to."

"Where's the dog?" Drew asked.

"He's at your clinic. Connie had to knock him out before you got there. He was getting a little nasty."

Ben pulled to a stop outside the vet clinic and Drew jumped out and ran toward the doors. As she was reaching for the door, Theo grabbed it first and held it open for her. Ruby greeted them, pushing her wet nose into her hands. Drew scooted Ruby out of the way, ordering her to sit down, and rushed to the exam room. As she went to enter the treatment room, Theo was there, blocking her view. She huffed and skirted around him. "Connie."

"Oh, you're back, good." She looked up warily. "I had to give him a sedative. He tried to bite Ben."

"Local mutts don't really like Ben, do they?" Drew chuckled as she moved around the table and pulled rubber gloves from a box. "That's okay, I'll fix him up and he can have another go at Ben."

There was complete silence in the exam room. Drew looked up at Connie's startled expression to Theo's frown. She tsked. "I was kidding. Geez! I'm not that nasty. Besides, God only knows what diseases Ben could give this poor boy."

Connie sighed and laughed softly. Theo just sighed.

"All right, let me have a look at what we have."

As she bent over the dog, Theo grasped her wrist and spoke like a cop. "I need pictures of this, a report and the bullet."

"No problem." She nodded to her bag. "Connie, get my phone out of my bag." She looked up at Theo. "It's all I have."

"It'll do." He frowned at the dog lying on the chrome table. "Do me a favor?"

"That's number three," she retorted.

"Keep Frankie sedated." Then he cautioned in a hard tone, "This guy isn't to be trusted."

"Got it." She took her phone from Connie and got ready to take a few pictures for the report she would have to write. "Drew," Theo snapped out her name. "Do *not* allow this dog to wake up until I'm here." His gaze burned straight into hers. "Am I clear?"

"Yes." She bit out. "I heard you the first time and I heard you say he could get nasty. This isn't my first time dealing with a wounded animal, so go do your cop thing and leave me to do my vet thing."

The muscle in his jaw flexed as he straightened. "I'll be back to collect my report."

"That's fine." She waved him out, focusing her attention on the dog. She didn't have time to get into it with him when there was an injured dog lying before her.

She didn't hear the door shut. "Whao!" Connie said across from her.

"What's whao?" She snapped a few shots of the entry wound from different angles.

"Theo really didn't like you being near this dog."

"That's too bad. This is why I became a vet, to help sick and injured animals." She passed the phone to Connie and prepared what she would need to remove the bullet.

"He didn't like the way you snapped at him either. I don't think I've ever heard someone talk to a cop that way."

She opened the cupboards behind her. "Cops are people too. When they say something stupid, they need to be put back in their place. In this case, Theo assumed I didn't know how to handle a wounded dog, which, of course, is bullshit. I've dealt with bigger and nastier dogs than this, and I told him so."

"You are one ballsy chick. First a pack of wolves and now a cop."

It was funny that Connie had mentioned that, because dealing with the wolves and Theo kinda felt like the same thing for some reason. Drew frowned at the sudden thought but pushed it aside. "Okay, my little helper, let's get this bullet out of Frankenstein here."

Chapter Seven

It was after midnight by the time Theo made it back to the clinic to see how Frankie was doing and to collect the report he'd asked Drew to make for him. He wasn't kidding himself, though. He wanted to go because he knew Drew would be there. He needed to see that she was okay, to make certain that Frankie hadn't woken up and bitten her.

Why it pissed him off that she had snapped back was beyond him. Why he had snapped at her in the first place was also a mystery. She was a vet, for God's sake, had been a vet in Vancouver for quite some time, so dealing with a difficult dog wasn't something new to her. Still it bothered him, but it bothered the wolf more. The damn beast had actually fought him as he had walked out of the clinic, made it hard for him to do his job. He had continually paced in circles in his mind and caused his muscles to twitch and flex at inappropriate times. The need to protect Drew from Frankie was so strong that he had begun whining, the high-pitched noise echoing around Theo's head. The behavior was unusual and the only thing he could come up with was that his wolf was feeding off his anxiety and was reacting when Theo couldn't. Which made sense, but, Jesus, whining didn't solve anything. It did, however, give him a bad headache.

He found the front door unlocked, which also annoyed him, and proceeded to lock it behind him. As he moved through the dimly lit clinic, he picked up Drew's scent and followed it. Ruby appeared in the doorway, blocking the entrance. He approached the dog and stopped, allowing her to sniff him over and before he registered that Drew was sitting on the floor. The dog nudged his thigh for a pat, leaning into his side. He obliged and scratched her ears as he scanned the back room that housed a few cages, storage and a small operating area. The room smelled of blood and dog, antiseptic and...chocolate. He searched and found a mug sitting by the sink. Correction, hot chocolate.

When he didn't pick up any other scents, he looked down at Drew sitting on the floor. She was resting against the wall and her legs were stretched out on old blankets and quilts piled together to form a makeshift bed for Frankie, whose head rested in her lap. The dog was lying peacefully in spite of the IV hook-up and bandages wrapped around one of its front legs and chest and Drew's arm draped over his neck.

She wasn't wearing her black dress pants or fitted purple blouse like she had earlier on Opitsat, but wore a white, oversized hooded sweatshirt, dark blue yoga pants and a pair of light blue, fuzzy slippers. And her hair no longer curled around her face but was pulled into a low ponytail, accenting her blonde highlights. He crossed the room and squatted down by her crossed feet and wiggled the top of her slippered foot.

All the tension that had built up over the past hours vanished when Drew opened her eyes and gave him a sleepy smile. "Hi." The greeting was soft with a husky edge.

He couldn't help but return the smile. "Things worked out okay, I see."

"Mmm." She shifted, arching her back slightly. "He was a good boy when I woke him. Got him to eat and drink a little, gave him some meds and sent him to sleep." Her eyes twinkled when she gazed at him. "Not one little growl."

He chuckled. "So you're saying he made a liar out of me."

"Sure did." She waved her free hand dismissing their difference of opinion. "It's okay. I appreciate the concern, although I hope you know it wasn't necessary."

He shrugged. "It came out anyways."

"Oh!" She raised her eyebrows and said slowly, "Okay."

"As ordered, I did my cop thing. Did you do your vet thing?"

"I did. Let me get it for you." He watched amazed as she lifted Frankie's head like it was a priceless jewel, shifted out from under the dog and gently rested the giant head on the quilts.

After checking his IV and giving him a quick pat, she stood up, resting her weight on one leg.

"You okay?" he asked as she limped to the door.

"Oh, yeah!" She chuckled. "I must have been there longer than I thought. My leg and butt cheek went numb."

He and Ruby followed her into her office, where he took note of the blanket and pillow sitting on the arm of the old loveseat Angus had bought. She hobbled over to her desk and as she reached to grab the report, Theo took in the nice view of her behind, thanks to the yoga pants she was wearing. That behind might be numb but—damn—the shape was perfect and he remembered how the soft flesh had fitted in his hands, as though it was created for him alone.

He raised his gaze in time to meet hers and accepted the folder she held out.

"I don't have a printer that will spit out photos, so I saved them to my hard drive and onto that memory card for you." She pointed to the tiny USB card taped to the inside of the folder.

"That's fine." He looked over the report and nodded approvingly. "This is perfect. Everything I need is on here. Though, I may have to call you in just to answer a few questions."

"No problem."

He lifted the top page and scanned down. "Where's the bullet?"

"Here." She grabbed a small clear bag that had the time and date written on it.

Theo held the clear bag up to the light and studied the bullet. *Shit!* He was hoping Frankie's and Molly's shootings were two separate incidents, but by the look of the bullet, both dogs had been shot with the same caliber gun.

"It kinda looks like the one I pulled out of Molly."

"Mmm," he agreed.

"Good thing this guy or whoever is doing this has a bad shot. It could have been much worse."

Theo met her amber stare. "How so?"

She shrugged. "I don't know anything about bullets or any of that ballistic stuff but the way the bullet went into Frankie's shoulder…" She frowned. "It only took out the layers of skin and a chunk of the deltoid and triceps. If he was a thinner dog it might have hit the scapula, which would have caused more damage..."

"I get the feeling there's more."

"I don't know." She wrinkled her nose. "Don't bullets leave big exit holes? I mean this should have been a lot worse, don't you think? This jackass must be a bad shot or...maybe killing Frankie wasn't the plan."

There was silence as both of them looked at the other. "But what the hell do I know? I'm just a vet. What do you think?"

"It's too soon to tell. I'll have to go through your report and both bullets will be sent to Forensic Identification in Vancouver."

She nodded and changed the subject. "Guess it's safe to assume you didn't find the person who shot Frankie."

"No, we didn't." He closed the folder. "Randall was incapacitated by the time we got there, so getting an accurate account was out."

"You mean he was drunk."

He felt his lips twitch but fought the urge to smile.

He nodded. "That's another way of putting it."

She crossed her arms. "Call it what it is. You don't have to be the polite cop around me."

He smirked. "That's easier said than done. Being a polite cop is a necessity. I have to be politically correct at all times. Blurting out that Randall was hammered isn't going to go over too well."

"You can't be a cop all the time. You must have some downtime?"

"I do." He inhaled her uncertainty. "Why so concerned with my downtime?"

Her ponytail swung back and forth when she shrugged. "You kissed me this afternoon," she reminded him. "You were working then, unless wearing a bulletproof vest has become the latest fashion trend."

Theo smiled. He had been wondering if she would bring that up. "Yes, I was working," he agreed as he placed the folder and the clear bag with the bullet on her desk.

"So it's okay to kiss while you're working, but you can't bad-mouth a guy who was too drunk to remember his friend's dog getting shot?" She held up her hands. "Sorry, I meant incapacitated."

One step had him looking down into her pretty face. "No, it's not okay for me to kiss while I'm working."

"So, kissing random women on the job is a big no-no?" She toyed with the string of her hood. "Then why did you kiss me?"

He pulled in her heat, her need. His lungs filled with her desire, a desire she had for him. He wrapped his fingers around hers as she continued to toy with the string, and tugged her forward. "Because you're not random." He bent his head, and pressed his mouth against those soft, upturned lips.

Christ, she was sweet. He could taste the hot chocolate she had drunk, but there was more, an underlying appeal that he couldn't place. He had tasted it this afternoon, and, like this afternoon, it was alluring and addictive and it created a need in him that he didn't quite understand. The wolf, on the other hand, didn't seem to be having any problems. He wasn't bothered by Theo's sudden need for Drew. The beast simply curled up into a ball and faded into the shadows.

The exact same thing had happened when he'd kissed Drew in the afternoon. He had become twisted with voracious need that heated his blood to boiling point and the wolf had calmed. Drew was the one responsible for these two different reactions, she had to be. He had never had this untamed desire to take a woman before and the wolf had never been so accepting of a woman he had wanted. It was Drew all right, Drew and her sinful sweet lips, that caused this inner conflict.

As he placed her hands on his chest, Drew ran the tip of her tongue along his bottom lip, then pressed her mouth harder against his, opening just wide enough so he could slip his tongue deep. He curled his arms around her, automatically reaching for her behind. He began gently squeezing and massaging both globes. He liked the way his touch caused her to clutch at his shirt. He liked how he could smell her arousal. But most importantly, he liked that he was the one who caused it.

With their mouths open and bodies glued tight, Theo took his time exploring the silky depths. As the kiss became deeper, Theo felt his desire grow, and with it was his need for her compliance. His kiss became hard, even demanding as he explored her sweet warmth. She teased him, sliding her pliant tongue along his teeth, purposely avoiding contact. He pulled her body tighter against his own, nipped at her bottom lip in retaliation for keeping her sweet taste to herself, but quickly soothed the ache when she whimpered.

With each kiss and touch, Drew responded by giving him a little moan or shifted her hips, rocking her behind firmly into his palms. He gripped tighter and pressed the tips of his fingers into the supple flesh between her thighs. He groaned when he felt the damp heat seep through her yoga pants.

Pulling away, Drew grasped his jacket. "Wow!" she puffed out, then, taking a shaky breath, insisted softly, "Please tell me you're not working now."

Grinning, he gave her the truth, "I'm not working now."

"Thank God," she huffed and clasped his wrist, dragging him over to the old leather loveseat. "I'm pretty sure this isn't what Angus had in mind when he bought this thing, but it's mine now so..." She gave him a wicked smile. "Want to help me christen it?"

Theo laughed. What else could he do except agree? He sat and tugged her down so she straddled his hips. He automatically cupped her behind as her lips met his. She didn't tease him this time. She simply met his tongue head-on and allowed him to take control of her mouth in a sensual frenzy. As she held on to his neck, he held onto her bottom tightly, thrusting his hips up as he slid her body along his now hard cock. Her low moan vibrated against his lips. He broke the heated contact and relaxed his hold. "Cheeks still numb?" he asked, kissing the side of her neck.

"A little." She sighed, resting her cheek against his head. "Feels good, though." Unexpectedly she pushed back. "Wait."

Before he could ask what was wrong, she unzipped her white hoodie to reveal lush breasts kept in check by a cream lacy bra with a pink trim. He groaned when he saw her tight nipples peeking through the material and how flushed her skin looked next to the lighter lace. "Please tell me you're wearing a matching thong." He pushed the sweatshirt over her shoulders and let it fall to the floor.

"Maybe," she teased, rocking her hips up and down his cock in slow strokes, her amber eyes locking with his. Her look turned thoughtful as she sucked the corner of her bottom lip into her mouth.

Fear, mixed with desire, filled his sinuses. "Drew?" he asked gently.

"I want to have sex with you, Theo," she blurted out.

That may have been true, yet something wasn't right. The sudden scent of fear and the hesitation spoke volumes. He ran his hands up her thighs, over her hips to her waist. "I want to have sex with you too." He narrowed his eyes. "But not if you're feeling unsure."

"I... I'm not unsure. I want to have sex...with you," she stressed. "But I don't usually jump a guy. Actually this is the first time I've ever jumped a guy." She lowered her gaze as she toyed with the buttons on his work shirt. "Usually, I go out on a few dates with the guy first and if I don't get the creepy vibe, I might kiss him goodnight. I only ever have sex with people I've spent time with and have got to know, I never have sex with a guy I just met."

"That shows good common sense — one-night stands have the potential to be dangerous." He mentally rolled his eyes. *What was that?* Acting like a cop when she was confessing personal information was a douche-bag move. What was the matter with him?

Drew, however, didn't seem to notice. "I'm not a slut," she announced. "I just wanted you to know that."

He smiled at her admission, running his fingers lightly up and down her waist. "I didn't think you were." And he didn't, hadn't before he'd done a background check on her and definitely not afterwards. A background check... That was another douche-bag move, but with the wolf acting up because of her, and her being new in town... He'd had to be sure she was who she had said she was.

"Okay," she breathed and undid a button on his shirt.

"Feel better now that you confessed?" he teased.

"Yes, as a matter of fact I do." She slid another button free.

"Good. Anything else you want to admit to while you're at it?"

She smirked as yet another button was freed. "I really do have unpaid speeding tickets." She met his stare. Bolts of gold lightening brought a mischievous glint to her amber gaze.

He gripped her hips and rocked her against his cock. "Come by the station and pay them off, or the next time you're caught speeding, your car will be impounded."

"Okay, I will." She sighed, rocking her hips of her own accord.

"Good. Now it's my turn." She blinked at him as she continued to pop the buttons free on his shirt, her hips now moving in a slow, steady rhythm. "I don't have relationships while I'm posted to small towns like Tofino."

She stilled. "Oh."

He squeezed her hips and forced her to move. "It caused a few problems at my last posting." Which wasn't a lie, it had caused problems because he had made the mistake of sleeping with a woman who wanted more than just sex. He, of course, hadn't been able to give her what she wanted and not simply because of the wolf, he just hadn't felt any connection to her.

He saw her lip twitch before she mumbled, "Who said anything about a relationship?"

He jerked her forward before he could stop himself, kissing her hard, forcing his tongue past her lips to taste the sweetness of her warm mouth, and only when she melted against him and trailed her fingers into his hair, did he finish. "I didn't tell you to tick you off," he whispered against her lips. "I told you so you would know this isn't a normal thing for me either and that I want this as much as you do."

She sighed, sliding that last button free, and opened his shirt, then spread her fingers wide over his chest. "That's nice to know." She gave him a sexy smile while she explored his skin with her fingers. "Anything else?"

He slipped his hands below the waistband of her yoga pants, felt the thin lace of her thong before gripping the bare flesh of her behind. "Yes." He massaged her soft skin. "I already knew about the speeding tickets."

She laughed softly as she lowered her head and swirled her tongue around his nipple. God, that felt good, but that wasn't where he wanted her mouth. He wanted those full lips circling his cock, he wanted to feel the moist heat wrapped around him, he wanted to feel the muscles tighten in her throat as she sucked him deep and he needed her to be open and submissive for him. He wanted to blame the wolf for that thought. It was a normal characteristic of one animal to want to dominate the other. But the wolf was still tucked away in the corner of his mind. There wasn't a single underlying influence from him at all.

This was strange. He had never wanted a woman to submit to him—he enjoyed women like Drew, confident enough to go after what she wanted. Was his male pride fighting her strength? Or maybe it had been kicked into overdrive when she had shown him her vulnerable side. He really liked that she trusted him to admit her fear to him.

Theo closed his eyes, did his best to push his new-found desire to the side and just enjoy Drew's hands and mouth on him. It was short-lived, however, when she kissed and nipped at his neck while she tugged on the belt to his pants. Before he would allow himself to think, he was tugging Drew off him and laying her on the empty end of the loveseat. He moved between her legs, bent over her, and covered her body with his own. He pressed his mouth to the swell of one breast, kissed it gently while he cupped both through the lacy material. She squirmed under him as he covered a stiff nipple and pulled it, lace and all, deep. Her stomach muscles clenched and her nipples hardened into small beads when he tormented the area with his tongue. She whimpered and tugged on his hair when he went to pay attention to the other breast.

When her other nipple was as pink and swollen as the first, he gazed up at her. "Time to see the full set?" he asked, running his thumbs over the sensitive peaks.

Drew could only nod. Theo was taking her over. First her mind and now he wanted her body and, God help her, she was more than willing to give it to him. This excited and terrified her at the same time. This wasn't her, she didn't just give out the goods to anyone, but with Theo she didn't want to hold anything back.

Theo reached for the top of her pants as she lifted her hips for him. He pulled them off in one fluid movement, dropping them onto the floor. Before he shrugged out of his work shirt, he stared down at her for a moment, his eyes glazed over with the same look of hunger she felt burning her on the inside.

Her voice shook when she asked, "Well?"

He met her stare as he ran his hands over her stomach and down to touch the transparent material of her thong. "My mouth is watering."

Cheeks heating, she pulled him down, running her fingers over his chest up to his shoulders taking his shirt along for the ride and let it fall to the floor. His body was lightly tanned, a slight covering of dark hair spanned his chest and his muscles were solid, well-defined and warm... So warm.

This was heaven. To be held and kissed by a man like Theo was one thing but to know he wanted her just as much as she wanted him was pure ecstasy. He tangled his fingers in her bra straps and tugged them over her shoulders, freeing her breasts from the lace. With a smirk, he cupped both mounds, and lowering his head, suckled gently on one taut nipple.

Drew tried to remain still, the loveseat not allowing them a lot of room to move, but her back arched anyway and she pulled at his short hair. She sucked in a breath when he ran his tongue around the tip, and in a swirling motion licked her entire breast before sliding over to pull the other straining nipple into his mouth. Wet heat collected in her scrap of lace thong when he closed his teeth around the puckered skin. Flicking it ruthlessly with his tongue, then blew cool air over it and the surrounding areola. She cried out, her body shaking, her insides moist and tender. "Theo," she whispered, not trusting that her voice wouldn't crack.

He gazed up at her, slipping his fingers into the sides of her thong. "Yes?"

"Do you…?" She shivered as he began sliding down her lace. "Do you have a condom?"

"No." He stopped and blinked. "You don't either?"

"No, I… I…" She shook her head, trembling once again, this time from disappointment. "I have some at home, but I never carry any with me." She sighed. "I don't suppose one of your many pockets has one?"

He shook his head. "Not the type of equipment I carry on the job." He lowered his forehead to her stomach. "Shit. I'm sorry."

"Don't be. It's not like this was planned." She ran her fingers along the tips of his ears and down his neck. *Damn it!* She wanted Theo so bad, but she couldn't have sex with him without a condom. There was no way she would take the chance. She wasn't ready to be a mum, didn't think she would ever be. There was too much she wanted to do and a baby wouldn't fit into the things she wanted for herself right now. Maybe someday… Maybe, but definitely not now.

He pushed up onto his arms and looked her in the eye. "We might not be able to christen Angus' loveseat, but we can still give it a good go."

She shook her head. "Theo, I can't."

He lowered his face only inches from hers. His breath was hot and sweet on her cool skin. "I'm not talking about intercourse." He gave her a mischievous smirk. "I'm talking about a little playtime."

"You mean…?" She trailed off, holding up two fingers.

"If that's what you want." He gave her a sexy smile.

"I want you," she revealed, straight-faced, then shrugged. "But that will do."

He laughed, then claimed her mouth in a hot kiss. He dragged his hand over her stomach and under her thong. "You will have me." He inched his fingers between her folds. "Soon."

He teased her damp mound as he kissed her again. He rubbed her clit in long-drawn-out moves, slid up and down in fast strokes, only to slow the movement and circle the swollen nub again. She gripped his shoulders, pulled on his hair, even nipped at his lips, anything to get him to slide inside and end her torment, and just when she was about to yell at him, he stole her breath when he drove his fingers deep.

She trembled as he pumped into her, cupping her mound as he went, rubbing his palm against her clit. She pulled away from his and wanted to tell him how unbelievable she was feeling but all she could do was moan. Hearing him groan as a response, Drew realized then that she was receiving this heavenly treat and she hadn't done a thing in return. Well, she could give as good as she got and wanted to. She reached for his pants, freeing the top button, and slid down his zipper.

He shifted his hips, allowing her to inch his pants down enough so she could slip inside and grasp his cock, which from the feel of it was generous in both thickness and length. She moaned in her head, *Oh God, this can't get any better.*

"What are you doing?" he breathed into her mouth.

"Playing." She stroked the silky length, squeezing gently as she went. She smiled, pleased with herself when his nostrils flared.

She gasped when his hips pushed against her mound, driving his fingers farther inside her body while he stroked her. She tried to keep up with him. Tried to give him some sort of pleasure, really wanted him to feel what she was feeling but he was relentless with his torment. She could barely breathe, let alone stroke his cock. As her limbs turned to jelly, he tugged her hand free from his pants and pinned it above her head in an almost painful grip. Then, thrusting his tongue deep as he worked his magic on her core.

As Theo continued his delicious torture, the tops of her thighs began to quiver and she knew that erotic pulsing would follow. It would consume her and send her spinning out of control. The weird thing was that Theo knew too—she wasn't sure how, but he knew and proved her theory right by breaking contact with her mouth, and pulling her nipple deep, he sucked hard, swirling his tongue as she came. No man she had ever been with had caused that sensation in her until now. It was incredible how his kiss and touch drew out that sinfully delicious throbbing of her body. It forced her hips to rock, her belly to tighten. She was pretty sure she moaned some really naughty things before the spinning ended.

When she was able to catch her breath and found the strength to open her eyes, Theo was there staring down at her, a smug grin pulling at his lips.

"You look pretty pleased with yourself." She ran her fingers into his hair, traced the outer shells of his ears.

"Of course." He shifted to the side and forced her to do the same so he was face to face with her. "A man isn't worth his weight if he can't satisfy a woman by making her come." She hadn't heard that saying in a long time, not the *come* part, but the *worth his weight* part. Her Gramps used to say that every once in a while.

"Would that be the male ego talking?" she teased with a sigh.

He scanned her face and flushed breasts as he touched her hip. "You came, therefore you're satisfied. Enough said."

"Who said I was satisfied?" She stared into his eyes, slipping her hand inside his dark pants, watching as the gray became polished silver when she gripped his cock and squeezed, pumping the silken length.

He reached for her behind and cupped the flesh hard as she continued to pump up and down. The defined muscles of his chest flexed, as did the muscles in his jaw, and the veins in his neck became visible. His hooded gaze trailed over her face, stopping on her mouth. The look was so intense and direct that a damp heat gathered in her thong and she ran her tongue along the seam of her lips at the titillating sensation. He groaned, watching the movement. "You have the perfect mouth." He held her face still as he traced her bottom lip with his thumb.

As she moved up his shaft and toyed with the head, she purposely touched the tip of his thumb with her tongue. He groaned again and cupped her cheek, pulling her lips to his.

She vaguely wondered why it was so easy for them to be this free with each other. They barely knew one another. But there was something about Theo, besides his good looks, that pulled her to him , she just didn't know what that something was and probably couldn't explain it if she did know.

His hot kiss suddenly blocked out her unease and she sighed, enjoying the pressure of his lips.

His breathing increased and so did the intensity of his kiss. It was searing and relentless. He held her tight, not allowing her to break contact and pressed on as she stroked his cock faster, clasped it tighter. He tore his mouth free and growled something out in a low voice, but with the combined noise from his ragged breathing, she couldn't make out what he had said. His hips jerked again and this time he yanked her hand away and pinned it to his chest. He rested his face next to hers, pulling her earlobe between his teeth and pinching the tender flesh.

Drew tried to free herself but he held firm. "Theo?"

"No!" He was shaking his head before she had finished his name. "Don't touch me... Not like this." He kissed her wrist then pushed away from her and stood up.

Not like what? What had just happened? What has she done...or not done?

She pulled her bra straps up and reached for her hoodie. "You don't want me to touch you?"

He left her question unanswered and reached for his shirt. He pulled it on and began buttoning it up, then adjusted his work pants.

Drew was beginning to get annoyed. First, she had done something to push him away and now he was ignoring her. "Could you at least do me the courtesy and tell me what I did to freak you out?" Was she that bad at jerking off a guy? It had only been a year since her last time, she couldn't have been that rusty. Unless she had always been that bad and Theo was the first to call her on it. Oh, Jesus, she didn't know which one was worse.

He turned to face her fully dressed, the stiff proof — that she hadn't been too bad — still very evident. He took a deep breath. "You did nothing wrong and you didn't freak me out." He picked up her yoga pants and handed them to her. He frowned, as he watched her tug them on.

"Then what did?"

He exhaled a slow breath as he studied her. "I don't want this old loveseat of Angus' to be the first place you touch me. I want you in my bed." He stepped in front of her and extended his hand to her. She accepted and he helped her to stand. "Your bed is also acceptable." His larger body was close but not touching hers. He gave her an evil smirk. "Mmm, I think I like that idea better."

All she could do was stare at him. She didn't know if she was pissed off because she hadn't gotten to finish what she had started or was flattered because he wanted to wait and have sex with her on a full-size bed instead of a cramped loveseat. Still, she couldn't shake the idea that she wasn't up to his normal standards, which was silly. And really, why should she care? She had gotten off, felt all yummy and, as he put it, *satisfied*. She shouldn't complain, she just couldn't help feeling…hurt. She wanted to touch him, *needed* to and she'd thought… She was positive he had said that he wanted her too… "Whatever." She waved away the hurt then moved to step around him. "At least you can't say I'm a tease."

He quickly reached for her and tugged her in front of him. A shadow crossed his face as he leaned down and kissed her sliding his lips smoothly over hers. "No. You are not a tease." Then, oh so softly, he informed, "You are a temptation, unlike any other."

Chapter Eight

Drew was a temptation, and the only one he'd ever had to deal with since joining with the wolf. Even now, he didn't really want anyone, except Drew. He wasn't sure how it had happened but in a short amount of time she had him and the wolf sitting up and begging.

Stopping in front of his house, Theo then threw the truck into park before shutting the engine off. He reached for his cap with the intent of pulling it on only to stop short when Drew's scent—still strong on his fingers—filled his head and lungs. The wolf, who had quieted since Theo had first seen Drew sitting on the floor with Frankie, snapped his head up and whined for the one person that Theo shouldn't let him whine for.

"I hear yah, bud." He threw the cap on and grabbed his bag. "But I need to sleep."

The wolf whined again, this time ending in a huff.

Theo chuckled, despite his growing concern over Drew and the wolf claiming she was their 'mate'. He wanted nothing more than to get into his truck and drive back to her but he had to try to keep her at a distance, it was better for both of them that way. How long he would be able to do that was still up in the air.

"We need to master the art of playing hard to get," he spoke out loud. The beast grunted his response and Theo chuckled again. "We'll see her tomorrow."

After entering his small house, Theo tossed his work bag and cap onto the kitchen counter and pulled out a chair which was tucked into a small table set. He sat and began untying his boots, thinking about what really had freaked him out with Drew.

It wasn't Drew herself who had alarmed him — it had been the overwhelming need to dominate her that had had him rushing to get out. The urge had risen from deep within him the second he had kissed her on Opitsat. But once he had been alone with her in her office and had inhaled her desire for him, he had become the wolf without actually swapping into the beast. He had become an animal that wanted nothing more than to pin his mate to the ground and assert his control over her mind, body and soul. And he had wanted her to give in to him, longed for it. He needed her to accept him as her lover, that he would be her only lover. It was an irrational thought, but he knew that if Drew hadn't cried out as she'd come, he would still be pinning her to the loveseat doing everything in his power to convince her otherwise.

Placing his boots next to the door, he crossed to the fridge, then pulled out a container with leftover sliced meatloaf, and a bag of rolls. The wolf raised his head when the aroma of meat reached him and licked his lips the precise moment that Theo's stomach growled. He threw a sandwich together in record time and after placing the food in the fridge, he grabbed a bottle of water then kicked the fridge closed.

Resting his hip against the counter, Theo groaned when the food reached his stomach. He had gone too long without eating, something he rarely did. He—and the wolf—needed a steady flow of food. It kept both of them from getting into trouble. Trouble he was all too familiar with.

The one and only time he had ignored the craving for food had been just shortly after the wolf had joined with him and it had not been a good experience.

They had been out scouting for a German sharpshooter, who'd been picking off British officers located behind the line. Theo had just returned from another patrol, and as scarce as food was, he would have found something to eat, but the urgency of his Commanding Officer had had him heading straight back out.

He'd tracked down the shooter with little effort and while the wolf had still been in control, he had killed the man, ripping his windpipe free from his neck. It had been when the taste of blood had flooded the animal's senses that the hunger gnawing at both of them had become too much and Theo had set the wolf free. The beast had prowled the forest searching for a rabbit or some other small creature, but there had been none to be found. As they'd drawn closer to the trenches, the wolf had caught the scent of rats, thousands of rats. They'd scurried across his path, unaware of the predator that stood in their midst, and within seconds the wolf was chewing on a disease-tainted rodent. After three more had been caught and ingested, the wolf had trotted into the forest so they could swap back without any spectators.

Once in human form, Theo had stumbled around looking for his clothes, fighting wave after wave of nausea. The taste of impure flesh had filled his mouth and his body temperature had suddenly risen in an effort to combat the infections that had polluted his system. Slumping to the ground, he'd quickly realized that remaining human would have only increased his chances of becoming ill, whereas the wolf could easily absorb the nutrient they'd needed and rid itself of the infections that would cripple his fragile human body. So he'd swapped back and hidden in the forest until the wolf had been able to completely digest the foul meat.

That had been the only time he'd allowed the wolf to control what they ate. Even during the war, when food had been limited or contaminated with parasites, he and the wolf had gone without unless they'd crossed paths with an animal that was free from disease, which hadn't been very often.

Jesus, that had seemed like a lifetime ago, it *was* a lifetime ago.

Now he made a habit of eating every couple of hours. Though the wolf preferred meat, he had quickly gotten used to the other foods that Theo forced upon him.

He downed his water and headed up the stairs to bed, his thoughts turning from the past to the present. To Drew.

She had been hurt by his pulling away, especially since he had confessed that he wanted her just as much as she wanted him. Even so, how could he tell her that he was sharing a body with the soul of a wolf, who had claimed she was their 'mate', and that he had a sudden urge to dominate her in every possible way. He smiled at the absurd idea as he threw his work uniform in the dirty clothes bin.

Both he and the wolf sighed as he stretched out on his bed. It wasn't just any sigh. It was a sigh filled with longing. Longing!

"Damn." He rubbed at his face then dropped his arms over his head.

He had to muzzle this obsession he had for her. His wants and the wolf's needs couldn't influence how he lived his life. He had lived with the wolf since 1915, and thanks to advancing technology, it had become increasingly more difficult to keep the wolf hidden. Exposing his tenant would bring nothing but a world of hurt to himself, the wolf and anyone that was tied to him, especially if they were tied to him romantically.

He could never let Drew find out about the wolf, even though his gut was telling him she would never betray him, if they became 'something'. He couldn't risk it. No matter what he felt in his gut or what the wolf claimed about her being their mate. He couldn't willingly risk her. But most of all he couldn't take the chance of what would happen if Drew ever found out the truth. How would she look at him when he swapped into the wolf? Fuck, he didn't even want to think about that.

He rubbed his face, stopped when he caught her scent again and grinned, remembering the way her body had moved under his, the taste of her skin, the enticing fragrance of her damp need. Jesus, she had been so wet and ready. Ready for him.

He sighed, flipping over onto his stomach, staunching the sudden ache in his groin. This was going to be very difficult for him and the wolf, but tomorrow was another day. That would be soon enough to begin restraining the desire he had for Drew, assuming that she wanted to see him.

The wolf released a low growl that mimicked his feeling precisely.

The upside was that she was angry because she hadn't gotten to jerk him off. That, he was going to take as a good sign. Good sign or not, he had to start to keep her at a distance. "Yeah right," he mumbled into the pillow.

* * * *

"That's it, I'm done." Drew looked over at Ruby who was stretched out on the loveseat in her office. She slouched into her chair and rubbed her eyes.

Man she was tired. She leaned into the armrest and propped her head up. She hadn't really slept, her time divided between taking care of Frankie and tending to her regular appointments. The only time she went home was to change and grab a quick bite for her and Ruby. The loveseat in her office was quickly turning into a bed. Sadly it was nowhere near as comfortable as it was when Theo had been there.

She focused on the untouched cardboard cup still sitting on her desk. Theo had dropped off the coffee early this morning. He'd placed it on her desk as he had asked her how Frankie was doing and if she had gotten any sleep. Of course she hadn't slept and it was his fault. To get her hot and horny then insult her by telling her he didn't want her to touch him then tell her she was a temptation, only to leave? She was hurt and confused and pissed off. And she hated that she couldn't stop thinking about him all through the night, and all day, thanks to that cup sitting on her desk. Every time she looked at the damn thing she thought about Theo. Just like now.

"Damn it!" She reached for the cup with the intent of throwing it in the garbage but stopped when she grabbed it. She popped off the lid and checked the contents. Yup, it was a cappuccino, just like he had said. He had bought this for her because he'd thought she could use it. Her stomach flipped unexpectedly.

"Damn it," she moaned. How the hell was she supposed to stay pissed off at him when he went out of his way to do something nice for her? It was probably to make up for last night, and he should be kissing up, she just wished he hadn't pulled away. The memory still had her feeling undesirable even though he had labeled her a temptation. She sighed, not enjoying how insecure she felt. It wasn't a normal thing and she really didn't like that a man had caused it.

Standing, Drew then walked to the small washroom and dumped the cold liquid down the drain then tossed the cup into the recycle bin. She was just heading back to her office to pack up when there was a knock at the front door.

Ruby beat her to it, her curled tail wagging in greeting to the person waiting outside. It was funny — before she even saw who was at the door she knew it was Theo. She flicked on the outer light and sighed when she saw him standing there.

She crossed her arms. "Can I help you, Officer?"

He laughed and crossed his own arms. "Let me in, Drew."

"Why? You have no reason to be here." She frowned, the memory of last night stirring those hurt feelings again. "I called the station and informed Ben that Randall took Frankie home a little while ago."

He stared back at her, his eyes flashing. "Let me in, Drew." She blinked when she heard a rumble mix with his words.

Despite what she thought she had heard, she reached for the lock. As she gripped the door handle, she paused when Theo moved closer to the door. A thin piece of glass separated them. He looked down at her. It was the same look the gray wolves on the beach had given her, as though they wanted to devour her.

She paused. What was she doing? This was stupid. She shouldn't open the door—he had given her self-esteem a good kick in the ass, would probably do so again. *Not* opening the door was for the best.

"Drew." Her name was spoken in a low pleading tone that locked onto her unsuspecting heart.

She sucked in a breath as she became lightheaded and unlocked the door. Holding it open, she informed him, "I was just about to lock up and head home."

He nodded and stepped inside. "I'll wait."

Her stomach tightened at the close contact. "Why?"

He ignored her question. "Go get your stuff, I'll wait here."

It wasn't long before she was back at the door with her bag and keys. Ruby, the traitor, was leaning into Theo's thigh getting her head scratched.

"Ready?"

"Mmm." She frowned at him and asked her question again. "Why are you waiting for me, Theo?"

He gave her a wink, leaving her question unanswered again, and reached for the door. Ruby bolted out and tore around the front giving everything a good sniff while Drew locked up.

Theo walked beside her as she crossed to her car, not touching her just walking quietly next to her. As she threw her bag into her car, Theo whistled for Ruby to come. When Ruby was settled in the back seat, Theo grabbed the car door and held it in place. Leaning in close, he informed, "I'll follow you," then he politely closed her door.

"Why?" she gritted into her rear-view mirror as she drove home. "So you can make me feel like shit again?" She didn't want that, but she wanted Theo. This strange mixture of hurt and infatuation confused the hell out of her. She wanted Theo, had wanted him last night. Yet she was worried about being rejected again. She felt like she was getting involved in something she didn't quite understand, namely Theo.

She had the sudden impulse to speed up and try to escape him. She even pressed her foot down on the accelerator, but, as though he knew what she was trying to do, he flashed his police lights once.

Sighing, she slowed and continued at a normal speed and arrived at her house shortly after.

Once in front of her house, she opened the car door and stood, coming face to face with Theo. "You need to get into the station and pay for those speeding tickets." He took her bag and closed her door, after Ruby had jumped from the car. "I'll set aside time for you tomorrow."

"Okay." She eyed him over her shoulder as she climbed the steps to her front porch.

"I'm serious, Drew." He was right behind her. "I could have given you a speeding ticket just now, but I didn't because your emotions are controlling your actions."

"Yeah, well," she huffed, opening the door. She whistled to Ruby and stepped inside, expecting Theo to follow. But when she looked back, he was still standing outside on the porch staring at her.

"Why?"

Drew felt the air between them still and become heavy, like a humid pause just before a thunderstorm. The muscles in her arms and legs squeezed in response to the lack of circulating air. "Why what?" she asked.

"Why are you upset with me?" His voice dropped. "Is it because of last night?"

She nodded, knowing instantly that he would know if she was lying, and grumbled, "I've never been told by a man not to touch him. It made me feel like I ..." She shook her head, annoyed that she had almost shared her true feelings. "Are you going to stand there or are you going to come in?"

"Are you going to ask me in?" he countered, holding out her bag to her.

She took the bag and dropped it next to the door. "Do you want to come in?"

He sighed. "Yes, Drew." He nodded. "I want to come in. I also want to finish what we started last night, but I was taught to enter a house only when invited by the owner."

A giddy feeling bubbled up at his formal statement, making her smile like an idiot. As the air around them became light once again, she did her best to remain cool and leaned into the door. "How do I know you won't pull the same thing as last night?"

He stepped to the threshold of the house but didn't cross the imaginary line. "I thought I made it pretty clear that I wanted to come back for more."

"Maybe I thought it was just a line." She looked at him in his cop uniform and sighed. Oh God, he was yummy. "That was the first time I was ever put into that situation. I felt..." She waved her hand, trying to make light of the circumstance. "It doesn't matter."

"It matters." He paused briefly as his nostrils flared. "Invite me in, Drew." His lips pulled into a sensual grin. "And I promise I will make it up to you."

A nervous giggle escaped and heat spread across her face. "Sounds as though I'm about to be satisfied...again."

The grin remained as he nodded.

She reached for the side of his vest and tugged him inside. He closed the door behind him and locked it. He enfolded her in his arms as she gripped the other side of his vest. She looked up, his silvery eyes startling thanks to his dark expression. "Have you had dinner?" He pulled up her raincoat then tugged up her shirt, flattening his palms against the bare skin of her back. He nuzzled her neck and kissed the skin just below her ear.

"Not yet," she mumbled, bracing herself just in case her knees gave out.

He unzipped her light raincoat and let it fall to the floor before tugging her shirt up. "Can you wait until after?" He reached for the hooks on her bra.

"Yeah," she breathed into his shoulder. "I can wait."

Chapter Nine

Drew's legs automatically circled Theo when he lifted her up. It hadn't occurred to her to tell him where she slept, but he seemed to find her room anyway.

He released her thighs as he stopped next to the bed. Her feet touched the floor as he finally moved his mouth over hers. The touch was light, not hard or demanding like the previous night, as though he was keeping his actions in check. The softer touch was nice—it sent shivers down her back, caused goose bumps to prickle at her skin, but she wanted that intense kiss and touch that set her body on fire.

She ran her fingers into his hair, tugged lightly at the short dark strands so her mouth was firm against his, then sucked on his bottom lip.

He groaned as he allowed her access and she slowly slid her tongue against his. She stroked the sides, made small circles over the tip and traced his straight white teeth before slowly licking the contour of his firm lips.

He groaned for a second time but this time his fingers dug into her skin as he encased her in his arms. His kiss became more urgent and his body became hard...everywhere. His arms and shoulders flexed. His thighs were solid and she could feel his cock lengthen, before he asked. "You said you have condoms?"

He released his hold on her, then, reaching under his arm, pulled at the Velcro straps that held the vest in place and tugged them loose before ripping the strap on his shoulder free.

"In my bathroom," she confirmed.

He turned from her, asking over his shoulder, "Under the sink?"

"Yes." A slow smile pulled at her lips as she watched him walk into her attached bathroom. Seconds later, the cupboard closed with a bang and Theo reappeared with a funky black and purple box.

"What are these?" Coming to a stop in front of her, he flipped the box over and read the back. "Designer condoms?"

"No." She tapped the cardboard, pointing to the swirly black tag line located on the bottom of the box. "Mind-blowing pleasure for the woman in your life."

"What's so mind-blowing about them?" he asked, peeling open the end.

Drew laughed. "I don't know. It's the first time I've bought this brand, but they look like fun and they're ribbed for my pleasure."

"I'm the old-fashioned type and prefer just a plain old extra-large condom," he teased, tossing the box on the bed. He spread his fingers wide as he moved his hands along her waist and slipped them under hem of her shirt and caressed her bare skin. "But those will do. Although..." He traced the outer edge of her breast with his thumbs as he steadily removed her shirt, finally tugging it over her head and dropping it to the floor next to his bulletproof vest. "I doubt you'll need all that extra stimulation." He skimmed his fingers down her back and smoothly unhooked her bra. Then he guided the silky straps down her arms.

When her bra was added to the growing pile of clothes on the floor, Drew pulled his long-sleeved T-shirt free from his pants and petted the heated muscles of his stomach up to his chest where she could feel the hard outline to his defined pecs.

"Mmm." She moaned lightly when he cupped her breasts. She liked that his hands were slightly callused. The rough skin intensified his touch, and it caused her nipples to pull into tight pink beads.

He allowed her to pull his work shirt over his head and she dropped it, not caring where it landed. She was too enthralled with his body. He was tall and athletic, with just enough muscle mass so that it was obvious that he took care of himself, but not so much that he looked like he was into body-building. Perfect.

She felt her mouth beginning to water. Theo was all male and deliciously so. She loved the chest hair and his rough touch, the deep voice and the strength that accompanied it. She trailed her palms up his chest to his shoulders and she inched closer so she could press her breasts into his heated skin. Then, without thought, she lifted her face just as Theo claimed her mouth once again.

His kiss was slow and coaxing. He traced her waist then popped the button on her pants free before lowering the zipper. He forced them over her backside and down her thighs where they slid the rest of the way down. She stepped out of the pants and flicked them with her foot across the room without breaking contact with Theo's lips.

For a long time they stood together, kissing. Theo caressed the soft skin of her shoulders and back, down to her bottom where he kneaded the supple flesh. She was ready for him, he could sense the need in her. It was almost as strong as the scent that clung to her body. God, he liked her smell of arousal. It was fresh, with a unique mixture of spicy and sweet, and Theo knew she would taste the same way.

He forced her to step back, pinning her legs against the bed and he sat her down before leaning into her. She looped her arms around his neck as she lay on her bed. He raised her face and trailed his tongue around the outer edge of her ear then sucked the dainty lobe between his teeth. She exhaled slowly and rested her cheek against his head when he kissed her collar bone and down to the swell of her breasts.

Caressing them gently, Theo grinned. They fitted his hands perfectly. Not too big so they spilled over the sides, and not too small so they disappeared when he cupped them. The petit nipples were delicate with a lush rosy hue to them. He cupped both at the same time holding them firmly in place, and proceeded to kiss his way between the creamy mounds. He circled the tips with his thumbs and he felt the skin become taut and push against his touch. He kissed the underside of a single breast, and she shifted impatiently, her breathing quickening.

As he brushed his lips against her tender skin, she pulled at his hair, trying to force him to the tightly puckered nipple. He held firm and teased the outer pink ring, and almost smiled when she arched her thrusting her breast up. He finally gave in and drew the sweet tip deep, sucking it gently at first, then harder when she moaned his name. His trigger point was when she locked her legs around his waist. He ground his body down onto hers. Nipped at her breast, clamped his teeth around her small peak and flicked it with his tongue before sucking it deep. She cried out, but not from his ministrations. She cried out only when he pulled away and moved to the other breast. Her lusty groan quickly followed and she continued to hold his head to her breast as he thrust his hips, grinding his cock against her.

When he finally did pull away from her breast it was to kiss his way down her stomach. He held her waist in his hands, rubbed his thumbs along her sides when he licked a long trail to her neat little belly button. He raised his head and touched the cute pink angel ring pierced through her skin.

He wasn't a big fan of body piercings or even tattoos. He was from a time when decorating the skin came in the form of women putting on rouge and lipstick and that hadn't started until the 1920s. He didn't understand why people wanted to mark and in some cases scar their own bodies with the intent of wanting to appear more attractive. He had a deep respect for the human form, especially the female form, but he had to admit, this tiny piece of jewelry nestling against Drew's silky skin was quite nice to look at.

"I can't believe I missed this yesterday."

She giggled. "You were busy." She skimmed her fingers along the outer edge of his ear. "What do you think? A bit girly?"

"No." He shook his head. "It looks pretty on you." He kissed it.

She closed her eyes and dropped her head back when he kissed her stomach again. He hooked his fingers in the sides of her black panties and eased them over her hips and down her legs. Then he ran his hands along the outside until he reached her hips where he clamped around the smooth skin and yanked her to the edge of the bed.

"Theo!" she gasped as she grabbed at the bed to stop from sliding off the edge.

"Shhh," Theo cooed, holding her by the backs of her thighs. "You're safe. Now open your legs for me."

He locked eyes with her as he knelt down between her parted thighs. Her face flushed and he drew in her embarrassment and lust. He wanted to tell her that she had no reason to feel embarrassed, that he wanted to see her like this, open and exposed to him. Any man did, it was a turn-on to know your lover trusted you enough to let you see the most intimate parts of their body. He held her gaze as he slid the backs of two fingers through her wet folds. He repeated the stroke again but stopped alongside her clit and circled it slowly.

She sucked in a breath as her hips jerked. "Theo."

He could still sense her embarrassment, and, though he wanted to keep teasing her glistening pink skin, he opted for tasting her instead.

She groaned as she ran her fingers through his hair, traced his ears. God damn, he liked when she touched his ears — there was something very sensual and soothing about it. A low growl vibrated from his chest and he was unsure where it had come from. As he licked Drew in long slow strokes he searched for the wolf. Theo found the beast curled up in the back of his mind not quite awake but not sleeping either, but he was calm and that alone spoke volumes. He was content now that Theo was finally with Drew, whereas during the day he had been a bloody nuisance.

Drew bucked her hips when he sucked the swollen bud into his mouth and pulled gently. He rubbed his tongue along the side in quick succession before giving her another long stroke that covered every inch of her spicy core right up to the tip of her thin strip of tight curly blonde hair.

"Theo." This time she called to him in frustration. "Stop making me wait."

He answered her plea and he slid two fingers into her wet opening and began a slow pumping as he covered her body. He grinned when he saw that her face was flushed, her nipples erect into little points, and her sinful lips were dark pink and swollen from her nibbling on them. She was sin and purity rolled into one beautiful package.

Her lids were lust-filled and heavy and the gold of her irises flashed brilliantly next to the stark black of the pupils. She scraped her nail down his cheek. "Why do you get to have all the fun?"

"Because you're the one who's naked." She sucked in a breath when he curved his fingers up to caress her sweet spot and rubbed his palm against her clit.

"Oh my God!" She pressed her face into his shoulder and nipped at the skin. "I-I… Want to… Oh!"

He repeated the graze to both sweet spots as he kissed her neck. "What do you want?"

"I want to… To touch you too. Make you feel this." She covered his hand, resting between her thighs.

"You will have my undivided attention after. But for now, hold on to me."

Drew did as he commanded and pressed her face into his chest. He pumped faster, flicked her delicate earlobe with his tongue as he stroked harder. "You feel so wet. I love touching your body. Inside." He rubbed his thumb in teasing circles. "And out." He sucked the soft skin under her ear between his lips.

Drew clung to him, shaking. Her fast and choppy breathing heated his chest, her rocking hips were in perfect sync with his pumping fingers, and she dug her fingernails into his hair when she finally cried out. Her body pulsed around his digits, and his palm became damp with her lust. God this was perfect, and so fucking sexy.

Theo held tight as her convulsing slowed. She panted next to his ear, a shiver enveloping her entire body. "How do you do that?"

He kissed her shoulder as he rolled her onto her back. "Do what?"

"That... Make me shiver like that."

She still held him tightly, stroking the skin at the top of his shoulders. "I've never had an orgasm that...crazy, overwhelming."

"Would you be willing to freely admit that I was the one who triggered said orgasm?" he teased.

Her sexy laugh caused an ache deep in his body and, not caring that he should give her a few minutes to recuperate, he lowered his head so that his mouth was a breath away from hers. Resting his hips between her legs, he slowly thrust forward, the pressure and moist heat from her body teasing his all-too-ready cock.

She ran her hand down between their bodies and rubbed the bulge through his pants. "No more playtime?" she asked in a pout.

His nostrils flared as he watched the liquid gold of her unique eyes darken to a rich amber color. Her long black lashes lowered slightly as she tugged on his pants. He lifted his hips for her and her pout turned into a sly smile. "Maybe a little playtime…" She licked her sinful lips. "Please."

He nodded without thinking. He wanted her lips wrapped around his cock, but if she was willing to touch him, who was he to argue?

She slipped inside his pants where she curled her fingers around him, and in slow strokes, began stroking his hard length. She ran the tip of her tongue along the seam of her lips, making the plump skin glisten. He groaned, tangling his fingers in her silky hair and, holding her still, slanted his mouth over hers.

She nipped at his lips and he thrust his shaft further into her palm. "Drew." He closed his eyes, his hips rocking. "You're killing me."

She continued to squeeze him tight and breathed into his ear. "Good." She flicked his ear with her wet tongue. "Now you know how it feels."

His grin quickly disappeared when she swirled her finger over the head. "Fuck," he growled. He quickly reached for the condoms, then pulled one free from the box. While he tore open the purple wrapper, Drew tugged on his cock. He gazed down just in time to see her wet lips cover his shaft.

He let out a long shaky breath as the moist heat of her mouth surrounded him, and she sucked him deep. Oh God, this was perfect. She was perfect. They were perfect. He was still unsure about this whole 'mate' thing, but he wanted her…badly. The desire to dominate her was so strong. He wanted to fist his hands in her hair—not caring if she cried out—and thrust uncontrollably into her hot mouth. He fisted his hands at his sides instead while he fought a natural instinct that he'd had no idea he even had.

When his muscles tensed and his groin became heavy, he jerked away cursing. He watched her, fighting his body as a frown wrinkled her brow. Then she did something he wished she hadn't... She licked at her lips like a contented kitten. A low growl echoed around his head as he watched her pink tongue trace along her bottom lip. Theo was well aware that the wolf was still curled up in the back of his mind, which meant that it was he, himself, that had been the cause of the feral sound. And that scared him because this... This feeling of raw need and possessiveness was new.

"Is everything okay?"

Squeezing his jaw tight, he cupped her cheek gently and bent to kiss her. He brushed his lips over hers, kissed the tip of her delicate nose. He forced his pants down his thighs, and quickly covered himself. Then hooking his arms under her legs, he yanked her to the edge of the bed where he didn't bother waiting for her approval and drove between her flushed skin and into her narrow body.

Theo sighed, closing his eyes. The feeling was unbelievable. Her warm muscles clung to him as he pulled from her. Drew whimpered as though pleading for his return and exhaled lightly when he did. As he began moving his hips in a steady rhythm, Drew wrapped her legs around his waist, locking them tight. She ran her hands up his chest to his face where she cupped his cheeks. Her breath was shallow and sweet and he bent down so he could draw her exhale deeper into his lungs as she urged him on.

"Faster, Theo."

He pushed farther into her, pounding hard. She scraped his neck with her nails, ran her tongue along his shoulder, nipping at the skin, and squeezed her legs tighter around his waist. Every touch to his skin, every shift of her hips, every breath she took set his body on fire with a need so deep he couldn't quite understand it.

Releasing her thighs, he then pulled her arms from his neck and forced them above her head, pinning her by the wrists. He pushed up onto his arms, easily overshadowing her smaller frame, and looked down into her face. Her wicked mouth, red and swollen, was parted erotically. Her eyes were swirling pools of gold, and her body, her smooth, sweet-tasting body flushed as he continued to pin her to the bed. He gazed down the length of her. She was so slender, so feminine and so incredibly enticing... Another growl bounced around the inside of his head, and Theo found himself in the middle of a silent struggle — the battle between his desire to be the gentle lover and the need to devour this woman from the inside out.

He tightened his grip on her as his frenzied pace began rocking their bodies and the bed. She tried to free herself but he wouldn't let her go, couldn't let her go. He threaded his fingers with hers instead and ordered against the corner of her mouth, "Squeeze me, baby. I need to feel you tight around me." He slowed his pace and growled out loud when he felt her legs and every other silky muscle squeeze him. He drew his hips back and drove his cock so deep he pressed against her inner thighs, sealing their sweat-coated bodies.

She cried out as the brush of his body stroked her swollen clit. He kept on with the steady thrusts, pulling out and driving deep, tormenting her. She tangled her fingers with his, her nails scratching the flesh on the backs. Her inner muscles gripped him so strongly it felt almost painful. "Raise your hips, Drew... That's it. Ah, God."

Her breathing became sporadic and her body shook. He fought hard not to come, but then again so did she. He didn't want her to hold back—he wanted her to shiver in his arms, he wanted to hear her cry out. "Don't fight it. Let go."

"I... I'll wait..." She was waiting for him, she wanted to come with him. He was strangely touched by that.

He nuzzled her cheek, kissed the side of her mouth as he thrust into her faster. "Let go, Drew."

And she did, the same moment he did. The orgasm was long and intense and so utterly mind-blowing that he hoped it would never end. They shook and trembled as he pinned her to the bed.

Her breath warmed his neck. Damn, he liked that. He liked how her body went all soft and pliant after their trembling had subsided, and he liked the way she sighed as he tucked her into her bed. But most of all, he liked how their scents mixed together and hung heavily in the air.

Chapter Ten

Drew sat up in bed and looked around. The sun filtered through her windows and streaked across her face. Squinting she could see her room as she had left it the night before, blinds open, clothes dropped to the floor in a rushed manner, an open condom box sitting on her bedside table.

The only thing that she wanted to see was the one thing that wasn't there... Theo.

Her stomach dropped low, disappointment filling her chest.

Now this was a first. Usually she was relieved when the guy went home, even Jamie, whom she had dated for over a year. She always wanted him gone when they were done and never cared when the door hit him in the ass on the way out. Jamie was always cool about it, though some guys... Not so much. It was completely personal and completely selfish. She wanted to sleep by herself, in her own bed, and she did *not* want to wake up next to the guy she had just slept with. She wasn't the type of woman that woke up before the guy the next morning and fixed her hair and reapplied makeup, just so she looked as appealing as the night before. Screw that—that was way too much work.

Besides, she enjoyed her space in the morning. She liked to stumble around with her messy hair pinned up, liked wearing her baggy pajamas. She didn't want to make coffee for anyone but herself and she liked beginning her day by getting breathed on by a dog with stinky breath. She had no desire to tamper with her normal routine because she had had a 'sleepover'. But this morning... There was no desire to stumble around and get her coffee, no Ruby to breathe in her face and no satisfaction that she was alone.

She was swamped by a rush of different emotions. She felt disappointed again because she wanted to see him, and hurt because he was gone. Even after he had called her a temptation and promised to make up for his actions the night before at the clinic, which he had... And then some. He hadn't said he would be here in the morning and she'd never asked him to be, so she had no reason to feel this way.

Then a sudden realization slapped her on the ass.

"So this is what it feels like when someone sneaks out after a night of incredible sex." This was what her friends had felt when their dates left in the middle of the night. *Wow*. Her shoulders slumped. She should have been more sympathetic while listening to her girlfriends bitch, because they were right... This really sucked.

Sighing, she gazed at her alarm clock and swore. "Shit." She had forgotten to turn on her alarm last night—for obvious reasons—and now she was late. She had twenty minutes to shower, dress and drive to the clinic before her first appointment of the day.

She jumped from the bed, crossed into the bathroom and froze when she saw a note stuck to the mirror.

Tonight you'll get to eat. Promise.

Theo's handwriting was elegant, almost old-worldly, as though he had been taught to write in a specific manner.

There was a stupid smile covering her face when she looked at her reflection in the mirror and that sucky disappointed feeling slowly faded.

She readied herself in record time and grabbed her bag and keys, calling for Ruby to follow. She was speeding down the road in a matter of minutes, thinking about her morning appointments and how she could fit in a run to Milk & Sugar to grab a coffee, when she heard the siren. She automatically glanced at her speed. "Shit." She looked in her rear-view mirror and she noticed the flashing lights behind her. "Shit, shit."

Pulling over to the side of the road, Drew then stopped before shifting the car into park then gaped when she looked again, she saw Theo climbing out of his police truck. She rolled down the window, a mixture of excitement and dread filling her stomach. He stopped at her window and without so much as a greeting said, "Driver's license, please."

Drew sat for a moment just staring at the name tag pinned to the left side of his bulletproof vest. She gripped the wheel and tried to explain, "I was running late... I didn't..."

"Give me your license, Drew," he demanded quietly.

"Why?" She frowned when he lowered his head. She couldn't see his expression because of his dark sunglasses, but boy, did they look good on him.

"I told you to get into the station and pay for those speeding tickets." She looked at his mouth as he lectured her and she remembered how hot those firm lips had felt against her skin. "Drew!" he snapped. "Are you listening to me?"

She nodded, trying to focus on what he was saying.

"I stopped you from speeding last night, but I will not ignore the fact that you just flew past me twenty-five kilometers over the limit."

Drew shook her head when he mentioned how fast she had been going. "What? No way. I wasn't going that—"

He took a deep breath and straightened. "Close your window and get out."

"What?" she asked for a second time.

"Get out of your car, Drew."

She opened the door, the dread now overpowering any memory of their night together.

"Get your bag."

She threw her wallet into her bag, then climbed out.

"Stand back there." He pointed to the trunk of her car.

She gaped up at him. Was he going to...? Was she under...? "No!" The word burst from her before she had time to stop it.

"Excuse me?" Theo asked quietly.

"You can't arrest me, I..." She stuttered on her explanation. "I-I have Ruby with me... And I have patients waiting for me too!"

His nostrils flared as he pointed to the back of her car again. "Stand by the trunk of your car, *off* of the road."

She blinked, stepped away from him and watched as he slid her license into the pocket on one thigh. He closed her front door and opened the back. He locked onto Ruby's collar. He then urged the dog out of the car, closed the door, and walked past her to the tailgate of his truck.

"Hey, what are you doing?" Drew quickly followed. "You can't take my dog. I'd rather you arrested me."

This time Theo shook his head. "Stop overreacting."

She watched as he opened the tailgate and coaxed Ruby into jumping into the large kennel secured inside. After giving her a pat he closed the cage door then the tailgate and ordered. "Lock your car and get in."

"What...? Why?"

"Now, Drew." He walked away and got into the truck.

Oh my God! This could not be happening because of speeding tickets. No way! Theo wasn't that kind of dick... Was he? Just because she'd had sex with him didn't mean she knew him. What she did know he was that he was a hottie cop, knew he had a good relationship with the locals and with the Reserve over on Opitsat, plus he was friends with Angus.

"Drew," Theo called from his truck.

She slowly walked to the passenger side door and gripped the handle. When she looked up, Theo was staring at her, his dark sunglasses now on top of his head. He was pissed off, she could see it, but she could see something else. God, she hoped this didn't change things between them. Last night had been so great. She ran her tongue along her suddenly dry lips as apprehension swirled around her belly.

He lowered his gaze to her mouth and followed her tongue and there was a new expression. Heat? As in, 'I want you now'? She couldn't help but smile, feeling a little relieved. His eyes flashed once again but this time it was anger. "Get in."

She opened the door and hopped in. They drove in silence until the suspense got the better of her. "So... What, you haul my ass to jail and keep my dog?"

"You have a bad habit of jumping to conclusions." He turned down the chatter on the police scanner.

"Yah well, what do you expect? You took my license and locked my dog up in your truck." She clutched at her bag on her lap.

Theo shook his head. "I'm driving you to work. I put Ruby in the back kennel because it is the safest place for her and I will keep your license until you pay off your speeding tickets." He looked at her. "Which will be today."

She opened her mouth but he stopped her when he asked a quiet question, "Won't it?"

She clicked her tongue. "It's not like you're giving me choice."

He pulled to a stop just outside the clinic. "No, I'm not."

"Fine, whatever. I'll go over when I have a break." She threw open the door, hopped out then slammed it shut. Marching to the rear of the truck to set Ruby free, she mumbled to herself about how stupid men were. She wasn't expecting Theo to answer her.

"We have our moments." He opened the tailgate and reached for the lock on the kennel. "But more times than not, when a woman thinks a man is acting stupid, it's because things aren't going in her favor. Those are the times when our *stupidity* has a solid reason behind it, like keeping your car from being impounded." He opened the kennel door and Ruby, the traitor, wriggled right to Theo and nuzzled his chin. Drew stood and looked at the scene, then in a huff that even she considered quite dramatic, turned and stomped to the door not bothering to wait for Ruby.

* * * *

The morning didn't go any better after Theo had dropped her off. She ended up being late for her first appointment, which had her running behind all morning. She called a patient by the wrong name—twice—never got her coffee and had forgotten to pack her lunch. Not that she had time for lunch. She had to get to the police station so she could pay off her speeding tickets, get her license and get her ass back in time for her afternoon patients and she had only twenty minutes to do it.

Thankfully, the station wasn't far and she walked over with her wallet in hand. She pulled open the door, praying that Theo wasn't there. She really had no desire to see him after this morning. *Argh, the jerk.* If she saw him while paying off her tickets, she was pretty sure her head might just explode.

As it was, she was helped by a woman in her mid-fifties who knew exactly who she was when she walked in, calling her by name. Which meant that Theo had told her why she was coming in. What a jackass. What made things worse, the woman, Joanne, was so damn pleasant and actually really nice about the whole thing that Drew felt a little guilty about being snippy with her.

She placed her wallet on the counter and smiled, listening to the woman talk.

"Theo said you would be in a hurry when you finally came by. So I printed up everything you would need so we can get you in and out as fast as possible."

That was the only nice thing he had done. His thoughtful gesture, however, wouldn't help his case. He was still being a dick, but she didn't have the time to think about it. She filled out the paperwork, paid off the tickets and got her license. She was on her way back when she spotted Theo leaning against the front of his truck outside the clinic. She crossed the parking lot and walked past him.

"Thank you," was all he said.

Drew stopped and turned to face him. "What for?"

"For paying off your speeding fines. Now you can start with a clean slate."

Her mouth dropped open. "You're thanking me for paying off my tickets?" He nodded. "Are you stoned?" she asked.

There was a slight twitch at the bottom corner of his right eye. "I beg your pardon?"

My God, he was so polite, it drove her nuts. She gripped her wallet. "You heard me. I said last night that I would come by today and pay them off. You didn't have to be a tool and pull me over and then take my license."

She studied him as he rested against his police truck, waiting for his response. Besides the twitch, he calmly waited for her to finish venting. And man did she need to vent, it made her feel better. "And why do you care if I have speeding tickets or not?" she snapped. "It's none of your business."

He folded his arms across his chest and took a deep breath before he spoke. "As a police officer, it *is* my business because you were speeding." He then lowered his voice. "And this has nothing to do with last night. I didn't set out to do this. I know why you were running late this morning and I know I was the cause, but you can't use that as an excuse for your mistakes."

First he's polite and now he's logical. Great! "You're right. I shouldn't have used it as an excuse," she agreed, her voice a little high. "But you were being a dick. That's the second time you've done that, you know."

He raised a single, dark eyebrow. "Done what?"

She quickly scanned the parking lot, making sure no one was listening, then whispered, "Make me com—" She hesitated on the word then substituted, "Feel…great. Then you do a one-eighty and turn into an ass-hat. So from where I stand, it looks deliberate."

A frown darkened his expression, as he looked her dead in the eye. "It wasn't."

Drew knew right away he wasn't lying to her but she still felt hurt, she couldn't help it. "Well, it sure felt like it."

"There won't be a third." He gave her an accepting nod. The serious expression turned into a cheeky smirk. "Feel better now that you got to screech like a hen?"

She felt her mouth drop open in surprise at his choice of words. Then snapping it shut she hissed, "Screw you."

With a chuckle, he pushed off the truck and issued an order as he moved to the driver side door. "I want you to call me when you're ready to go home and I'll take you to your car. It's not safe walking along the highway at night."

"Ha! Now you care?" She shook her head at the twists and turns her emotions were going through as she spoke to him. Angry because of his actions this morning, hurt because she felt it was deliberate, · confused because she now wasn't sure what to think, and desire. Lord, she still wanted him even after this bizarre morning.

A dry laugh to escaped, as she walked away. "No thanks, Officer Grey," she called over her shoulder, hoping her rebellious attitude would piss him off. "I can find my own way home." And with that said, she went back to work.

* * * *

Drew's rebellious attitude did piss Theo off. He had told her to call him, but knew deep in his gut that she wouldn't, so he really shouldn't be this annoyed. He just couldn't help it. He hated the idea of her walking along the highway. It was only single-lane but it still had a high rate of traffic — and she was alone — and it was dark. She shouldn't have walked alone. He inhaled a deep breath. The damp earthy smell of the forest filled his head and body and helped to clear his mind. What the hell was the matter with her? Was she trying to get herself killed just to spite him? She was acting like a spoiled brat.

The beast agreed with a low grunt.

The wolf easily cleared a log and continued its course. The forest was black but he could see clearly through the wolf's eyes. He could smell what the wolf smelled — the damp ground, the pine trees, the salt from the ocean, the other animals that lived in the area. He could hear what the wolf heard — the rain hitting the leaves on the tops of the trees, the crash of the waves in the distance and the music coming from Drew's house.

The wolf came to a stop just before breaking through the trees that surrounded the back of Drew's house. In the shadows, the beast sat panting and looked up at the light streaming through the open door that led to the small Juliet balcony. Thankfully, the curtains were open so he could see clearly into her bedroom.

As he watched and wondered what Drew was doing, music drifted down. The female singer had a low, sultry voice. The kind of voice that conjured images of tangled, sweat-covered bodies. Of blonde hair brushing his chest, lust-filled amber eyes staring up at him, silky muscles squeezing his cock, and husky cries of ecstasy.

A low, exasperated groan vibrated in the wolf's throat.

Christ. What the hell does the thing expect? He was attracted to her.

The wolf's snort almost sounded like the beginning of a chuckle. Theo realized then that the beast was taking the piss out of him.

Theo smiled inside the animal. *"Okay."* He sighed. *"I'm more than attracted to her."*

"Drew mate," the wolf agreed with a mental shrug.

"Maybe."

The beast shifted its front paws, adjusting its weight and, for the first time in a long time, teased Theo. *"Maybe good mate. Just Drew."*

Theo outright laughed this time. Wolf had obviously remembered their first discussion about Drew's name, when they had followed her to the beach. Theo laughed again. It had been decades since their relationship had been this easy. Dealing with the daily threat that someone might find out what they were put a great deal of strain on their partnership. They functioned well together under pressure, but it was nice not to have to worry about things, for a while at least.

A shadow crossed Drew's room and she appeared at the balcony door. She wore a tight-fitting pink tank top and white cotton panties. She stepped through the door onto the balcony and leaned her hip into the black iron railing. *My God, she's breathtaking.* Her lightly tanned skin looked smooth and her blonde hair fell about her shoulders like a silky cloak. She took a deep breath, and exhale slowly. She looked puzzled and he had a feeling that he was the cause. He didn't want to be and he should have come here tonight to set things right, but he thought she needed time. Maybe that had been the wrong thing to do. Maybe he should have come here, instead. He wasn't one to second-guess himself but when it came to Drew—hell, he second-guessed everything.

He had jumped the gun when he'd seen her fly past him this morning. He would admit that. But he had told her twice to get into the station and pay off her tickets. He should have had her car towed to the impound yard in Port Alberni. That was what he was supposed to do, what any other cop would have done. But he hadn't. He couldn't do that to her. He couldn't stand the idea of her being that angry with him. Oh, and she would have been fuming, there was no doubt about that now. Most of all he couldn't stand the idea of her being away from him, even for one day. Therefore he had taken the ribbing from the guys at the station for letting the new hot vet off the hook, tried to look repentant when his boss had lectured him about doing favors for the locals and tolerated the bitterness in Drew's voice as she'd walked away.

Drew turned from the balcony door and he focused on her sweet behind as she walked into her room. He let out a long content sigh, deep within the wolf. All of today's aggravation was worth it, because she was still close. He would set things right with her tomorrow.

Movement from behind had the wolf stiffening. He froze in place. The hair on the back of his neck rose and continued all the way to his tail. Theo held his breath, as did the wolf. Both blocked out the music from Drew's room and focused on the sounds in the forest. Leaves rustled. The wolf slowly turned his head, his long body following until he stood with his back to Drew's house and his eyes to the shadowed forest.

Chapter Eleven

Ken watched as the wolf circled the house and headed back in his direction. He aimed his rifle, his sight locked on the animal's head, and mentally pulled the trigger. He hated that he had to wait for Hendrik. An animal this prized shouldn't be left to a fucking amateur who would blow a gaping hole in it. A delicate touch was needed to preserve this beautiful creature. Nonetheless he wasn't getting paid to kill it, he was getting paid to track it. He would keep his skills sharp, though, just in case, and there was no better place than Tofino, with its ample supply of wild and domestic life.

The wolf slowed to a walk as it approached. It was the third time the black beast had searched this part of the forest. He was still pissed off at himself for making a rookie mistake. He never made mistakes—ever. It had been beaten, literally, into him not to move once in position, even if it was an uncomfortable position. Still, he wasn't hunting with his father, and he was no longer in the Marines and it was only a stupid animal for fuck's sake. Right?

Wrong. This was no ordinary wolf. It was a British Colombian wolf, the last of an extinct species. It was a rare find, a find that would cost him one and a half million if he had to shoot the damn thing in self-defense. Yet his prize for tracking the wolf wasn't the only thing different about this particular wolf. This wolf was protective of a human. He had, for some strange reason, latched onto Drew, the new vet in town. Not that Ken could blame him. That woman was a spectacular piece of ass and got him hard with just a single look.

Yet there was more going on. Ken had witnessed first-hand how the wolf had protected Drew from the pack roaming the area. It had sat next to her on the beach, followed her to her house and left only after it had checked out the perimeter. He had also seen the thing come back almost nightly to perform sweeps of the area with military precision.

Ken blinked, yet remained frozen. His muscles became tense to hold his position when the beast stared up at him.

He knew the wolf wouldn't be able to spot his scent—he had been doing this far too long to get caught. And he knew the wolf wouldn't be able to see him. He had used this very same tree multiple times and had taken great care to blend his ghillie suit in with the local vegetation. What startled him was the fact that the animal knew to look up for a possible target. Wolves didn't do things like that.

He focused on the animal. It turned from him and began sniffing the ground of another tree and up the bark. It even hopped up, its front claws digging into the wood so it could sniff higher up. Ken was amazed by the way the thing swept his head back and forth over the area in a slow, disciplined manner. It looked back up in his direction then off into the distance toward Drew's house. For some strange reason it shook its head in an irritated manner, and with a low almost aggravated snort, leaped into the cover of low hanging branches.

The rain started and after another hour of getting wet, Ken finally left his position from high up the tree and climbed his way to the ground. There was no sign of the wolf—the rain had washed almost everything away. This animal never left many prints, which wasn't natural—everything left prints. The thing was light on its feet, eerily so.

He squatted, tucking his rifle tight against his thighs, and studied the one shallow print next to the base of the tree. It was barely recognizable and the rain was doing a good job of erasing what evidence was left, which meant that he wouldn't be able to follow the damn thing to see where its den was located. His tracks were covered. Again if he wasn't sane, he would think the thing was acting like a trained solider.

He stood then shouldered his rifle and looked up, the rain soaking his face in seconds. "Fucking rain." He scanned the forest for any trace of the wolf. Nothing. *Son of a bitch*, he had never had this hard of a time tracking. Then again he wasn't used to dealing with all this rain and animals that acted like humans. Of course, he was always up for a challenge. He grinned. This was going to be a good hunt.

* * * *

Drew was fumbling with her keys in the door to the clinic and struggling to hold on to her bag when Theo suddenly spoke from behind her. "Can I help?"

She looked over his shoulder just enough to see him holding two foam cups covered with plastic lids. "I don't see how."

He chuckled before balancing one cup on the other then took her bag with his free hand.

She mumbled her thanks and opened the door to the clinic, holding it so Ruby and Theo could enter. She took her bag back and walked into her office. She didn't want to make eye contact with him. She was still confused over her reaction to him. Her emotions seemed to be all over the map where Theo was concerned and she had no idea why. She was never this touchy. She wasn't an ice princess or anything, she had feelings, they were just never this dominant before she had met him.

Man, she had been so angry after seeing him yesterday, yet by the time the afternoon was over and it was time to go home, all she could think about was him. She'd wanted him to come over, wanted him to pin her to her bed again and do naughty things to her but she was still angry at how he had treated her. She wasn't a child, she was an adult—a very angry and, apparently, horny adult. He never did come by and that had upset her too. She didn't know if it was because she was so horny or because she hadn't gotten to yell at him.

He placed the foam cup on her desk next to her bag, and as though he had been reading her thoughts he said, "I wanted to come over last night but I thought you might need to be alone."

"You were right." She glanced down when she muttered the lie. "I did."

"Mmm."

She could hear the doubt in his voice. There was silence as she looked at her desk.

Then he was beside her. The heat from his body warmed her shoulder and arm. "I did what I did so you wouldn't have lost your license or your car. I was only thinking about you. I'm sorry if you don't see it the same way, but I wouldn't change what I did if the opportunity presented itself."

Always so damn proper. Drew was about to roll her eyes but she nervously toyed with a file folder sitting on her desk instead. "You made me feel like a child. I'm really pissed at you."

"I know and I apologize." The radio attached to his vest crackled and a man urgently called out for him. He answered the call then looked at her. "I have to go."

She nodded, locking eyes with him—that was a big mistake. She could see the determination mingle with his handsome features. He meant what he said, he wasn't lying to her and he wasn't playing her, he was only thinking about her.

He gave her a boyish grin and teased. "Do you think if I stop by tonight you might invite me in?"

She fought a smile and shrugged. "I don't know. Why don't you come by and we'll see what happens?"

"I can do that." His radio crackled again. "Time to go." He went to leave then suddenly stopped. He closed the gap between them and, cupping her cheek gently, he pulled her close and kissed the corner of her mouth. It was only a quick kiss but damn, it was nice...and warm...and so nice. He pulled away, brushing her chin lightly with the backs of his fingers. As he stepped around her desk, he tapped the lid of one of the foam cups. "Coffee, two cream, two sugar?" Then pointed to the other. "Or cappuccino?"

She blinked, fighting the urge to touch the side of her mouth where his lips had been.

"Drew?"

"Cappuccino, thanks."

He grabbed the other and jogged out of the door.

Drew fell into her chair, floored by her reaction. It had just been a little kiss and not even on the mouth, but it had turned all the muscles in her arms and legs into mush. She gave in to the urge now that she was alone and touched the spot where his lips had been. She smiled as heat covered her face and a giddy sensation filled her belly. Theo had come to apologize to her and twenty seconds after an apology she had forgiven him. She shook her head in disgust. What the hell was the matter with her?

Sighing, she reached for the cappuccino and pulled off the lid. It didn't matter that this was out of character for her, or that she felt like things were moving beyond her control where Theo was concerned, it felt only right to forgive him. It had really bothered her when she hadn't gotten a chance to battle it out with him—and boy, she did enjoy a good argument—but life suddenly slowed and all she could focus on was setting things right with him. She couldn't eat, couldn't sleep, her thoughts were consumed with Theo. Now that he had explained his reasoning and she had told him how angry she had been, she felt like a heavy weight had been lifted off her shoulders. That confused her too. She didn't understand why it was so easy to be with him or why she *needed* to be with him. She just did and that really frightened her.

She wouldn't think about that now. Her day was about to start, Connie would be in any minute and patients shortly after that. She had other things to think about, she would worry about Theo later.

The front door suddenly crashed open.

"Drew!" Kevin bellowed. "You here?"

She jumped from her desk at his urgent tone and nearly crashed into him as he entered her office.

She stumbled back, gaining her balance and spotted blood on his shirt and arms.

"Whose blood is that?"

He didn't answer and instead locked onto her arm and began dragging her out of the office. "Come on."

She tried to free herself but he tightened his grip. "Ouch! Kevin, you're hurting my arm."

"Sorry," he rushed out. "I really need your help."

"Why? What's going on?" She looked him over as they stood in the middle of her reception area. Fresh blood streamed down his arm. "You're bleeding?" She reached for his wrist and pulled it closer to have a look at it, and gasped. "Who bit you?"

"That's why I came to get you. Remember those three gray wolves you saw?"

"Yeah." She pulled him into the exam room. Opening up a cupboard, she then pulled out a basket of gauze and dropped it on the table. As she held up his arm to help slow the bleeding, she tore the sterile package open with her teeth, then pressed the white square to the wound. "What about them—?" She stopped abruptly. "Did they attack you?"

"No." He held the square gauze in place as she reached for a roller bandage to wrap around the bite. "One of the males was hurt bad. He bit me when I tried to help him." He shook his head. "But you can still help her."

"Help who?" She wove the dressing around his forearm. "What are you talking about?"

"The female wolf, she was shot." Kevin looked her dead in the eye as he relayed the information. As though he was waiting to see what her reaction would be. "So were the two males."

She couldn't help but gasp again. "Oh my God!" She tied off the dressing. "Are they okay?"

"We tracked the males into the forest. One was already dead and the other was... The female survived and somehow managed to crawl to the main road. That's where I found her and how we found the males." He moved to the door. "I tried to help him but he bit me. And then the cops had to put him down. Fuck, I wish I had been more careful."

He looked at her, regret mixing in with his concern. "I'll get my backpack."

"Thanks." He sighed.

They were in his truck racing to the wounded animal minutes later.

Drew looked at Kevin. His expression was grim and his face was pale. "You're going to have to go to the clinic and get that arm looked at." He nodded. She continued to talk because she hated the silence in the cab. "Kevin, there is also a possibility that the wolf might have rabies."

"I know." He looked at her and smiled when she frowned. "Hey." He grabbed her hand and gave it a squeeze. "Don't look so worried." Then he rubbed his thumb over her knuckles. It felt nice in an innocent, intimate sort of way. "Everything will be fine and so will the female now that you're coming to help."

"I'm not concerned about the wolf... Well I am," she conceded. "But I'm more concerned about you. That's quite the bite and it's still bleeding pretty heavily."

He watched the road, a mischievous grin crossing his tanned face. "You're worried about me? That's promising."

She rolled her eyes. "Nothing is promising. I just don't want you to get sick or black out from blood loss. I'm not in the mood to crash into a tree."

He gripped her knee and slid down her thigh. "I would never let that happen." She turned at his serious tone. He was looking at her with honesty and longing in his blue eyes. He squeezed her thigh as though asking her to believe him.

She clasped his hand, and, lifting it away from her leg, returned the squeeze. "I know." She moved it to the safety of the console that sat between them but he refused to let go of her. "I'm just a serious control freak. So, focus on the road."

He laughed as he slowed the truck

"Is this where you found her?" She blinked. "So close to town?" There were cops everywhere, including Theo. She recognized his truck right away.

He nodded. "Apparently a couple of the locals heard the shots sometime last night but didn't bother to call it in." Drew could hear the bite to his words. "If they had, the males might have survived. God knows how long the female was lying there." He shook his head as he opened the door. "Fuck, people are stupid."

She agreed. It was for that reason that she had gone into veterinary medicine instead of becoming a lawyer—animals were easier to get along with and the risk of being bombarded with stupid people committing asinine crimes was low.

Kevin joined her on the shoulder of the road and pointed toward a shallow ditch. "She's over here."

There was no need to show her, Drew saw the animal the moment her feet hit the gravel on the side of the road. As she got closer, she could see the blood matting the beautiful fur. She stopped next to an officer who was trying to hold her still.

They had thrown a blanket over her in an effort to make their job easier and also to keep from being bitten. The girl was feisty, though, struggling and growling as the men tried to keep her from making her injury worse. Her growl was weak but she was fighting and that was a good sign.

Ben suddenly appeared then knelt down next to her and reached to help hold the animal still. The growl that rumbled in the wolf's throat became quite deep.

"Easy, slow movements, Ben," she instructed. "She's not a happy camper."

Drew didn't take her eyes off the wolf as he answered. "I wouldn't be either if I had been shot."

She gently laid her hands on the animal, one on its ribs and the other on the back of its neck, behind its ears. The animal calmed almost at once, which considering her condition was good, but this pretty girl was wild. Everything Drew had ever read said that this animal should be trying to attack her, yet she had quieted when Drew had touched her. Strange.

Drew pushed the odd behavior aside and began to speak to the animal in soft tones. Nothing she said made any sense, it was pure gibberish, but she kept her voice low and non-threatening. This lovely lady needed to know she wasn't there to hurt her and Drew also needed her to become familiar with her touch and smell. It would make treating her that much easier.

After a little while of Drew still cooing to the beast, Ben made a bold move and tried to stroke the animal's face. The wolf growled, exposing her teeth, then jerked her head, and snapped at Ben.

Drew quickly stilled the wolf. "Shhh! None of that now. Ben won't hurt you. But to be on the safe side he won't try to touch you again." She looked up at the cop sitting across from her. "Isn't that right?"

Ben nodded, and Drew asked the other officer to move away as well. She thought maybe that the strain of the blanket tugging on her wound might be causing the aggressive behavior. She was proven correct when the men released the blanket and the growling stopped.

Drew sighed and leaned over the wolf to get a good look at her. She was beautiful even with the blood covering her. "Don't worry," Drew whispered to the wolf. "I'm here to help you." The wolf answered by curling back her lips and displaying her vivid -white fangs.

Theo's heart pounded when he spotted Drew next to the female. He almost shouted out to her, demanded that she get away from it, but his panic was suddenly overshadowed by the wolf as it started to whine and snap inside his head.

Gritting his teeth, he ignored the wolf and headed straight for her.

Something had been up with the wolf from the second he had arrived on the scene. The low whimpering and occasional whine didn't make any sense. It still didn't.

As he crossed to Drew, his muscles shifted and jerked and he had to fight to hold the wolf inside. The damn thing was so strong and he understood that it wanted to protect their mate, even if it meant exposing their secret. Theo, however, was a little more level-headed.

"*Enough!*" He bellowed the command in his head as he fought the beast for control. "*Calm down. Drew is okay.*"

The only response he got was another high-pitched whine.

With the beast somewhat held in check, he made his way to Drew. He squatted down facing her, the wounded animal's face and exposed fangs only inches away. He did it on purpose, of course. The animal would catch his wolf's scent and would either calm down or attack. If it was the latter of the two then he would take the brunt of it and Drew would be safe.

Now that he was close to Drew, the wolf calmed fully.

"Drew."

"Isn't she gorgeous?" She smiled, stroking the female's neck. "Look at the traces of red in her fur." She was doing a great job at controlling her fear for the wolf because he had a difficult time picking it up but he knew she was concerned.

"I see it."

He looked up at Ben. "Where'd you go?"

"Back toward town to see if I could find any other trails."

"And?"

"Not a damn thing." Ben shook his head. "So I came back and saw that Drew needed some help."

"It's true. Ben was trying to help. But this little lady didn't like him helping. She's still a nervous."

Funny. He couldn't pick up much nervousness, and only a trace amount of fear. Something more was going on here but Theo didn't have the time to investigate.

He nodded. "I think we need to get her to your clinic so you can help her there."

"Okay." She slowly reached for her bag but Ben, trying to help, grabbed her knapsack and unzipped it for her. The animal began to struggle again and her growls became deep and aggressive.

Puzzled by the sudden aggression, Theo gave Ben a shrug and calmly placed his hand on the animal as Drew politely told him why he needed to go. "I think it's you, Ben. Are you nervous?"

"Damn straight. I don't want her to bite you, or Theo or me."

Drew smiled as she tried to calm the animal. "She doesn't like it and probably thinks you're going to hurt her. You have to go. We can handle it from here."

"Right." He nodded and moved away watching.

As soon as Ben had moved, the growling stopped and the beast stilled. Theo spent all of ten seconds thinking about its reaction to Ben, until his wolf suddenly did a whining-growl thing in his head. He focused on the beast inside and realized that he was watching Drew and the syringe she was now holding. The wolf let out a low whimper when Drew gathered the loose skin at the back of the wounded animal's neck and delivered the shot.

If he hadn't known better, he would've thought his wolf wanted to protect the injured female. What made things even more confusing was when the gray wolf whimpered in reaction to the injection and his wolf whined back as though confused. It was as if his wolf wanted to protect both females. That was a first, but then again, this thing with Drew and mates was new to both of them and he didn't know what to make of his wolf's response to the female. Theo knew first-hand that wolves were instinctively protective of their pack and would attack and kill any outsiders. Yet, Theo and his wolf were the only one of their kind—they didn't belong to a pack, so it made the wolf's reaction all the more bizarre.

"She's out now." Drew interrupted his thoughts. "Can you help me lift her into Kevin's truck?"

Theo nodded and lifted the animal. He stilled when he smelled Kevin but didn't see the man anywhere. That meant Kevin's scent was on Drew...again.

He took another breath. No... Not all. Kevin's blood was on Drew too. How'd he missed that? Jesus, he was easily distracted when it came to Drew. He needed to fix that.

"Where's Kevin?" He looked around and saw him step out from behind the cab of an ambulance. "What happened?"

"He was bitten when he tried to help." She frowned at him while he lifted the wolf. "Weren't you here?"

"I was sent into the forest to...search for tracks." He walked toward his truck. "We'll take mine."

"Okay." She stayed by his side, stroking the female's head. "Did you find any tracks?"

He left her question unanswered and gave her an order. "Open the back, please."

She huffed at his demand but still opened the tailgate. She climbed in and knelt down, facing him and spread a blanket she found inside. He placed the wolf on the blanket and pushed while Drew pulled the animal inside.

Adjusting the animal just so, Drew sat down and adjusted herself against the side of the truck bed. "Okay, I'm good."

He knew she wanted to stay in the back with the female, but there was no way *that* was going to happen. "What the hell are you doing?"

"Waiting for you to drive us to the clinic."

"I am not driving anywhere until you get out of there."

"Well that's interesting, because I'm not getting out."

"Drew." He squeezed his fists. "Get out."

"No. I won't take the chance that she will get hurt further. I'm staying here."

He gave her a hard stare.

She returned it.

"Fine." He slammed the bottom half of his tailgate closed and, looking her in the eye, gave her a warning. "But if that wolf wakes up and hurts you, I'm not going to be so nice."

She sighed. "She's not going to wake up. I gave her—"

"I don't care," he whispered between clenched teeth. "If she hurts you, she dies. It's that simple."

Her eyes grew wide while she shook her head. "Theo—"

"No." He snapped. "I've given you my warning. Hang on."

Chapter Twelve

The better part of the day was spent tending to the female wolf. Theo had pulled the massive kennel out of his truck and brought it into the clinic for the female to rest in—actually he had insisted—and once the animal was resting peacefully in the secured kennel, Drew was asked to give the two males a once-over before their bodies were sent to Vancouver. She had a real hard time doing her exams and reports. She didn't find anything surprising, besides the bullet holes, that is. It was heartbreaking that some dickwad had found it necessary to kill two beautiful creatures and almost a third, just for funsies. She just didn't understand people.

In the late afternoon, she called Kevin to see how he was doing.

"Just thought I'd call to see how your arm is."

"Hmmm. I think I would rather have you come by in person and check up on me. Do you own a naughty nurse costume, with fishnet stockings?"

Drew laughed at his suggestive comment even though it bordered on pig-ish. "Yeah... That's not going to happen. I don't do fishnets."

"But you do naughty nurse?"

"Kevin!"

He laughed. "Okay, sorry, go ahead, check up on me."

"How's the arm?"

"It's all right." She could almost hear him shrug through the phone.

Now for the bad news. "Listen, the BCPP want to fly the wolves to Vancouver to get looked at, so you won't know for a couple days if they have rabies or not."

"Okay."

She felt so bad that she began to ramble. "I don't think they have it, and I looked it up. The last known case in BC involved a bat, not a wolf."

"Okay."

"You don't seem too worried."

"I don't need to be. You're worried enough for the both of us."

She really was—rabies was not a nice disease and neither was the treatment. "Well, you—"

"It's fine, it was my fuck-up, not yours, I'll live with the consequences. But, if you want to make me feel better you could come by my office in the nurse outfit. I promise to be a good patient," he teased again. Or was he serious? She found it hard to read Kevin sometimes, except when they had been in his truck and he had laid things out for her to see. Wow! That still shocked her and made her a little nervous. Not because she didn't like his concern—who wouldn't want a hot guy to care for them?—but it felt like she was going behind Theo's back. Which was strange because it wasn't like they were an item or dating—she just couldn't stop thinking about him or the strange pull he had over her.

"Like I said," she clicked her tongue. "Not happening." Then she couldn't help but giggle. "You are nuts. I'll call you when I hear something from Vancouver."

"Ha! You like that idea. I can hear the interest."

"Goodbye, Kevin." She hung up as he laughed into the phone.

Just as she was hanging up from Kevin, Connie walked in. "How's my stud-a-saurus?" she asked plopping down on the loveseat. "Does he need me to kiss him better?"

Drew pushed her chair out and propped her feet up on her desk, laughing. "Maybe. Why don't you go by his office and ask him?"

"Like that's going to happen," she huffed. "He doesn't even know I exist. Besides..." Connie stretched out on the loveseat. "If I go to see him then I can't stay here and watch wolfy in the back. Huh! Not a bad fit."

Drew wasn't all that surprised by the gesture. She could never allow it, of course. She'd hate herself if something happened to Connie. "No. You're going home and Ruby and I are staying here."

Connie pushed up onto her elbows. "I can look after her, Drew. I know I can."

"I know you can too. The simple fact is that I have insurance and you don't. But that's not my main concern. I'm worried you'll get hurt."

"But she probably won't even wake up."

She shook her head. "Sorry, kiddo. I like you in one piece."

Connie flopped down. "Well, that sucks ass. I canceled my plans. Now, it's Friday night, I don't have anything to do and I did my hair."

Drew looked at the young woman studying her. Her hair appeared the normal shiny black. She didn't see anything special except for the blue. "Looks the same to me."

"Oh no, it's not." Connie shot from the couch with a giggle. "Looky-looky." She turned her head to the left and showed Drew her new pink highlights. It wasn't a subtle pink either, it was bright and bold and reminded her of a stick of bubble gum.

Drew laughed. "How in the hell did I miss that?"

"Ah." Connie sat on the edge of her desk and crossed her legs. "You had a busy day. Besides, it's easier to spot in the light." She began swinging her feet. "Seeing how I'm now bored, how about I grab us some food?"

Drew's stomach rumbled at the thought. "Sounds good. But no meat." She pressed her on her stomach. "It makes me feel queasy."

"Really? I didn't know you were a vegetarian?"

"Yeah! I've been off meat about six months now."

"And how's that working out?"

"Not bad. I've had a few relapses." Drew grinned. "Wish I had a sponsor to talk me down."

Connie laughed. "Well don't ask me. I'm a meat-a-tarian."

This time Drew laughed.

"No worries, Ms Veg-head, I'll get you something meatless." Connie clapped her hands. "Sweet. I love girlie nights." Connie hopped off the desk and skipped into the front office calling out, "You can nibble on cardboard, while I enjoy my bacon cheeseburger." Drew chuckled at the dig. "Then..."

Connie continued from the outer office. "We can play truth or dare and I'll color your hair."

"What?" Drew sat forward.

Connie stuck her head around the corner as she pulled on her coat. "I said I'll color your hair. Don't worry. I'll choose a color that Theo will like."

"What?" Her voice went a little higher when Connie brought up Theo. She cleared her throat. "I don't care what Theo likes. But I'm still not sure about the color."

"Don't panic." Connie disappeared again. "It's not too permanent."

Drew heard the front door open and Connie call out, "And by the way... You may not care about Theo, but he sure as hell cares about you." The door closed behind her soon-to-be-fired receptionist.

Did Theo care about her? If he did, he sure had a weird way of showing it. The idea frustrated the hell out of her and made her feel giddy at the same time.

She really liked the idea of Theo caring for her, because she already knew she cared for him. Actually it worried her because it had happened so fast. She had no desire to be with anyone else. She only wanted Theo, she craved him. Man, that scared the shit out of her.

* * * *

Once again, Theo was annoyed when he found that the front door to Drew's clinic was unlocked. He walked in and immediately pulled in Drew's scent, then the female wolf and—Connie. He stopped and listened as Ruby approached him. Connie wasn't here but she had been recently because her scent was fresh. He locked the door and followed Drew's scent toward her office, not hearing anything other than Ruby's nails clicking on the floor. God, he needed to see Drew, to touch her, to taste her. The muscles in his neck and shoulders had become tight the second he'd walked out of the clinic door and had been all day. It had been hard to leave her here earlier today when she'd been caring for the female wolf, even when his boss had ordered him back to the scene.

Something was very wrong in Tofino and his gut told him it was more than just random shootings. Things like that did not happen in a town as close-knit as Tofino. What disturbed him the most was the odd scent he had picked up while searching the forest for clues with the others. It had been very subtle and kind of reminded him of grease or maybe oil used for frying food, but...not. There was also a metallic quality to it, but again he wasn't sure. The scent was familiar, though, they had caught wind of it last night outside Drew's house. In fact, he had traced the scent all the way back to the tree where his wolf had first caught hold of it. Damn it! The beast had known something wasn't right and after letting him inspect the area and not finding anything, Theo had finally called it a night, ordering him home. He should have listened, should have paid closer attention. Now three more animals had been shot and Drew was getting pulled into it.

Damn. He stopped in the middle of her reception area and unclenched his fists. He stared at Drew's open office door, knowing full well that she was in there and that she was sleeping. He could hear her slow, even breathing from where he stood. He forced his muscles to relax and took a breath. It didn't help. He knew that she was safe, but it didn't matter—only being with her and touching her would calm this sudden fury he had. "Shit."

He tugged off his cap and ran his hand through his hair.

"Drew? Mate?" The concerned tone was unusual for the wolf and it stirred, nervously pushing at Theo's insides to keep him moving toward Drew.

"Yes." He gave the beast the truth, because it would know if he was lying and there was no point in lying to himself anymore. *"Drew is our mate."*

The wolf settled, but kept a watchful eye on his thoughts and emotions.

Theo sighed. He knew deep in his soul that he would never be able to escape this overwhelming feeling he had for Drew, or this need to protect her at all cost. The wolf wouldn't let him and he wasn't entirely sure he would want to escape it. What bothered him was that there was more to this.

With another sigh, Theo walked away from Drew's office door.

The wolf stood to attention, and squeezed the muscles in Theo's thighs tight, keeping him in place.

"Easy," Theo soothed. *"I was going to check on the female gray."*

The wolf released him and paced around inside his head, almost excited.

When he approached the kennel, he noticed that the animal was sleeping on her side, atop thick blankets. Her neck was wrapped up and IV hook-ups were taped to her leg. He also noticed that Drew had taken the time to clean the animal as well, as there wasn't one speck of blood marring her beautiful coat.

Kneeling down, Theo reached his fingers through the sidebars and stroked the soft fur. "Drew's right, you are a beautiful girl." Then he added with a smile, "When you're sleeping."

His wolf snorted in agreement but he was also intensely focused on her and Theo could feel him struggle to pull in her scent. He accommodated him, and right then as the female's scent hit the wolf, Theo could have sworn his wolf sighed.

Theo entered Drew's office a few minutes later and stopped next to the loveseat, staring down at Drew. Her head was turned to the side facing him and he could see, even in the dimly lit room, how her pouty lips were slightly parted. He smiled when he saw her crossed feet peeking out from under her blanket. He liked the way she rested one arm over her breasts while the other arm was draped above her head. She looked so beautiful and peaceful, but he knew if she'd been awake she would have either been scowling at him or giving him hell. God, he liked her feisty attitude and that made him smile too. She turned her head in the opposite direction and he watched amazed as silky pink highlights slid down and skimmed her cheek.

He blinked. *What the – ?*

He squatted next to her and gently threaded the pink strands through his fingers. Drew had the ability to be unpredictable – that trait worried him because it would push him and the wolf beyond their normal limits of control while trying to protect her – yet he found he was looking forward to seeing what she would do next. He chuckled softly as he toyed with her new pink highlights.

He closed the small gap between them with the intent of tasting her sweet lips, but he froze instead. Kevin Beauchamp's scent suddenly filled his head. A protective instinct had him curling his lips in a snarl and it wasn't the wolf that pushed for the action. Oh no! It was all Theo. He hated smelling Beauchamp on

Drew. She belonged to him, no one else, and it didn't matter that she was only trying to help Kevin. He had touched her and that was something he could not tolerate. He would have to find a way to let Beauchamp know Drew was his without killing him. But how in the hell was he going to do that when every fiber of his being wanted to rip the man to shreds?

Drew stirred at that moment, shifting fully onto her side and tucked her feet under the blanket. Her lips puckered then relaxed. The action was so feminine, so unbelievably sexy, that Theo had to fight every urge to climb onto that loveseat and join her.

She sighed then. The sound, a mixture of sweet and innocent, which reeled his desire for her back in. He lightly brushed his mouth over hers then tucked her new highlights behind her ear. "What am I going to do with you?"

With the question left unanswered, Theo settled himself on the floor, resting his back against the small couch, where he spent the night watching over her.

Chapter Thirteen

It amazed Drew that after only three days, the female wolf was up and pacing in her kennel. What was more amazing was the fact that she allowed Drew to touch her, adjust her bandage without the aid of a muzzle, plus she would lean into the side of the cage welcoming Drew's pats. Then again, wolves were very smart—the female was probably just playing the sweet girl while she was locked up. If Drew was to meet her out in the forest, she might finally become that dinner for one.

The wound the female had sustained wasn't all that bad. Drew's concerns lay with dehydration and blood loss. However, just like Frankie and Molly, the gray would have a scar but wouldn't have any lasting effects from her injury—which was great but at the same time confusing because the potential for a fatal wound was there, she just didn't think killing had been the intent. Of course, the two males were dead, which blew her theory all to hell.

She sighed out loud in a huff. This was crazy. Who in their right mind would want to shoot an animal in the hopes of only wounding it? Thing was, this person was *not* in their right mind so guessing at the reasons behind these acts was useless. "Who knows?" She looked down at Ruby while she fixed herself a sandwich for dinner. "If we're lucky, the dude is simply a lousy shot." Although for some reason she knew accuracy had had nothing to do with it.

"Well?" she asked. "What do you think?" Ruby's bark echoed throughout the main level of the house, her dark stare never leaving the sliced cheese sitting on the kitchen counter. "You're not paying attention. You're supposed to be looking at me, not the cheese." Drew laughed when Ruby barked a second time.

"Fine," she caved. "Take it." She tossed a slice of cheese and nodded when Ruby snatched it out of mid-air. "Nice catch."

Drew picked up her plate and she marched into the living room and flicked on the TV. She was just about to bite into her veggie sub when headlights streamed through the windows. She checked her watch—a visitor at seven in the evening? That was weird. The only person to come here was Theo and that one time had been much later. Could it be Theo now? Her heart jumped at the idea—it seemed like forever since they had spent the night together. She hadn't helped, thanks to her having a hissy over his forcing her to pay for her speeding tickets. Later, she had heard from Ben that Theo's boss hadn't been happy with him about letting her off and how the other cops had heckled him about getting soft. That, of course, had made her feel like a real tool, but despite all of that, they really hadn't seen much of each other. She had spent the last three nights sleeping at the clinic and had worked during the day, so she hadn't seen him at all except when he'd come into the clinic today to collect the female.

Theo and Kevin had taken the animal over to Stockham Island. It was a smaller island that was joined by a strip of land to the larger island that the Opitsat Reservation was located on.

"She'll be safe over there," Theo had said and Kevin had nodded his agreement. "The people over on the island respect the wolf as one of their spiritual leaders."

Spiritual leaders? She had no idea what that meant.

A smile pulled at her lips as she heard the engine turn off.

She quickly stood then snapped her fingers at Ruby and lectured, "Don't touch my sandwich or you're toast."

She opened the front door after the second knock and found herself eyes to chin with Theo. She slowly scanned his face, full lips, straight nose, and finally locked on his intense gaze. The dark look on Theo's face stirred up a bubbly feeling in her stomach and within seconds, her limbs felt like mush.

She leaned into the frame, doing her best to act composed while her heart did double flips. "How did it go this afternoon?"

He narrowed his turbulent eyes on her and smirked. "Do you really care, or would you rather ask me in?" He took a deep breath and answered for her, "You want me to come in." And like the last time, he stepped to the threshold of the house but didn't enter. "Don't you?"

That was strange. She nodded, then drew out her answer teasingly, "I care."

He laughed. "It went well. She's better off on the island. Few chances at getting shot."

"Thank you for thinking of her well-being and taking her over there." She stepped back, allowing him room to enter. "And yes, I do want you to come in."

He followed her in and reached for her and the door at the same time. There was a loud bang just as she was pulled into his arms... Or maybe she threw herself at him. Whatever. All she knew was that it had been too long since the last time they had been together. Too long since their last kiss and too long since they had made love.

He pressed his mouth down on hers, bruising her lips and she loved the urgent way he pulled at her T-shirt, tugging it over her head. He was touching her everywhere, her face, exploring her back, squeezing her bum. All the while, he made love to her mouth. He was ravaging her and, Lord help her, she loved it. Loved the way her nipples tightened from his kiss, and the way his touch caused her to ache and that he was here with her, making her feel this way.

She nipped at his ear when he kissed her neck. She flicked her tongue over his lobe and drew it into her mouth. He slid his hands down her back and over her behind, and stopped when he reached the top of her thighs. He gripped tight and lifted her off the floor. She circled his neck with her arms and wrapped her legs around his waist as he carried her to the couch. She clung to him, she couldn't help it, but not because she was afraid he would drop her—no way, Theo was strong, really strong—but because it intensified the greedy throbbing in her core. She rolled her hips, dragging her moist body against his. Her name rumbled deep in his throat. He stopped by the couch, lowering her so that she stood in front of him. He pulled off his jacket and his black T-shirt.

"No cop outfit," she mumbled, touching his chest.

"Changed before I came over," he added, unbuckling his jeans.

"I like you in jeans. You have a great ass for them." She blew on his nipples, teased them into hard points. "But I like the cop stuff too. It was like acting out a kinky fantasy. I don't suppose you brought your handcuffs with you, Officer Grey?"

His laugh was deep and unbelievably sexy. "Another time. Right now I need you to take those jogging pants off."

"And why is that, Officer?" She stepped back, the coffee table catching her just below the backs of her knees.

He quickly grabbed her waist and pushed the table away with his foot. "Because I want you naked so I can…" He looked down. She followed his gaze, noticing that Ruby's attention was still focused on the sandwich and that she had simply moved when the table had moved.

"Is Ruby drooling over your dinner?"

"Yeah." She sighed, pressing her face into his chest.

He pushed her back and gave her a frown. "You haven't eaten yet?"

She shook her head at his serious tone. "I can wait." She tried to move into his arms again.

The grip on her waist became tight. "You have to eat." He'd dropped his voice low.

Drew blinked at him, speechless. He *was* concerned for her. Connie was right, he did care for —

Wow!

Her heart did this happy-flip thing when she accepted the fact that Theo cared for her and that she returned the feeling.

She cupped his cheek and smiled. "I will eat. Promise. If you want, you can sit down with me after and make sure I do. Okay?" She ran her thumb over his lips.

He drew out a sigh when he nodded.

"Good because there is no way I could stop now that you have me all hot and juicy." She stepped back and gave him a wink. "Now where were we? Ah yes, you had ordered me to take off my jogging pants so you could see me naked." She hooked her thumbs in the waistband and inched the material slowly down her legs. "Was that all you wanted?"

The concern Theo had displayed vanished and a dark longing that bordered on the aggressive side appeared instead. He pulled her into his chest a scant second after she had stepped out of her pants, and once again he lifted her high around his waist. He brushed her ear with his warm breath. "What do I want?" He nipped at the lobe. "I want you wet. I want you hot. I want you so far out of your mind that you lose all sense of time and I want to fuck you until you can't stand."

A shiver ran through her as she opened her mouth for him, their tongues tangling in a hot, open-mouthed kiss. Theo sat on the couch and cradled her backside in his big hands as they continued to kiss. With callused fingers, he gripped her bum, forcing her to rock her hips. She groaned. The bulge of his cock and the rough texture of his jeans magnified every sensation. Her clit throbbed, her nipples felt raw, her breasts ached and her lips tingled. Then things sped up. Theo removed her bra without breaking their kiss and tossed it aside, then after forcing her to stand he tugged down her panties in a swift calculated move. He greedily pressed his mouth to her stomach, flicking her belly button ring with his tongue. She grabbed the back of his head as he slid two fingers inside her, pumping slowly, deeply, teasing her sweet spot like a pro until her legs shook and her knees buckled.

He held her tight as he withdrew his fingers then he licked her juices from one finger, then the other. *Oh, wow!* She leaned into him, wishing he was licking her instead, but she was too impatient. It seemed like he was torturing her by making her wait for him. She tried to slide down his chest, but he stopped her by pulling a nipple deep. He sucked, he licked, and he took his damn time and it was killing her. "Theo!" she cried rocking her hips. "You said you were going to fuck me."

"I am," he mumbled licking a wet trail up between her breasts.

"Then please." She raised her hips giving him room to push down his jeans. "Do it."

He forced her hips down. "Baby," he groaned in her ear. "I'm not wearing a condom."

Drew dropped her head onto his shoulder and sighed. "Crap."

He chuckled. "Unlike the last time, this time we can fix it." He lifted her off and was about to stand when she stopped him. She bent and captured his mouth then whispered against his lips, "I'm the desperate one. Stay here, I'll be right back." And after another quick kiss, she hopped off him and flew up the stairs and was in her bedroom seconds later. She rushed to her nightstand, only to remember that she'd thrown the box of condoms under the sink. She moved to the bathroom and threw open the cupboard doors. She panicked when she didn't find them right away, and dropped down on all fours to get a better look. She sighed when she caught sight of the box.

As she reached for the condoms, a rough hand spread wide over her behind. "You're taking too long." She sighed and pushed back when he repeated the caress. "You have a beautifully curved bottom." He tugged on her waist. "You'd better come out of there before I forget why we're up here."

He assisted her to her feet. She was about to face him but he stopped her. "Don't move," he cautioned, taking the box from her. Drew looked at his reflection in the mirror and sucked in a breath. He stared at her as he pulled a foil-wrapped condom free. After tossing the box aside, he pushed his jeans and boxers down his hard muscled thighs. The soft light coming from her room played with the shadows on his face and brought the silver in his eyes to life. If she didn't know better she would have thought his expression had changed from desire to an animalistic hunger. The look he gave her set her skin on fire, made her clit throb and her core ache. She flushed and bit her lip when she felt her need slowly trickle down her leg. The muscles of his chest and shoulders flexed as he tore open the condom wrapper and covered his cock. Then, gripping one thigh, he lifted it so her knee rested on the bathroom counter, opening her wide for him. He stopped then, his nostrils flaring as he drew in a deep breath, and setting his jaw, he thrust into her.

Drew bit her lip to keep from crying out. The sensations that flew through her body as Theo made love to her were lightning-quick and just as powerful. They sparked a need so deep that she could do nothing else but fully immerse herself. She pushed back as Theo entered her, determined to give as good as she got. He wasn't gentle as he grasped her hips. His tight grip bordered on pain as did the slap he delivered to her butt cheek. She cried out as the throbbing in her body mixed with the sting on her behind. He bent, slowing his pace, drawing each thrust into long, delicious strokes, and placed a soft kiss on her spine then followed it with a gentle nip. His hot ragged breath flowed over the skin, heating then cooling, triggering goose bumps.

He slowed his thrusts and took his time as he explored her body, seemingly in control whereas seconds before he had been untamed. It was wonderful and sweet, except she didn't want that, not right now. "Theo," she begged through choppy breaths. "Faster."

He grunted. Keeping his mouth pressed to her shoulder, he ordered, "Give me your hand."

"What?" She pushed back trying to get him to move.

"Give me your hand." This time he growled as he pulled on her arm.

She obeyed and allowed him to place her fingers between her thighs, against her moist lips to the sensitive bud nestled within. He covered her hand with his own, directing the circular movement. It was so wonderfully intimate and her stomach squeezed in reaction.

When he pulled away, she sighed and braced herself on the counter for support.

His hand was back on hers in a flash. "No," he snapped. "Don't stop."

Once again, she followed his instructions and petted her achy clit. Her reward was exactly what she had asked for. He fucked her fast. Hard. So incredibly deep that within minutes she was crying out to him, bucking against him. The orgasm was so wild that she might have — maybe — pleaded with him to *never stop*.

He growled aloud and followed her orgasm with his own, his slamming thrusts slowing as he trembled against her. After a minute, he pulled away. Her legs shook as she straightened and her arms felt like jelly but, wow, did she feel good, real good. She turned and found herself pinned against his chest. He was damp, a light film of sweat covering his body, and he smelled so fantastic that she couldn't help but bury into his chest and hug him. He kissed her head, gently stroked her back. God she loved how he curled his arms around her and squeezed her tight.

"That was fun," Theo teased. He could feel goose bumps rise to the surface of her heated skin as he touched her.

"Sure was. I'm glad I invited you in." Her husky laugh made his cock spark back to life. "Mmm," she cooed, noticing his thickening shaft. "Guess fun's not over yet." She pulled away and walked to her bed, calling over her shoulder, "I don't suppose I have to tell you to hurry, do I?"

He grinned, watching her luscious bottom, his handprint bright in contrast to her creamy skin. Her desire hung heavy in the air and he remembered how he'd enjoyed watching how her wet sex had welcomed him, could still feel her tight opening holding him snug. He wouldn't apologize for the red welts marring her delicate skin — the animal in him, and not the wolf, wanted to claim her for his own, so no other would try to take her.

She pulled back the covers and climbed onto the bed. "You're taking too long," she repeated his statement from earlier as she brushed her fingers down the cleft between her breasts, then down her belly circling her belly button ring and continuing lower as she slowly parted her legs.

* * * *

Theo stepped onto Drew's front porch three hours later. He was relaxed and thoroughly sated. He chuckled. He had felt the same after the first time they'd had sex, but apparently where Drew was concerned he would never be completely satisfied. After forcing her to eat her veggie sandwich—which was not enough nourishment for the night he'd had in mind—he'd dragged her back upstairs and proceeded to snack on her. In between, they'd rested in her bed, just talking. It had been nice and effortless. Drew was an easy person to be around. He liked how she'd blushed and giggled when he'd teased her about the pink in her hair. And he liked that she hadn't pressed him for anything, and hadn't asked that dreaded question 'what are you thinking?'. She hadn't tried to snuggle with him either, which normally he would have liked. But he didn't this time, not with her—he'd wanted her next to him, touching him and he wanted her to need his touch. Thankfully, she hadn't pulled away when he'd caressed her hip and stomach, she'd just exhaled a little sigh that told him she enjoyed his touch.

Though she hadn't pressed him for any life tragedies or romantic sonnets, she had answered all of *his* questions. She'd told him how her grandfather had left the house in Cox Bay for her in his will, and that she'd spent many summers here in Tofino. He wondered if he might have seen her at some point during those summers. He had traveled here often—

spending two, sometimes three weeks at a time. Maybe he had seen her...when she was a little girl. Was this why the wolf had pushed at him to come back here? Had he caught Drew's scent, knowing she was his mate that long ago, when she was just a child?

"Is that why you always whined to come back here? Did you know Drew was here? Did you know, even back then, that she would be our mate?"

He never did receive an answer — the wolf simply gave him an indignant snort and turned his back. It wasn't until the fresh night air hit him that the wolf stirred in Theo's mind.

"Answer me now."

The animal yawned.

"All right." Theo sighed. *"No run until you tell me."* He didn't withhold runs from the wolf because the damn animal usually took it out on him while he was working, making his life a living hell until he was freed. But he *needed* to know — he deserved to know.

A low growl echoed through his head.

"Pathetic." Theo held firm. *"I've heard better from you."*

The muscles in his thigh tightened and his leg jerked forward. His foot hovered over the steps that descended from Drew's front porch. The beast was trying to make him move.

Theo laughed and forced his leg back to where it had been. *"No. Tell me. You knew Drew would be here, didn't you?"*

The beast ruffled its fur, irritated that Theo was his equal in strength. Then, in a huff, the wolf revealed, *"No, just Drew. Just mate."*

"You knew my mate — " The beast's low growl was a clear warning. Theo corrected his thoughts, *"You knew our mate would be here."*

"Mate here." Then in a low, frustrated growl, the wolf informed, *"Mate gone."*

Now what did that mean? *"No,"* Theo corrected. *"Drew is inside sleeping."*

There was another irritated grumble and Theo recognized that the wolf wasn't happy and becoming impatient with their conversation.

Sighing, he stepped off the porch and marched around the house. When he reached the shadows of the forest, he stopped.

There it was again, that slight greasy stench. Not human. The oil and sweat secreted from humans was thick with their bodily odor, and any other fragrance they may have covered themselves with. This odd scent was solo, there were no attachments, and something metallic about it, which was unusual to find in the middle of a forest — at night. He drew the aroma deep into his lungs where the wolf could study it.

"Man?" the wolf asked, then said, *"Man make."*

"Man-made," Theo corrected. *"Has to be, it doesn't fit in here. What the hell is that?"*

"Smell before," the wolf suddenly announced. *"At tree."*

"I remember."

"Hurt mate. Drew." The wolf growled.

What? *"Calm down. We'll go check it out,"* Theo reasoned. *"Then you can go for a run."*

The wolf paced around in his head nervously as he quickly removed his clothes and tossed them next to Drew's house. He looked up at Drew's balcony window and smiled. They would check out the area as normal and try to follow that scent, then the wolf could have his run.

Theo flexed his shoulders as he walked into the forest. Once the beast was content, he would come back and check to see that Drew was safe, and maybe make love to her one more time before heading home.

The wolf snorted again, his attempt at animal mockery.

Theo grinned, feeling the wolf push from the inside out, his muscles beginning to pull and stretch as he continued deeper into the woods. *"Hey, you were the one who called mate. I'm just taking full advantage of your gifts."*

"Run!" The wolf barked out the demand.

"Run," Theo agreed with a chuckle.

Chapter Fourteen

Ken still couldn't believe what he had seen. His palms were still sweating from his run back from the vet's house and he almost dropped his phone. He had gone to Drew's knowing the wolf would show up, as it had every other night. Except this night, he wanted to catch it on his phone and send the images to Linde so he could see what his money was paying for.

He hit the play button one more time. He needed to be sure he had seen what he had seen and that he wasn't going crazy.

Ken let out a long breath when he watched Theo Grey transform into the wolf. It was a horrific process and made him want to gag, but he couldn't bring himself to look away. He was fascinated and disgusted by the idea of Theo becoming this one-of-a-kind animal, yet he wanted to know more. He wanted to know if there were any others like him and how this creature-human had come to be. Had Grey been born this way or had he been bitten? Could he transform on a whim or did he follow a lunar cycle? But the most pressing question — could Grey be killed?

Ken sat in his chair. What would Linde think about this? His prize wolf was actually a man — or werewolf? Or whatever the fuck he was. He needed to make a decision. Tell Linde... Or not tell Linde. Either way the old man would get his prize. He might, however, pay more if he could display the world's only known werewolf.

Decision made, he quickly forwarded the video to Linde's private phone and attached a brief sentence.

The price has just doubled.

Less than five minutes passed before his cell rang.

"Don't send trash to my private phone." Hendrik's harsh words were almost drowned out by background noise coming from his end.

"Trash." Ken laughed.

"This isn't funny, you childish fuck. I don't have time to watch fantasy movies."

Ken laughed harder.

"Are you drunk?" Hendrik demanded.

"I wish." He swiped a hand down his face. "You're right, though, it isn't funny, but it is also not a fantasy."

"What are you on about?" Hendrik snapped.

"The footage I just sent was taken a half hour ago. I was hidden in my normal post when I filmed it." He sighed heavily into his cell. "And believe me, it is very real."

"Stop wasting my time." Linde whispered the command.

Fuck, he wasn't in the mood to argue with this senile old fuck. "Listen to me," Ken barked. "I have been tracking this thing for weeks. I have seen how this...creature behaves. It's smart and it knows something is going on. It also has the potential to be very dangerous." Ken gripped the phone. "You have known me for a long time. I *do not* joke about anything, especially about money. And I meant what I said. The price for your prize has just doubled."

There was dead air for a few seconds as if Linde was trying to decide whether he believed him or not.

An arrogant snort broke the silence. "I'll give you the benefit of the doubt. And because I want my wolf, I will be there in seven days when my business here has concluded." He lowered his voice and calmly stated, "If I find out that you are trying to fuck me, Ken, I will bury you in that forest."

Ken laughed when he was cut off. The man was delusional. He would never allow anybody to bury him anywhere, his father and the US Marine Corps had made sure of that and if it happened then he deserved it.

He rested his head on the top of the chair. Jesus, the sooner Linde got up here, the sooner this shit-show would be over. He would have to go back to Drew's house again tomorrow night, watch for Grey. As surprised as he was, he didn't like the idea of killing a cop and even though he had seen Theo change into that wolf, he was still a cop and a good one at that. He was also a good guy. He shook his head. Yeah. A good guy, who just happened to be a werewolf. A good werewolf?

Was there such a thing?

It didn't matter. Good guy or not, cop or not, Theo Grey would die and be displayed in the center of Hendrik Linde's trophy room.

* * * *

The next week flew by in a blur. The town was abuzz with gossip about some big wig who had flown in on his private jet and was renting out the old Red Cedar Cottage. Red Cedar Cottage was huge and newly renovated and was usually being rented out by the TV and film studios in Vancouver. Despite all the excitement around town, Drew's days were full of sick animals and worried owners. It wasn't until she was on her way home, that her body came alive with an intense hunger that filled every cell with anticipation.

That was Theo's fault. He had come over every single night and had done wonderful thing to her, with her. Although, there were a couple of times he hadn't made it over before she had gone to bed. She had tried not to be disappointed — the man had a job after all, and an important one at that. Yet she still went to bed thinking about him, wanting him, missing him. Then during the middle of those nights, she had been woken by his hot kisses, and whispered pleas for her to wake.

Her breath caught at the memories. The tender way he'd touched her, kissed her. The way his body had been hard and hot, and pushing at hers.

"Drew." His sweet breath had been warm against her ear. "Lift your hips, baby." Her skin had already been on fire when he'd whispered that command. Her inner thighs damp as he'd pulled down her panties, her core hot when he'd pushed her legs apart. Then he'd been above her, kissing her face, saying the sweetest things against her mouth as he drove his hips forward, claiming her. She'd held onto him as their slow passion had ignited into a frenzied tangle of sweaty bodies and cries for more.

Then again, they could have been erotic dreams. Dreams that got her wet, dreams that had her crying out and dreams that left her buck-naked.

Those hours were a dark and seductive heaven, until the morning when she woke and she was alone. She stared blankly at the TV. God that hurt and sucked big time. She wanted to go to sleep just once and wake to find him next to her, but the reality was she wouldn't. He had his own house and his job had odd shifts. Besides, he had never asked to stay and she had never asked him to stay, her pride would never allow it. She was a creature of habit and having him here in the morning might not be a good thing. He might not enjoy the bitchy side to her morning personality.

She wanted this man so much, yet she was allowing her stupid pride to rule her actions. Pathetic!

The insecure feeling had her jumping up from her couch, knocking Ruby in the process. Her sleepy BFF sat up and followed her movement as she paced around her living room.

"There is no way I'm the only one who feels this." She tapped her breastbone. She thought about the tender way he'd kissed her, held her, how he always asked if she had had time to eat, and would order her to if she said no. She wasn't a mind reader but she knew Theo cared for her. She looked down at Ruby's beautiful soulful eyes. "What if I'm wrong? What if it's...just me?"

Ruby blinked.

"Do you think I'm wrong?"

Ruby groaned and dropped her head onto the couch pillow.

"Sorry if my inner torment is boring you."

Drew turned toward the door, her nervous energy needing to be expelled. "Come on. Get your furry butt off my couch. We're going to the beach." She needed to get out, clear her mind of all this...stuff.

Ruby groaned a second time.

She pulled on her coat. "Get up," she ordered. "Every time I go down to the beach alone, someone lectures me. So you're coming with me." She walked over to the dog and scratched her butt. "Come on, fur-face. Time for a walk."

Ruby jumped off the couch when she said the magic word.

They were out of the door and down on the beach minutes later. Ruby ran in front of her, nose to the ground, tail wagging. Drew walked to the far end of the beach and back, holding her flip-flops. When she was parallel to the stairs, she hunted for a dry spot and sat, watching Ruby sniff the sand.

Nothing helped, though. She thought about Theo the entire time. Groaning, she dropped her head into her hands. This was nuts, she couldn't let him do this to her, she had a life to live. She didn't have room for a relationship. She wanted one, and she wanted it with Theo. Even though he could be a bit overbearing and had a weird formal manner, he wasn't perfect, he was only human. Those flaws didn't bother her—in fact they made her want him all the more.

Ruby sauntered over, nose and feet wet and covered in sand. The wide toothy grin made her smile and Drew reached out to give her neck a scratch. As Drew was wiping the sand from the tip of Ruby's nose, the dog's ears twitched and her head jerked out from under Drew's ministrations. Then she was off, racing toward the stairs.

Drew turned, yelling at her to 'come', but the words got caught in her throat when she saw the huge black wolf making its way down the old wooden steps.

Theo's heart melted when he heard Drew's desperate plea for Ruby to 'come'. She was terrified for her dog and normally there would be just cause, but Theo would never allow the wolf to hurt Ruby, any more than the wolf would actually hurt her.

"No, Ruby! Come." Her voice shook and so did the rest of her. Then Drew caught and held their stare as Ruby approached. "Please. Please don't hurt her."

Ruby's low growl caught their attention and the wolf casually walked up to the dog and stopped. Theo commanded the wolf to remain calm as the dog sniffed him over. He knew the moment that Ruby caught his scent—her curly tail began to flop back and forth and her ears went a little limp. Satisfied with the inspection, the wolf quickly bent at his front legs and gave a high-pitched bark that screamed 'come and chase me'.

Theo laughed as Ruby returned the bark and chased the wolf down the beach. This was good for the wolf—he didn't get much social interaction on the basic animal level. Theo was his only social contact, and that was difficult for him. Wolves were social creatures by nature, but his wolf had been denied that basic need when he had joined with Jonathan all those years ago. So, he didn't interfere as the wolf played with Ruby.

The wolf led Ruby down the beach and back, running in the waves. They slowed as they approached Drew and Theo couldn't help but notice how her mouth was hanging open but twisted her fingers nervously together.

"*Not too close,*" Theo cautioned. "*Drew is still nervous of us.*"

The wolf picked up his angst, slowed to a stop and sat, keeping a good space between them and Drew.

Ruby, who was still in play mode, kept on with the nudges and a few nips trying to get the wolf to continue playing. Unfortunately for Ruby, the wolf was done, and nothing would persuade him otherwise. He allowed only one more nip before the beast took control of the dog. The snap didn't even touch Ruby, but it was enough for her to realize that the wolf was boss and that playtime was over.

Drew, however, didn't see things as straightforward as the wolf or Theo did. "Hey! Watch it, beast." Drew snapped her fingers to Ruby and the dog bounded over to her side. "Or you'll end up like the rest of your species – extinct."

The animal sat unaffected by the threat, as Theo chuckled.

She automatically reached for Ruby's head and scratched her between the fur pointed ears. "Okay. Now I know there is something different about you."

Drew was keeping strong eye contact with the wolf and she was acting her normal cheeky self. Her ease with the entire situation spoke volumes.

"Just Drew not much scared."

Theo smiled deep within the wolf. *"No, she's not."*

"Proud of Just Drew."

He was too. It had been a while since the first time they'd seen her here on the beach. She had been scared then, but now she seemed able to deal with his wolf without too much difficulty.

Theo noticed the odd expression she was giving them. "I can't believe Ruby played with you. She never plays with other dogs." Her laugh was a little high. "Then again you're not a dog, are you?"

She was silent for a few minutes as she studied them. The waves drowned out everything excluding the panting from the wolf and Ruby.

"Why are you here, wolf?" Apprehension crept into her expression. "You'd better not be looking for a midnight snack?"

All Drew could see was the animal snorting at her assumption. What she didn't know was how insulted the wolf was. Theo did and he shared the animal's feelings. The idea was completely absurd. How could they willingly hurt the one person who held their souls in her hand?

She widened her eyes in surprise. "You understood that."

The beast gave another low snort and jerked his head in an attempt to nod.

"Whoa!" Drew breathed out.

"*Enough*," Theo ordered. "*She may be our mate but she is still human.*"

"*Just Drew mate*," the wolf reminded.

"*Yes*," Theo agreed. "*But she could unknowingly bring danger to herself as well as to us. It is safer for Drew if she doesn't know about us.*"

"*Danger always with us.*"

Theo couldn't argue with that.

"This has got to be a first." She slowly dropped to her knees, using Ruby's head for support. "Unless... You were trained for the circus or something."

"*Circus?*" The wolf raised his nose sniffing the air while he kept a close eye on her movement.

Theo shared his memory of himself as a young boy at a circus his father had taken him to in London. Appalled by the idea, the beast mentally rolled his eyes.

"Nah. Didn't think so. Guess that makes you one of those rare creatures that is too smart for its own good." She smiled and reached out to him. "You like my Ruby. Can we be friends too?" The wolf looked from her hand to her face. "I promise I won't hurt you. Just a little scratch, that's all, promise."

Theo couldn't resist that face, with those golden eyes and lush mouth, and his wolf couldn't resist the idea of being petted by another living being. She had both of them wrapped around her fingers and she wasn't even aware of it.

The beast stood and took a step toward her. He lowered his head with the intent of placing it under her outstretched hand, but a sudden hiss and the stirring of the air around them caused Theo to force the wolf to stop in motion.

Thanks to the crash of the waves, Drew was unaware of the muted disturbance, her and was still reaching toward him, until the crack of the bullet finally hit the beach.

She jumped. "What was that?" She looked toward the forest.

Theo heard the second bullet as it was fired. The wolf leaped on top of Drew, knocking her to the ground as the bullet flew over them.

Despite the fact that his intention was only to protect Drew, the wolf had inadvertently scratched her in the process as well as scared her. Her startled cry shot Ruby into a protective rage and within seconds, they were fighting off the dog while trying not to hurt her in the process.

"No, Ruby, stop!" Drew called.

The black beast was only trying to protect her from the gunfire but Ruby didn't understand. Gunfire. That was something she had never thought she would say let alone think. *My God, what the hell is happening? Why is someone shooting at us?* This was quiet little Tofino, not Vancouver. Shit like this didn't happen here.

The snapping and growling grew more aggressive and she knew that it was coming from Ruby. If she didn't step in and stop this, Ruby would die.

Keeping her head as low as possible, she chased after the ball of black fur rolling on the beach and did the unthinkable—she reached into the middle of a fight between a wolf and a dog. She fought like hell to pull Ruby away and wasn't really surprised when she was bitten for her effort. Who bit her was still up in the air, but, damn, her arm throbbed like a son of a bitch. She gripped her arm tight, trying to stop the blood when the wolf suddenly hit Ruby with enough force to knock her back onto the sand. He trotted closer, his nose twitching, and she knew he smelled the blood. She prayed silently that the stench wouldn't pique his natural instinct and have him move in for the kill, because she knew she wouldn't be able to defend herself, if that was what it decided.

The second the wolf had clamped down on the soft skin of Drew's arm, Theo roared, ordering the wolf to release her. It was unnecessary—the wolf was already backing away and trying to fight off Ruby at the same time. Theo could taste her blood, that metallic, tangy-sweetness filled the wolf's mouth.

Theo swore. They had done that, they'd hurt her. They had hurt their own mate. Theo roared again, this time in anger, and the wolf flung Ruby to the side, uncaring if she got hurt or not.

Theo ordered the wolf to go to Drew so he could see the extent of her injury. The beast did as he was told and closed the distance quickly, the strong scent of her blood flooding both his and the wolf's head. Dark blood slipped through her fingers and ran over her knuckles. She gripped her arm tightly and did a good job of slowing the blood flow.

The wolf stepped closer, both of them wanting to give her some sort of comfort. Nothing else mattered but Drew. Not Ruby, not the gunfire, nothing. Drew was the only important thing in his — their — life.

Drew's eyes grew wide and her face paled as she screamed. "Ruby! No!"

The wolf turned in time to see Ruby launch herself at him. The bullet hit Ruby a second after that in mid-air, her black body jerking to the side with the force of the impact, sending her splashing into the waves.

Drew cried out again, this time in anguish. She struggled to her feet and ran to the limp body. Grabbing the dog by the scruff of the neck, she then dragged it out of the water and onto the dry sand. She fell to her knees and pressed into the small hole on the side of Ruby's chest. Theo knew it wouldn't do any good — the bullet had passed through and through. He saw it through the wolf's eyes.

As he watched Drew, another bullet flew past only inches from them. That was it. He didn't know who the target was or why, but he was damn certain it wouldn't be Drew.

He turned from her, blocking out her soft crying, and bolted across the beach to the old wooden steps. The wolf couldn't help Drew but he could track and kill the ones responsible for breaking Drew's heart and killing Ruby. And Theo would enjoy every bloody second of it.

The moment the wolf hit the forest, he hid in the shadows of the trees and stopped dead in his tracks. He pulled in the different smells and stopped breathing long enough to listen. Theo held his breath too. He didn't want to miss any sound that might give away the assailant's position.

The wolf snapped his head to the left when it heard movement. The beast tensed, every muscle shaking with anticipation and anger.

"*No,*" Theo ordered in a sharp tone.

The growl that rumbled from the wolf was low and menacing. "*Kill.*"

"*Not yet.*" There was more to this, Theo was certain.

If this was the person who had been using the local dogs as target practice, then they needed to be careful. But he was confused. With the lack of evidence at the scene of the other shootings, Theo was under the assumption that the assailant was a good shot. Then why had it taken him two shots to kill Ruby? Why was he still shooting after Ruby had gone down? And why was he shooting when there were people nearby? There were no reports of the last shootings happening so close to civilians. Sure Randall had heard the shot that had hit Frankie, but he hadn't been close to the dog when it had happened. So why do that now? And why suddenly kill, when the MO before had been to wound, with the exception of the wolves of course?

Shit! The wolves. His wolf. This didn't feel right. Uncertainty ran through his veins and settled like a stone in his stomach. Were wolves the target?

Once again, the wolf caught movement in the distance to the left. Luckily this time it was accompanied with a low curse. Before Theo could stop him, the wolf took off in the direction of the noise. He jumped over some low-lying bushes just as another shot was fired. This shot, however, was not aimed at Drew down on the beach with Ruby, but at him. It grazed the wolf's front leg, taking a chunk of fur and skin with it.

He was right. Wolves *were* the target.

The wolf ducked behind a tree at Theo's command and froze, listening as the attackers ran through the forest. They were heading north toward town. There was an old beat-up lane in that direction, it ran to the far end of Cox Beach from the main highway. That was where they were going, Theo was sure of it.

"Go."

The wolf gave the wound on his front leg a quick lick and bolted after them. He quickly caught up to a man. Only one. Which confused Theo because he could have sworn he had heard two people running. He was older in appearance and his hands shook as he fumbled with the door to the car that sat in the middle of the narrow lane. There was a smirk on his rounded face as the wolf stepped out into the open. They were a good fifteen feet away from him but they could still smell his fear and excitement. It poured off him in waves and it mixed with cigarettes, garlic and his sweat—the combination of scents almost made Theo gag.

He saw the rifle and they both smelled the discharge from the bullet.

Oh yes. This was the man who had killed Ruby. Had almost killed Drew.

"Kill." The demand mixed with a deep growl as the beast lowered his head. He fixed his sights and began stalking his prey.

The shooter slowly turned and faced the wolf. The smirk was still there. It annoyed the hell out of Theo that this sorry excuse for a human found killing an innocent animal amusing.

"That's it," the bastard cooed in a heavily accented voice. "Come a little closer."

"Stop!"

The wolf continued forward despite the urgent command.

"*Stop!*" Theo used all of his strength to slow the wolf. "*It's a trap. There's another shooter.*"

The beast froze to the spot and watched the man by the car as they both listened — nothing but the normal sounds. The wolf inhaled deeply and Theo caught the same scent of grease and metal that they had noticed during their runs in the forest numerous times before. Except this time, it was stronger, and a sudden recognition hit Theo. *Son of a bitch!* He knew that smell — it was G-Tac gun cleaner. It reminded him of Propert's leather soap and wood polish. It was a cleaning solvent used for a gun and the oil stench was the firing pin lube. He cleaned and lubed his sidearm on a regular basis, so he was used to its low odor. Of course, it was strong to him and the wolf, but it wasn't bad considering...

A disturbing thought had Theo snapping out an order. "*Back up,*" Theo said quickly. "*We have to get out of here now!*"

"*Kill,*" the wolf demanded. "*Kill!*"

"*No.*" The other man hiding in the woods was a cop. One of his friends. Someone just like him. "*We have to get out of here and get to Drew.*"

The wolf caught his thoughts and moved into the shadow of a large evergreen.

The bastard standing next to the car laughed as sweat rolled down his face and into the first roll of fat on his neck. "You can run, cop, but you can't hide. Not from me." He taunted. "Go on." He waved his meaty hand. "Go back to your little cunt. And I'll see you both in town."

As the wolf tore into the forest and ran as fast as he could back to Drew, Theo's gut twisted. That man knew who and what he was.

Fuck.

Chapter Fifteen

No matter how hard Drew pressed, the blood didn't stop. It was everywhere. On Ruby, on her, it soaked into the sand and mixed with the water. She felt for a pulse on the left side of Ruby's chest. Nothing.

She bit her lip, holding back a cry, and felt for the femoral artery on the inside of Ruby's back leg. She sucked in a breath and dug her fingers deep, searching for a sign. There was nothing. No pulse beating under her finger, no breathing, no movement.

Ruby was gone. She buried her face in the black fur and cried.

She didn't know how long she stayed there like that, it could have been minutes or an hour. She would have stayed like that longer if Theo hadn't called to her.

"Drew," he said quietly next to her. He gripped her shoulders and pulled her away.

She looked up at him, her face feeling damp and swollen. "Somebody was shooting at us. They killed Ruby."

"I know. I heard the shots." He squatted on the sand next to her. "We can't stay here and you need to have that arm looked at."

She shook her head and sniffed. "I can't leave her here. The tide is coming in. She'll get washed away." It was completely unreasonable. She knew that, and she understood that Ruby was dead and that her body was only a shell that held a loving soul. It didn't matter. She couldn't stomach the thought of Ruby being left alone on a deserted beach, where other animals would feed on her.

"I'll take care of Ruby." His voice wasn't hard but there was a no-nonsense bite to it. He stood. "Get up, Drew. We have to move."

She clasped his hand and allowed him to pull her up. She looked down at her best friend and fought the tears that wanted to fall. She watched as Theo easily lifted Ruby's lifeless body walked across the beach.

"Drew." She flinched at his sharp tone. "You walk with me. Stay one pace behind on my right side." He didn't move until she was next to him and began a quick march up the beach toward her house. "I want to move fast so hold onto the waistband of my jeans and do not let go. If I tell you to run, do not question me—just do it. Do you understand?"

What? "Why? 'Cause of the shoo—"

"Quiet. They could still be out here," he ordered in a harsh whisper. "Do you understand me?"

"Yes." She nodded as she meet his intense glare.

He quickened his pace but she was able to keep up and they were standing next to his truck minutes later.

"Open the back, please." His words were spoken just above a whisper.

She did as he had asked and scanned the area as he gently laid Ruby on a blanket in the tailgate. He grabbed a small first aid kit fastened to the inside wall of the flatbed.

"Let me see your arm," he instructed, tearing open a square piece of white gauze.

"It's fine." She sniffed again.

He reached for her arm. "It is not fine." He pressed the dressing tightly against the bite. "Hold it tight." He indicated to her wound and next opened a roll of gauze that he wrapped over and around the bite on her arm and secured it with a knot.

"It's too tight." She tugged at the sides, trying to adjust the bandage.

"It's meant to be. Get in. I want to take you to the clinic."

She didn't respond to his command but instead gave him a good once-over. He wore only a pair of faded jeans and a T-shirt and his feet were bare until she watched as he quickly stooped and pulled on a pair of casual black sneakers and swiftly tied them up.

"How did you know we were on the beach?"

He was scanning the forest when he answered her. "You didn't answer the door. And then I heard the shots. I put two and two together." He pulled her to the passenger side of the cab. "I'm taking you to the health clinic to get that arm looked at."

"No." She stopped pulling away as he opened the door. "I want to take Ruby to my clinic first."

"No."

"Yes!" She cut him off, suddenly feeling panicked. "Please, Theo. I want to take Ruby to my clinic. I don't want her sitting in your truck like a sack of meat." She sucked in a breath, trying desperately to control her emotions.

"Damn it, Drew." He looked past her into the forest again. His nostrils flared as he shook his head. "Ruby's dead. You can't fix her."

"Don't you think I know that?" She jammed her fist against her breastbone, shaking from grief, and anger and fear. "I know that better than anybody."

He put up his hands and slowly closed the gap between them. "Okay, easy." He pulled her close to his heat, then threading his fingers through her hair, forced her head to his chest. "We drop her off, then I take you to the clinic."

She fisted her hands in his shirt and nodded. "Thanks."

"But I swear," his words were harsh, "if you argue with me or try to postpone treatment... I will not be fucking happy. Clear?"

"You're not happy now." She sniffed. "How much worse can you get?"

He nuzzled the top of her head. "You have no idea."

She shivered and she didn't know if it was from the situation or his words.

He gave her a tight squeeze and kissed her temple when she shivered. "Let's go. I don't like keeping you out here, when I don't know where the shooter is." He gently pushed her toward the truck and opened the door. "Here." He yanked a light rain jacket off the front seat. "Put this on." He waited for her to tug it on and climb into the cab before closing the door.

* * * *

Ken walked out of the forest cradling his rifle in his arms. He stopped when he reached the side of the black Mercedes where Linde was waiting. "Why didn't you shoot it?" Ken noticed a lit cigarette wedged between his fingers as he waved his hand out in front of him. "He was right there in the open. I could have had him."

"I saw."

"Then why the fuck didn't you shoot him?"

"Because you moved after I told you *not* to."

"So?"

"He heard you move."

Linde raised his head and looked down his nose. "You're not afraid of a wolf, are you?"

"We both know I'm not the one who has fear issues. Then again, he's not all wolf, is he? He's part man and that man...is a cop. A very smart cop, who now knows what you look like." Ken exhaled a long breath and made a decision. "You FUBAR'ed this hunt. It's time you moved onto the next prize."

"No." Linde raised a cigarette to his lips and pulled deeply. "I want this bastard added to my trophy case." He exhaled the smoke and pointed a chubby finger at him. "And you'd better mind your fucking attitude or you'll find yourself hanging on my wall next to that man-wolf."

Ken closed the distance, easily towering over Linde. Sweat gleamed on the obese man's forehead, nose and chin. "That threat is getting old in a hurry, but if you would like to try..." He lowered his head so he was nose to nose with Linde. "By all means."

He held Linde's stare until the greasy perspiration covering the older man's forehead trickled down the sides of his cheeks. He cleared his throat and looked the other way. Satisfied, Ken took two steps back and, bracing his legs apart, stood watching his employer in silence.

Linde finally faced him and with a nod said, "I'll double your fee as you asked, plus throw in a bonus of one million. And as a thank you, I'll fly you down to my private villa in Costa Rica for as long as you like."

Ken laughed. "Your private villa, huh? Is this the same private villa where your last two trackers went and were never heard from again?" Ken laughed harder when Linde's eyes grew wide. "No thanks. But you can wire the money to my account first. Not the bonus, of course, I should only receive that after you collect Grey's head."

Linde went to open his mouth, but Ken held up his hand silencing him. "Your prize has become that much harder to capture thanks to you. Therefore, if you want your trophy, you'll do exactly what I tell you. Are you tracking?"

Linde's face turned red. The man hated when he wasn't in the driver's seat, that much was clear, but Ken still got his nod of agreement.

"Good. I'll call you when I get word from my bank that the money has been deposited." Ken walked around the Mercedes and stopped just before entering the forest when Linde called out to him.

"Where are you going?"

"Home." He turned slinging the rifle over his shoulder.

"If he knows who I am, he'll know you too. There was no way he missed your scent." An arrogant edge clung to Linde's statement. "He'll recognize you."

Ken shook his head. There was a reason why he didn't smoke and he used odorless soaps. He was damn good at what he did. Hiding a human scent was the most challenging part of his job. Keeping his hunting gear in trash bags filled with local dirt, leaves and pine needles was a daily routine that paid off. It was what he was trained to do and it worked. Linde had no idea what it took to be a hunter. He didn't have the patience or the stamina. "He knows who you are, not me. Remember, I'm the one who plays this game professionally."

Chapter Sixteen

Life was a blur for the next day and a half. Drew did everything in her power to block out what had happened on the beach and to *not* think about Ruby and the only way she could do that was to work. It was weird — working with other dogs and animals in general probably should have made Ruby's death more painful for her, but it didn't. She had always been able to separate her feelings for her own pets from those of her patients.

Nevertheless, she was beginning to feel the effects of working almost non-stop. She felt awful, looked awful. She hadn't slept and she hadn't gone home to shower because she didn't want to be reminded that Ruby wasn't there and she was probably beginning to smell pretty ripe. Washing in the small bathroom at the clinic could only help so much.

She rested in her chair and scrubbed the sleep from her eyes. She needed to wake up. Mr Darcy, the cat, was due in for a follow-up to check his weight.

She looked at the time on the bottom-right corner of her computer. She had twenty minutes. Just enough time to grab a coffee.

She grabbed her jacket and her arm throbbed from the bite as she pulled on her light raincoat, and just like the other times she flexed her hand, trying to loosen up the muscle. When that didn't work she reached inside her sleeve and grabbed at the dressing that had been applied the night before.

She really hadn't wanted to go to the clinic, even though she knew it was the right thing to do. The bite was pretty deep in some areas—she just didn't want to talk about how she had gotten it and she didn't want to talk about Ruby. She needed to fill out the paperwork for Ruby and get things into motion to have her picked up and taken into Port Alberni, where a vet friend of Angus' would handle her cremation. She needed to be a vet, to do something that she could control, to do something that she could hide in.

Theo, however, had insisted that she get her arm looked at. So, he had dragged her to the medical clinic. When the doc had asked what had happened, Theo had answered for her. Which normally she would have hated, but she was glad he did. The cop in him had risen to the surface and he was very diplomatic about his answer, telling the truth but not giving away too much information then ending the conversation. If she had been the one to answer she probably would have blurted out that her dog had been shot to death then burst into tears. She had felt like she was going to break apart at any second. She hadn't, though. And she had no idea if that was good or bad.

She mumbled on her way out of the door, not bothering to ask if Connie wanted anything, and made her way to the local coffee shop, Milk & Sugar.

Today was a 'fuck the calories day', so a mochachino with extra whipped cream and butter tart was on the menu. As sad as it was, she had a feeling that she would be drowning her sorrows in sweets for a long time to come.

She looked both ways before crossing the street and quickly made her way to the other side. She squeezed between a large black sedan with tinted windows and a small pink compact car that had three bobble-head cats on the front dashboard.

The line inside Milk & Sugar was short and she was out with her large mochachino and homemade butter tart in no time. She was just about to cut between the two cars when a deep voice called her.

"Excuse me."

Turning at the heavy accent Drew watched as the rear window of the black sedan slid open and a man with a round face became visible.

"Yes."

"I was wondering if I could have a word with you, Dr O'Bannion?"

Drew stepped closer to the car, studying the man. "I'm sorry, have we met?"

"No." The man flashed a charming smile and waved to her to step closer, but her gut told her to walk away instead.

"I'm good right here, thanks." She smiled and took a sip of her mochachino. "What can I do for you?"

"I heard you were a vet."

"True."

He leaned forward, exposing more of his face to her. White streaks ran through the sides of his thinning brown hair and mixed into his thick eyebrows. "I also heard you were a very good vet."

"That's also true."

His booming laugh caused passers-by to turn their heads. "I like a woman who is confident in her abilities." His thick accent became very apparent when his voice dropped and he said, "I also like very beautiful women and you, Dr O'Bannion, are both."

She didn't know whether to laugh in his face or tell him to screw off. Either way it was a pathetic attempt from a man old enough to be her father. She didn't do that older man and young chicky thing. It was gross. Then again, she didn't need that to stop her in this case. This guy — whatever his name was — was creepy on so many levels.

"Thanks, Mr..."

"Linde. Hendrik Linde." His accent became apparent once again.

She nodded a greeting. "Not from around here, are you, Mr Linde?"

"Hendrik is fine and, no, I'm from South Africa."

She caught movement out of the corner of her eye and saw Theo's police truck pull in behind the bobble-head car. He threw the truck into park and shut off the engine, then casually rested his arm on the inside of his door, simply watching her. She hated that she couldn't see his eyes, but damn, those dark sunglasses always looked so good on him. She gave him a smile and expected one in return but got nothing.

Linde said something to her but she missed it. "I'm sorry, I got distracted. What can I do to help you?"

"Distracted?" He looked over his shoulder and out of the rear window then laughed. "Ah!" He chuckled as he faced her. "Your boyfriend's here."

"My what...? No, he's not my boyfriend. We're just friends." She fairly choked on the words. She had never thought of Theo as her boyfriend, because the man was no boy. Lover. Now she liked that label. Theo was her lover.

"Come now, Drew. We're both adults here. There is no point in hiding the fact that Police Sergeant Grey makes nightly visits to your house. You're not embarrassed to have him as your lover, are you?" He paused and flashed stained yellow teeth when he grinned at her. "Even with his extraordinary abilities I would think he is a fantastic lover. Great ramming power, I bet. Or maybe you can't admit that you prefer freaks?"

Her face heated over his rude comment. "What the hell are you talking about?" She pushed the repugnant remark aside for now because she was still trying to process the fact that this creep knew that Theo came over to her house and that they were lovers.

"Wait now." He studied her briefly then chuckled as he withdrew a packet of cigarettes from his breast pocket. "You don't know, do you?"

His chuckling continued as he lit his cigarette. "That's very interesting," he mumbled then puffed out a mouthful of smoke.

Dislike swirled in her belly. Not to mention shock and that the very idea of this man watching her and Theo made her sick to her stomach.

"Listen up, old man." She stepped toward the sedan as a ring of smoke floated from the window. "I don't know who the hell you think you are, but my love life is none of your goddamn business. And FYI stalking is considered a crime here in Canada. So fuc —"

"Is everything all right here?" Theo asked, pulling her from the car.

"No. It's not. This ass-hat seems to know a lot about me and you and I don't like it."

"Easy. Come on." He began leading her away, when he suddenly stopped and addressed Linde. "Wait there please, Mr Linde." Without waiting for a response, he escorted Drew over to his truck.

"Ass-hat?" He smothered a grin. "That's good." He took his sunglasses off and rested them on top of his head. "Are you okay?" Concern shone silver in his eyes.

"I'm fine," she snapped. "Just pissed off and freaked out that someone has been spying on us. That guy is a huge dick. In fact I think I'm giving him too much credit." The anger drained out of her when Theo raised a single dark eyebrow.

She sighed and pressed her palm to her forehead. "I'm sorry. I'm just tired."

He stepped closer and blocked her view of the black car and of the man who was most likely watching them. "I know." He grabbed her light raincoat then tugged her close. "You didn't go home last night." His breath warmed her cheek. "Or the night before."

"No. I had work..." She didn't want to lie to him, and besides she had a feeling that he already knew why she hadn't gone home. She lowered her head. "Ruby wasn't there."

Theo smiled, tucking a strand of silky hair behind her ear. "I figured that was the reason."

In fact, he hadn't even bothered going to her house when he was done working late the previous night. He had gone to her clinic instead to make sure she was safe and that the front door was locked, which it was—for the first time. He didn't bother going in, he went hunting instead. He hunted down Linde, and watched from the forest as the criminal of the hour moved around Red Cedar Cottage. His two assistants—or bodyguards—were constantly by his side, even inside the sprawling cottage. If he hadn't done a search on the infamous Hendrik Linde, he would have guessed that the man was using the guards for appearances' sakes, but as it was, the man had actually made quite a few enemies. First was his hobby of illegal big game hunting. Two was the mysterious way his business dealings didn't always turn out as predicted—in other words, the other party had a strange way of ending up dead. However, according to some of the other reports, he was well liked, in the United States in particular, thanks to his large donations to the film studios in California as well as here in BC. Yet interestingly enough he had been banned from entering the UK over ten years ago, which had nothing to do with his hobbies or charitable donations. It would seem that the UK didn't tolerate smuggling or human trafficking. Fortunately, for Linde, there was never enough proof to convict him. *Then again, you couldn't convict someone when all the proof against them was dead and buried.*

Human trafficking. Theo's stomach rolled when he thought about it.

He focused on the beauty in front of him. "You are going home tonight." He didn't ask her, he was telling her. She needed a proper night's rest and she would never get that sleeping in her office.

He stopped her as she shook her head. "You can't sleep another night on the sad excuse for a couch."

"But... She's not—" Her voice spiked as the coffee cup in her hand began to shake and she finished with, "there."

"Hey." He pulled her close. "Take it easy." He brushed his lips against her forehead. When she calmed, he pushed her back, careful not to jar her sore arm or the coffee and tart she was holding. "Wait for me tonight and I'll follow you home."

Once again, she shook her head.

"Drew." He hardened his voice. "I have given you two days to deal with Ruby's death because I knew how hard it was for you and then you had to answer all the questions from the guys over at the station. But it's done. I can't stand by and let you wear yourself down like this. You will go home tonight and if I have to, I will take you home myself — in a cruiser. Understood?"

She scowled as she lifted her chin. "Are you threatening me, Officer?"

He couldn't help but smile. He loved that fearless attitude of hers. "Yes." And before she could comment he gave her a hard kiss meant to shut her up. When the kiss ended, she looked around, avoiding his gaze, and licked her lips. "You shouldn't have done that. Someone could have seen."

"So? I don't care who sees us and neither should you."

She got his meaning right away. "I don't, not with anyone here, but that Linde guy gives me the creeps. He knew my name and that I was a vet." She glared over his shoulder at the black car. "He also tried to hit on me. It made me want to ralph all over that Hugo Boss he's wearing."

He hid his smile and rubbed her shoulders. "Don't worry about it. I'll take care of him."

She wrinkled her eyebrows. "But he said I preferred freaks."

"What do you mean?"

"He asked if I was embarrassed to admit you were my lover. Then said that I couldn't admit that I like freaks. Which means he called you a freak." She was getting worked up again.

He lightly gripped her upper arms. "It's just a word. No reason to get upset." He stared into her concerned frown and gave her a smile. Linde wasn't far off the mark. He was the only one of his kind, which did make him a freak. Tom and the other elders of the *Nuu-Chah-Nulth* would say he had been given a gift by the wolf, but the reality of it was that Linde was right, he was a freak.

"I can't help it. Why would he say such a thing? Do you know him?"

He shook his head. "I met him the other night." Of course, he couldn't tell her it was the same night that Ruby had been shot. The very same night he'd realized that two men knew his secret. One, the head of a human trafficking ring and lover of illegal big game hunting, and the other—was still to be determined but his gut was telling him he knew the other man. "Don't worry about it." He turned her gently in the direction of her clinic. "Get back to work."

"But I—"

"Hey," he whispered next to her ear. "This officer has no problem issuing another threat, and I've been itching to use my handcuffs."

She angled her face toward his, putting her mouth in the perfect position for a kiss. "Well in that case, don't be surprised when you get a nine-one-one call about a crazed vet robbing the bank."

She finally cracked a smile at her own joke and Theo chuckled, relaxing a bit. He would have preferred that she had laughed out right, but considering what life had dealt her in the past couple of days, she wasn't doing too badly. "That's better. I love the curve of your mouth when you smile."

"Thanks." She pressed her lips together then asked, "See you later... If you're not working or something...?" Without waiting for his answer she quickly stepped between his truck and the compact car in front of him and jogged across the street.

He frowned to himself as he pulled his glasses off his head and slid them up his nose. Of course he would see her later, it was the main reason he had ordered her to go home tonight. He needed to be with her, to touch her, and to offer her some sort of comfort for losing Ruby. Damn, he felt guilty about Ruby getting killed. It didn't matter that he'd had no idea at the time that he was the target—Drew loved Ruby and that made the guilt sit heavy next to his anger.

And he was angry. He was mad because someone he knew was keeping company with a dirt-bag criminal that wanted his head as a trophy, and mad because he should have been more careful when he swapped with the wolf. Most of all, he was mad at himself for putting Drew in a dangerous situation.

He snorted to himself. There was no way he would allow someone like Hendrik Linde to end his life. Yet how could he allow this man to leave this area alive after learning what Linde was involved in? He knew killing Linde wouldn't stop the atrocities he was involved in, but with the way the world was today, every little piece of justice was needed.

The wolf stirred, ruffling his fur, and grunted in agreement.

Straightening, he set his jaw and walked back to the black car that held said dirt-bag. The window was still open and smoke floated free. Theo stopped next to the window and raised his forearm onto the roof of the car.

Like the smug bastard Theo had imagined him to be, Linde chuckled and expelled another puff of smoke.

The wolf stirred beneath his skin, agitated by the foul smell.

"So your little cunt has left you, has she? Gone back to treat sick animals? How very noble of her."

The wolf growled and Theo fought the urge to reach through the window and haul Linde's fat ass to the ground and beat some manners into him. He knew Linde was trying to prick at his temper, wanted him to make a mistake, and if Theo did that as a police officer, there would be repercussions. This was when living for well over a hundred and twenty years came in handy, dealing with—as Drew liked to call them—ass-hats.

"Very good, Mr Linde. Hitting where you believe you can cause the most damage."

"Thank you. I've been playing this game a long time." Linde grinned.

"That would make two of us."

"Now that is intriguing." Linde sat forward and rested his elbows on his knees. "And how long would that be exactly?"

Theo snorted despite the anger that swirled in his belly.

The wolf pushed to the surface of his face. Theo's skin prickled and his eyes burned. The beast had done this very thing a few times before to warn off potential threats, so Theo recognized the sensation right away. This behavior wasn't something he allowed very often, but in this case he went with the flow. He took off his sunglasses, and bending at the waist, he leveled his stare at the older man. "It's time for you to leave this area, Mr Linde," Theo said with a smile.

Linde's eyes suddenly grew wide as Theo's eyes flashed a silvery-white.

Linde blinked as Theo chuckled and once again covered his eyes with his sunglasses. Linde didn't appear overly nervous, but the wolf pulled in his fear. Satisfaction hummed through his veins. *Damn, that felt good.*

Still, Linde shook his head and was stupid enough to taunt him further.

"I'm not ready to leave yet. I haven't got what I came here for. There are two things I want now." He lowered his voice. "One will decorate my wall and the other will make me lots of money when I sell her to the highest bidder."

Theo cocked his head, studying Linde while he fought to keep his fury and the wolf contained. If Theo had any second thoughts about letting Linde go they had just been kicked aside when he'd said that he would 'sell' Drew.

A low growl he couldn't contain rumbled in his throat.

"Ah! There it is." A slight sheen of sweat coated Linde's upper lip. "The protective nature of a wolf for its mate, and Dr O'Bannion is your mate, isn't she, Officer?"

He could tell Linde the truth, but the fact was that even if Drew hadn't been his mate, Linde would still believe she was and he would still go after her. He couldn't allow anything to happen to Drew. If she was taken from him, bad things would happen, and not to just Linde, but to anyone who came near him. The rage was simmering just below the surface of his skin, mixing with the wolf's need to kill this man. He would go mad if that happened. He would toss his control of the wolf aside as he had in the war and allow the animal to roam free and become the feral creature it once had been and when that happened, people would die.

Theo straightened, leaving Linde's question unanswered. "You're parked next to a fire hydrant, Mr Linde." He casually tapped the window frame. "You'd better move along before I have you towed."

Linde laughed. "Of course, Officer – if I'm anything I'm a law-abiding citizen."

"Yeah." Theo snorted. "Right."

He walked to his truck and hopped in, watching as Linde's black sedan pulled out onto the main road mixing in with the local traffic.

Theo rested his elbow against the window and waited. A couple of minutes passed before he saw Linde's car coming back toward him and heading out of town. He needed to know who was working with Linde and how dangerous they were. He started his truck and pulled a U-turn in the middle of the main street with the intent of following Linde. Not in a stalking way, but in a more protecting the public from a monster kind of way.

Staying a couple of cars behind Linde, he noticed the car slow as it passed the street leading toward the police station. He could make out the front end of a cruiser and a second later Ben came into view. He was sitting in his patrol car waiting for a gap in the traffic so he could turn right. Then he did something Theo hadn't expected. He nodded to the driver of Linde's car as it passed.

Theo frowned as he drew closer to Ben. He didn't know if Ben was just being his normal friendly self or if he had been acknowledging someone he knew. Theo hoped he was just being paranoid and that Ben was just being outgoing Ben. Still he couldn't help but wonder if he was the one who was working for Linde.

Theo focused on his friend and before he realized it, he had turned the corner, his focus now on Ben, and stopped next to Ben's cruiser and rolled down his window.

"Hey." Theo nodded. "Where you headed?"

"Got a noise complaint out on Cedarwood Lane."

Theo nodded casually. Red Cedar Cottage was located on Cedarwood Lane, and Linde was headed in that direction this very moment. Not good.

Theo drew in a slow breath in the hopes that the wolf might smell—something—anything that might indicate that Ben was in bed with Linde. Of course, if he hadn't detected any strong emotions when he was out in the woods, why would he expect to sense them now?

Ben continued talking. "Mr Pine called it in. He says the neighbors are 'whooping it up' and it's interrupting his nap. What are the odds that he has his TV turned up full bore again?"

Theo smiled. "Probably pretty good."

"Better go, or he'll be calling the station again. What are you doing tonight? Want to grab a beer?"

Theo paused. He wanted to go to Drew's tonight, keep her safe. But if there was a chance that Ben was Linde's invisible shooter, he might get a chance to prove it tonight. Then again, it could also be a set-up. Drew would be alone and an easy target. Capture the girl to draw out the beast.

"Not tonight, I have other plans."

Ben gave him a crooked grin. "Going to see the hot vet? Nice!"

Theo raised a single eyebrow. Ben knew about him and Drew. Linde knew about him and Drew. He was either letting his desire for Drew blind him at every turn or Ben was the other gun in the forest. Theo gave him a careless shrug. "It has its moments."

Ben's chest radio squawked. "Ben!" Joanne the dispatcher called. "Are you on your way to Pine's house? He just called again."

Ben shook his head and spoke into the radio. "I'm on my way."

"Good, I don't think I have the patience to talk to the man again."

"Shit." Ben sighed. "Later."

"Yeah." Theo nodded. "See you later."

Theo headed the short distance to the station, pulled into his stall then shut off the engine. He rested his arm alongside the window and sat for a minute, staring off into space, thinking about what Linde had said. He had threatened Drew. His Drew.

Our Drew, the wolf reminded. The beast was still close to the surface. He shifted under Theo's skin, the restless movement proof of his unease over Linde's threat.

Then there was Ben. Jesus, was his gut feeling right? Was Ben working for Linde? Did he know about the wolf and was just hiding it?

A memory, sharp and clear, came out of nowhere of Ruby growling at Ben. The fact that animals didn't particularly like Ben was nothing new, even in the short amount of time he had known Ruby, but Ben was the only person he had heard Ruby growl at. The injured gray female had growled at Ben too. Another thought occurred — why had Ben been searching away from the others the day the three wolves were found shot? He hadn't given much thought at the time but now it appeared as though Ben was... What?

Theo rubbed his chin.

Why would Ben have purposely headed in the opposite direction as the others? Hiding evidence that put him at the scene? Making sure his tracks were covered? Jesus. He just didn't know and he sure as hell wouldn't accuse his friend of any wrongdoing when he only had a couple of growling dogs to go on.

But...

What if Ben was the invisible shooter? Did that mean he was also gunning for Drew? He hoped not. He didn't want to kill him but if he tried to hurt Drew – he was a dead man.

As Theo watched the wind whip around the trees next to the station, a plan began to develop. It wasn't the safest solution, nor was it the tidiest, but it was straightforward. The downside to this simple plan, even though Drew would be safe, was that she might also be terrified of him. The same images he'd had before of her running from him in terror played once again in his head.

Jesus. He had replayed those thoughts in his head so many times that he should have been used to them by now, yet they still caused his chest to tighten painfully.

He sighed, opening the door and stepping out just as the rain began to fall.

Even if she was terrified of him, at least she would be alive and in the end that was all that mattered.

He closed the door and walked around his truck, heading toward the station when Kevin drove by. He gave Theo a wave and turned in the direction of Drew's clinic. Theo stopped for a moment and studied Kevin's taillights. He hated the thought of Kevin being there with Drew. That beach-boy smile of his had suckered in locals and tourists alike. But he had other things to worry about right now, like Drew's safety.

He continued inside, making a mental list of the calls he needed to make and the personnel file he needed to find on Ben.

Chapter Seventeen

Drew walked from the exam room into the front reception and sighed. "No, Miss Evans. I didn't read the scale wrong. Mr Darcy has gained three pounds."

Kevin was leaning against the front desk chatting to Connie. Both of them stared at her as she crossed the small space.

"Well that can't be right." The older woman followed behind, holding the cat. "I followed the feeding instructions you gave me. How could he have gained weight?"

Drew closed her eyes and took a deep breath, before dropping the file onto Connie's desk then asked. "Do you give your cat treats, Miss Evans?" She knew her voice was a bit harsh, but after being accused of not knowing how to read a scale for the past fifteen minutes, her patience had finally reached its limits.

"Well, yes. Mr Darcy is a good boy and deserves his goodies."

"Yes of course. A pet deserves a treat every once in a while, but not all the time."

"It's not all the time," the older woman snapped.

"You know what?" Drew snapped. "It doesn't matter because soon he will be dead and we won't be having this conversation again. That is, until you bring your next overweight cat in here." She could see Kevin straighten out of the corner of her eye, and frown. He probably didn't like the fact that she was getting snippy with Miss Evans. She just couldn't help it. She hated seeing animals abused by their owners, and whether Miss Evans' behavior was intentional or not, she was still abusing her cat.

"Mr Darcy is going to die if you don't stop feeding him crap. Do you want him to die?"

The older woman gasped, her old weathered hands shaking as she petted the orange calico in her arms. "No, of course not. I just thought a few treats wouldn't hurt if he was already on a diet."

Drew sighed again and stepped forward, touching the woman's shoulder. "Well, it is hurting him. He needs to be on low fat food until his weight is back to normal." She reminded again, "And no treats."

Miss Evans met her stare, her eyes rimmed with unshed tears. "Okay." She nodded in defeat and turned to the shelving unit that held a few lines of specialty dog and cat food. "Which food do you recommend?"

Drew sighed quietly. She didn't mean for the old girl to cry. "Connie knows which one, she'll help you out." Drew scribbled out another set of feeding instructions for Mr Darcy. "I want you to give him a few more meals. But" — she handed the instructions over to Miss Evans — "you will notice that each of those meals is very small. This way he won't go hungry throughout the day, which will eliminate the need to give him treats."

"Yes, that makes sense. Thank you."

"You're welcome." She marched to her office door and stopped. "I want to see him in a month, but come by every week to check his weight—you don't need an appointment for that. Connie here will weigh him and track his progress for you."

The woman nodded her understanding and smiled at Connie.

Drew looked to Kevin. "Did you need to see me?" *Please say no.*

"Yeah." His frowned deepened as he moved around the desk and entered her office.

She closed the door behind him. "So what's—?"

Kevin suddenly loomed over her. She tried to step around him but he blocked her and when she moved back he followed her until she was pressed against the door. "Wh-what are you doing?"

"I'm trying to figure out what the hell is the matter with you." His eyes softened as he traced her jaw with a single finger. "But I think I already know." He then cupped her cheek. "Ruby?"

She pressed her lips together to keep them from trembling. She looked at the top of his T-shirt—she didn't want to think about Ruby—a heartbreaking weight filled her chest every time she did and she just wasn't— Couldn't...

She exhaled a shaky breath.

"Hey, it's okay." Kevin pulled her into the warmth of his body and wrapped his arms around her. She struggled once again to draw air into her lungs when the image of Ruby lying dead in her arms flashed behind her eyes. He squeezed her tighter and brushed his lips against the top of her head. "It's tough now but it will lessen each day. Just breathe through it."

They stood like that for quite some time, Kevin holding her and she simply breathing. She liked his heat and she liked the smell of the rain that clung to him. It reminded her of Theo. She wished that Theo was the one holding her instead of Kevin but this was okay too.

Kevin lowered his head and rubbed his cheek against the side of her face. "Feel better?"

The rough texture of his stubble against her skin was a bit more intimate but still pleasant. "Yes." She pushed away but not too far—Kevin still held her tight. "Thank you."

He brushed his lips against the corner of hers. "No problem."

Ohhh! That was way too intimate and pleasant, but not— Kevin's mouth covered hers as his hand slid to the back of her head to hold her still. He moved his lips against hers with precision. The man could kiss like nobody's business. He was gentle when he teased and caressed her mouth into opening but he wasn't Theo. Kissing Kevin was nice, real nice, but there was no overpowering pull to him, no drive to rip his clothes off, no need to have him bury his body in hers. She had never felt that with anyone else, nor did she feel it with Kevin. Only Theo caused that hunger.

She pulled away and licked at her lips. He touched his forehead to hers.

"You taste so good." He sighed, trying to recapture her mouth.

She turned her head away. "Thank you for helping me. I felt like I was about to snap apart and take Miss Evans with me."

"Welcome." He adjusted and moved in once more.

"No." She shook her head. "I'm sorry, Kevin. I can't let that happen again."

"Why?" He frowned. "'Cause of Theo?"

Her cheeks heated. Did everyone know she was having sex with Theo? "Yeah." She nodded.

"I don't mind a bit of friendly competition." He narrowed his eyes. "You liked kissing me?"

"Yes… I mean no… It's just that—"

"Just what? What's the problem?" He gave her a sly smile. "If you still want Theo, that's fine, I don't mind sharing."

Sharing! He wanted to share her with Theo! She had never slept with two men at the same time and the idea kind of thrilled her in a kinky dot com kind of way. But— She frowned at him. She didn't want to have sex with Kevin. Period. Why? That was easy. He wasn't Theo. She only wanted Theo.

"I gather by the frown you don't like that idea?"

"Well…" Her cheeks flushed. "I guess I'm kind of flattered that you would be willing to share me. But I don't want to have sex with you." She blinked, suddenly worried, and placed a hand on his chest. "I'm sorry, Kevin. I just… I want Theo. It doesn't mean I don't like you, I just don't want to have sex with you. I hope I haven't hurt you. I just don't want any misunderstandings between us."

He laughed. "Cute and cruel at the same time." He laughed again and pulled her in close, giving her a hard squeeze. "Just you remember what I said in case you change your mind. And if you don't, that's okay." He cupped her cheek and grinned. "I have more than enough patience to wait you out or for you and Theo to come to an end."

He gave her a hard kiss before she could pull away. He released her.

She blinked, stunned by his confession, and tried to focus on something else. "So…" She cleared her throat. "What did you want to see me about?"

He crossed his arms and smiled. "I wanted to see how you were doing. I heard about Ruby."

"Oh. I'm... Crappy."

"Yeah, I can see that. You don't look like you've slept either." He stared down at her. "Have you?"

"As much as I can get on that." She nodded toward the old loveseat.

Kevin eyed the small couch. "Guess that wouldn't be much then." He cocked his head to the side. "That's not good, Drew. You need to sleep and you need to eat. I know you're not feeling yourself right now but you can't continue on this way. Okay?"

"I know, you're right. And I already promised Theo that I would go home tonight."

Kevin stepped around her and reached for the door. "Good to see he's keeping you in line." He stopped and looked over his shoulder at her. "Sure you don't want me to help him?"

"Kevin," she sighed, exasperated.

He chuckled as he swung the door open and came face to face with Theo.

Only a few seconds passed as Theo and Kevin stared at each other but the room was already flooded with testosterone by then. There were no angry words, or glares or even threats of beatings to come... Just silence. *God, men are weird.*

Guilt ran through her the moment she saw Theo. She hadn't done anything but kiss Kevin and that kiss had helped her to solidify what she felt for Theo but he may not see things that way.

"Hey." She stepped between the men but faced Theo. "What are you doing here?"

His stare softened when he looked down. "Connie called. She thought you might need to talk to me. Are you okay?"

Drew noticed Connie kneeling on her desk in order to look over Theo's shoulder. "I'm sorry, Drew. I was worried and I saw that Kevin was worried." She tucked strands of black, blue and pink hair behind her ear. "You didn't look too good after you snapped at Miss Evans. So I called Theo. I guess I jumped the gun."

Drew smiled. "I appreciate your concern but I'm okay. Don't worry about me."

"I'll try." She struggled off the desk, quite the feat considering the pencil skirt and platforms she was wearing. She huffed as she gained her footing. "But I can't make you any promises."

Drew met Theo's stare. "I'm okay. Really. You can go back to work."

Theo shook his head silently then glanced over her shoulder at Kevin. The look suggested one thing and one thing only— *Get The Fuck Out.*

"I guess I'll be going then." Theo stepped to the side and pulled Drew with him, stationing himself between her and Kevin as he left the room.

He closed the door the second Kevin was gone and faced her.

"Should I be worried about you?" he asked quietly.

Okay, what did that mean? Worried how? Worried because she was still trying to deal with Ruby's death? Or worried because she had kissed another man? Except he couldn't know about that, unless he had been listening outside the door, and even then, his hearing would have to be acute.

"What do you mean?" she asked anyway.

He drew in a deep frustrated breath and frowned at her, his nostrils flared and the muscles in his jaw clenched. He narrowed his eyes and it was as though he saw straight into her soul. *Oh my God, he knows. He knows!*

Feeling the panic rise in her belly, she shook her head and stepped close. "I'm not myself today. I kind of snapped at Miss Evans. I didn't mean to. Then Kevin wanted to see how I was because he had heard about Ruby." She was babbling now and she didn't want to stop until she had told him everything. "And then I almost cried, and he hugged me to make me feel better. And then... And then we... He..." Oh shit, this was harder than she had thought.

"You kissed," Theo supplied. His eyes weren't gray anymore, they were silver, and looked as cold as a winter's day.

She couldn't look at him anymore and lowered her head after nodding. He took another deep breath and gripped her shoulders.

"That's all, isn't it?"

"Yes." She met his cold stare again. "I told Kevin I didn't want him. That I only wanted you."

"Good." His voice became hard. "In the future, if you are having a difficult time and you need help, you call me." He paused. "Do you understand, Drew?"

"Yes and I will." Uncertain, she stepped closer and he jerked her the rest of the way to his body. He nuzzled her hair and pressed a tender kiss on the top of her head. Then he lifted her face and kissed her forehead, then her cheek, and the corner of her mouth. He was kissing everywhere Kevin had touched or kissed her. But how could he know where Kevin had touched her? Theo hadn't been in the room. It was impossible. Or maybe the guilt over her actions was still riding her hard, playing tricks with her emotions. She was probably reading too much into it.

He cupped the sides of her face and angled it up to meet his. His breath warmed her skin and she shivered as she waited for him to kiss her.

"I want only you, Drew. There is nobody else on the planet for me. There is only you."

Her heart squeezed as her veins flooded with a sensation that bordered on love.

Love.

She was falling in love with Theo. She took a breath and enjoyed the way her body tingled with a warmth only he could cause. Her stomach turned into a mushy knot and she began to feel lightheaded. She had been in love a long time ago, when she was young. She always remembered how great the feeling was, but this awareness Theo stirred in her went way beyond anything she had ever experienced. It frightened her but she allowed it to sweep her up and carry her away.

With anticipation building, Drew wove her arms around his neck, parting her lips, then Theo was stealing her breath. He swept his tongue into her waiting mouth and skimmed over hers. Then he flicked the tip lightly against hers, teasing. The caress was lovely—the mixture of the moist heat of his mouth and the sweet taste of his tongue was addictive. Moaning, she pressed her lips firmly against his, needing more of him, all of him. Her body heated. Her nipples tightened, and her core, wet and aching, demanded him. Only he could satisfy this hunger growing inside her.

His kiss became overwhelming and hot. So hot.

"Theo." She breathed heavy as he nibbled on her neck. "You're working."

There was a low groan, or it could have been a growl. "I'm on a break."

She giggled just before she was suddenly weightless and pinned against the wall. She wrapped her legs around him. His gun and handcuff case dug into her leg on one side and his flashlight and pouch for gloves dug into the other. She ignored the pinch they caused and just squeezed her thighs tight to keep from falling. He moved his hands from the top of her thighs to her face. He held her head still as he took control and ravaged her mouth.

Theo pressed his lips against hers, while his tongue met hers in heated debate. The added weight of his bulletproof vest crushed her. But she loved it. She couldn't get close enough to him. She arched her back, her wet center coming into contact with the bulge in his pants. She sucked in a breath as the sensation flew through her. She squirmed against him again, rubbing her swollen clit over his restrained cock. She would have thought that the tight confines of her own pants would have hindered the feeling, but instead it increased, helped it to grow, until she was shaking in his arms. "Theo?" She almost begged the breathy question against his lips.

"No." He shook his head. "Can't. Working." He inhaled a deep breath and swore. "Fuck me, you smell wet... Ready."

"I am ready," she mumbled into his neck, nipped at the tender skin.

He did growl this time, out loud, she heard it. He smashed his lips down on hers and forced her hips to move. Up and down, up and down. The friction, the heat. He was rubbing her into a state of delirium. The hard length of his cock became her personal play toy. The best play toy ever.

Her body tightened with each stroke, the feeling growing, taking her higher and higher. He was going to make her come, her body clenched blissfully tight.

She gasped as her body jerked with the delicious throbbing. Theo's mouth covered hers completely, muffling any loud cries, and he held her while her body trembled and finally relaxed into his.

After her convulsions had died and the trembling had stopped, Theo lowered her feet to the floor. He still had her pinned between the wall and his body. He lightly brushed his lips over her ear. "Okay?"

"I guess."

He hooked a finger under her chin and raised her face. "You guess?"

She shrugged. "It was good. But I want more, I want you."

His cool gaze turned warm. "If I promise to rectify the situation tonight, will that please you?"

She grinned at him, feeling her heart swell, and gently traced the shell of his ear. "I would really like that."

He shivered. "Then you have my promise," he announced formally in a low voice.

He pushed her back and took hold of her arm. He inspected the dressing and, once satisfied it was still snug in place, he announced, "I need you to do me a favor."

Drew stepped around him and rolled her eyes. "You really like to abuse this favor thing, don't you?"

She walked to her chair and adjusted her pants. She felt warm and sticky, and her body was oversensitive, every movement a reminder of how badly she wanted the man standing in front of her desk.

She sat down and caught his scowl. "What?"

"Abuse is a harsh description. I ask you for favors because you are receptive to them, as are most people." He bent forward, leaning onto her desk, and looked her straight in the eye. "And I also ask only what I know you can give."

She blinked at him, his intense stare making her achy all over again. She licked her lips. "Okay, what do you want me to give?"

Please say my body. Please say my body.

"I want you to take Friday and Saturday off and come with me to my cabin."

"What?" Her heart fluttered as her body stiffened. "What did you ask me?"

"Come with me to my cabin on Opitsat. I'll have you back here by Sunday afternoon."

"I'm sorry… I have…" Why was she having such a hard time with this? She was shocked sure but two full days alone with Theo. *My God, that was a dream come true. But…* "I don't know. I've got appointments and…" Why was she hesitating?

"And?" He was still bent over her desk, watching her closely. He drew in a long breath and exhaled it on a sigh. "You're scared."

She almost gasped out loud. *How in the hell does he know that?* She shook her head.

He straightened and crossed his arms. "Yes, you are. Though I'm not sure I know why. Would you care to explain it to me so I understand?"

Drew opened her mouth but stopped, not knowing what to say.

"Are you worried about upsetting your patients?"

She shrugged. "A little." That was a lie.

Theo narrowed his eyes and sighed. "Okay." He reached to the door and pulled it open.

What? He was leaving. "No, wait. Theo, I'm sorry, I'm just a bit nervous."

She chased him into the front reception and stopped when she saw him leaning onto Connie's desk.

He searched her face. "Nervous about what?"

She looked at Connie, who gave her a cheeky smile and wiggled her eyebrows, then looked back to Theo. "Us, too. I mean as well as my patients," she finally admitted.

"Okay. Let's sort that out first. Connie, what does Dr O'Bannion's schedule look like tomorrow and Saturday?"

Giving Theo a knowing grin, Connie quickly pulled up the appointments for both days. "Oh, she's not busy at all, and what appointments she does have I can totally rebook for next week. No problem."

Both Theo and Connie faced her. Drew crossed her arms, irritated that Theo now had Connie conspiring against her.

"Connie." Theo stared at Drew. "I'm taking Drew to my cabin on Opitsat. We're going to leave tomorrow morning and we will be back Sunday afternoon."

Connie's grin grew wider. "Sounds like fun."

Theo chuckled. "There you have it. We're going for a fun getaway over to my cabin and Connie knows, my boss knows, as do other officers over at the station. Does that make you feel more comfortable?"

"Yes, but... That wasn't really... I didn't mean to imply that I didn't trust you." She was babbling again, damn it!

Theo was suddenly before her, gripping her arms. "Relax," he said quietly. "It's just a weekend. I'm not asking for a full-time commitment, just two days."

"I know." She exhaled a choppy breath. "Okay."

He gave her the sweetest smile then slowly, gently kissed her lips. He ended the kiss and whispered, "See you later." And he was gone before she could blink.

"What's going on?" Connie's frown drew attention to the piercing in her thin eyebrow. "I thought you were in serious 'like' with Theo?"

"Like?" She shook her head. She didn't like him, she loved him, and that scared the holy hell right out of her.

Connie caught on right away. "Oh wow!" She crossed to Drew then clasped her hands. "That's great!" She frowned again when she saw the concerned look on Drew's face. "Right? I mean, if what I heard was right, you both want only each other."

Drew's eyes flew to Connie's. "You heard us?"

Connie gave her a sympathetic smile. "Guess Angus didn't tell you the walls are super-thin."

Drew covered her face. "Oh my God, you could hear us." She groaned into her hands.

Connie giggled. "Man, you guys are so hot together, like mummy-porn hot."

Drew chuckled despite the situation but she hated knowing that Theo had heard Kevin with her. Although, he would now know that she didn't want Kevin and that she only wanted Theo. Right? Argh! She didn't know for sure because she didn't ask him.

But he was taking her to his cabin. That was good.

Oh boy, he was taking her to his cabin. Her anxiety built higher.

Holy shit! She groaned to herself.

Going on a weekend getaway was what real life couples did. She hadn't even spent an entire night with him and despite what she secretly wanted he was always gone in the morning. What if he didn't like what he saw when he woke up?

Holy shit!

Her heart pounded, which in turn caused her to breathe faster.

"Drew?" Connie asked. "You okay?"

"Yeah, fine." She turned to her office, on the verge of hyperventilating. Damn it, she was going to turn into one of her friends.

"Liar," Connie said from behind her. "What's wrong? Are you that nervous about being alone with Theo?"

Drew spun to face her friend and threw her arms up into the air. "I'm not a morning person, Connie, and I just don't think I have it in me to get up before him so I can fix my makeup."

"Wait, what?" Connie asked.

"I'm going to turn into my friends. They get up before their dates and reapply their makeup so they look good the next morning."

"That's what you're worried about?" Connie burst out laughing. "You're worried about a makeup hangover?"

"Yes!" Drew jammed her hands on her hips. "What if he doesn't like—?"

Me. She whispered the word in her head for fear that she would shout it out loud. *What if he doesn't like the real me?*

"Whoa." Connie smiled. "Theo is in serious 'like' with you, he's not going to care about your makeup. I thought you two already had sex?"

"We have." Drew crossed her arms as her cheeks flushed.

"Then what did you do the last time?"

Drew shrugged. "My makeup was already off and he never stays over."

"Then there you go. Take it off and let him see that beautiful skin. As for not being a morning person, that will change. Waking up next to a man is sweaty fun, trust me." Connie wiggled her eyebrows before sauntering over to her desk. "Besides," she called out, "there are a lot of other things you should worry about."

"Like?"

"You could always fart in your sleep."

Groaning, Drew covered her face.

Chapter Eighteen

Theo parked his truck next to Drew's house and climbed out. It was well past seven and the cloudy day was beginning to turn dark. He stopped next to Drew's car and studied the forest.

He'd wanted to come sooner but had needed to clear up his desk before he could go, plus he had reread Ben's personnel file one last time. The desire to be with Drew was great, but his need to protect her was greater. He needed to know everything there was on Ben, which wasn't anything new. Ben was a local BC boy, born and raised in Victoria. He'd gotten average grades in high school and business college after that. His stint in the army had taught him how to use many different weapons including rifles. He'd done two tours with his infantry unit before releasing and joining the BCPP. Nothing he didn't already know. The doubt was still there, even though Ben appeared normal—he couldn't shake the feeling that he knew the ghost shooter. Whom he hoped he learned the identity of asap, because the sooner he knew, the sooner this would be over.

Sitting at his desk with Ben's file in his hands was when the idea had hit him. Take Drew over to the cabin tonight, enjoy the night alone with her. Because when Linde and his shooter followed—and they would follow, Theo was certain of it—all hell would break loose.

He sighed to himself contemplating his new plan. Taking Drew earlier than expected had seemed like a good idea at the time but now he wasn't sure. So many things could go wrong. It was a selfish move too, considering that Drew was beyond exhausted. She needed to sleep and she needed to mourn but he was still going to go through with his plan. Her safety was more important than anything else at this point. Everything else would have to wait.

He looked deeper into the dark forest, seeing every tree, every fern. He heard the rustle of the leaves, the scurrying of smaller animals. Yet he still couldn't detect the ghost shooter or Linde.

His muscles flexed as the wolf rolled beneath his skin.

They were out there. In the forest. Watching him. Waiting for the wolf. He could feel it in his bones, even if he couldn't see or hear them.

"*Kill,*" the wolf demanded.

"*Soon,*" he soothed. "*We have to get Drew to a safe place first.*"

"*Drew. Mate,*" the wolf ended on a sigh. It sounded as though the wolf was pining for Drew. Which made no sense because she was right next to him.

Reaching for the handle on the driver's side door of Drew's car, he opened it. "Why are you sitting here?" He held out his hand for her.

She looked up at him before sliding her hand into his. "I don't know." She shrugged. "Scared to go in, I guess."

He helped her from the car and closed the door. Drew squinted, into the forest. "What were you looking at?"

"I thought I heard something," he lied. "Are you scared because there might be someone in your house or because Ruby isn't with you?"

"A little of column A and a little of column B." She shook her head. "How pathetic am I?"

All of his senses were on high alert but the idea of someone waiting inside Drew's house caused his already tight muscles to clench further. He allowed the wolf to sniff the surrounding air—dirt, leaves, moss, and a squirrel had investigated the area some time ago, but there was no leftover stench indicating a human threat.

He took her keys from her and tugged her up to the front porch. "You are not pathetic. Please, don't talk about yourself like that. I don't like it." He unlocked the door and held it open for her. He pulled in a second deep breath once inside the house and finally relaxed. Nothing.

Drew walked into the house and switched on the light next to the couch. She unzipped her coat and froze, staring at the blanket draped over the couch. It was thick with black fur and tucked in the cushions was a half-chewed bone. The room filled with heartache. Theo stepped next to her. The sad look nearly tore his heart from his chest. Then suddenly she reached down and yanked the blanket free revealing pristine white leather. She walked to the corner where a large dog bed sat and dropped the blanket and bone on top.

She brushed off her hands and sighed. "This is what my couch really looks like." She crossed the short distance and sat down, caressing the supple leather. "I spent a small fortune on this bad boy and the day it was delivered Ruby chewed on the arm." She leaned to the side pointing at the bite marks.

When she glanced up at him, her eyes glistened. Theo settled himself next to her and wrapped his arm around her pulling her close. He kissed the top of her head. "Can't say I'm surprised. It's practically a giant chew toy."

"Yeah." She chuckled and sniffed. "She loved this thing."

They were quiet for some time just sitting together, her head on his shoulder. He loved how easy it was to be with Drew.

A snapping noise in the forest caught both his and the wolf's attention. It wasn't by any means close to the house, but it stirred up his apprehension and his protective side followed suit.

"Listen." He pulled away and straightened. "I want to take you out to Opitsat tonight."

"I thought you wanted to leave tomorrow morning?"

He stood and pulled her to her feet. "Why wait?"

"Isn't it dangerous traveling to the island at night? I mean boats don't have headlights or whatever, do they?"

"Mine does." Though he wouldn't use them. His night vision was superb thanks to the wolf.

"Oh." She paused briefly before blurting out, "I haven't eaten yet."

He crossed his arms. "I have enough food in the truck to last us a week, plus stores of canned food over there. And if there is something you specifically want we can stop on the way."

"Okay." She shifted her eyes away from him then she announced, "But... I want to have a bath first. You probably don't have a bath or even running water over there."

He grinned at her. "No, I don't have a bath. "

She smiled, relieved.

He stepped closer and narrowed his eyes. "But I do have a shower, and a fully functioning bathroom."

The smile slowly vanished. "No outhouse?" She avoided eye contact again.

"No outhouse," he confirmed, a smile pulling at his lips. "I had a well put in a few years ago. I have a fireplace for heat. I have a generator for electricity, though to be honest I don't use it all that much. I prefer candles. I have a wide selection of books to read and there is a fantastic beach close by where you can go swimming if you like, so you might want to pack your suit if you can handle the cold. I have towels and soap and anything else you could possibly need."

She nodded.

"You're stalling. Why?"

"What do you mean?"

The innocent bit wasn't working, he knew she was nervous, her fear filled the room, yet he didn't understand why. "You're pulling reasons out of thin air as to why we shouldn't go yet."

"I'm not doing that." She snorted and headed into the kitchen. He grabbed her around the waist and pulled her back against his chest.

"Liar," he whispered next to her ear.

She gasped and fought for freedom. "I'm not lying."

He groaned when she inadvertently rubbed her bottom against his groin, the friction causing more than a desire for the truth. "You can fight me all you want, but I'm not letting go until you tell me."

She stopped struggling and snapped her mouth shut. They stood quietly for a few minutes. The gentle heat of her body was teasing his. His cock missed the contact and he pressed her closer. He kissed the base of her neck as he palmed a breast, massaging it, then turned her face with the other hand so he could tease her lips.

She sighed, tilting her head back, and relaxed her weight onto him.

He kissed her mouth lightly, then ran his tongue over her parted lips. Pulling away he asked, "Ready to tell me why you're so nervous?"

She dropped her head onto his shoulder. "We are going to be together, alone, for a few days. What if you...?" She pressed her lips tightly together.

"What if I...?" he prompted.

"Argh!" She struggled against him and he reluctantly let her go. She turned to face him. "What if you realize you can't stand me?"

He frowned.

"I've never done this relationship thing." She raised her shoulders. "Okay, that's not really true. I was in a relationship for over a year. But I was trying to figure out why going away with you was freaking me out so much and I realized that old relationship was only based on sex."

"Based on sex?" The muscles in his shoulder flexed.

"Yeah, you know, a friends with benefits sort of thing. Sure, we did things together, sometimes. But most of the time that I saw him was for sex."

Theo raised a single eyebrow. "I'm liking this explanation less and less."

"Well that's too bad. This is who I am."

"And who is that?"

"A woman who has never spent more than a few hours with a man. I have never spent the night at a man's house and never wanted him to stay the night at mine. I never wanted him there when I woke up, because I didn't want to have to reapply makeup and I didn't want to make him coffee and I didn't want that 'I'll call you' parting line as he left. I'm selfish, I fully admit it."

"Okay." He crossed his arms again. Not once had he ever gotten the impression that Drew was selfish. She was always willing to help and never came across as the self-centered type. He kept that thought to himself, though—one, because he knew she would argue with him about it and two, because he had a feeling that this rant was her way of working through her insecurities.

"No. It's not okay." She threw her arms into the air. "I want to spend the night with you. I want to spend the day with you. But I'm a horrible morning person and I'm just nervous that my old habit will kick into high gear and you will think I'm a raging bitch and I don't want to be like that. Not with you." She pointed at him. "You have to promise me that you won't let that happen."

"Done." He nodded, fighting to hide his smile.

"And I won't put on makeup for you in the morning. What you see is what you get, smudged mascara and all."

He laughed aloud. He had no idea where that came from but agreed anyway. "Done."

She blinked at him. "Okay!"

"Good." He smirked.

"Then I'll go pack a bag," she snapped.

"I think that would be a good idea."

"Fine."

Theo shook his head as she stomped up the stairs. That had to be the most interesting one-sided argument he had ever witnessed and something in his gut told him that they would become a common occurrence where Drew was concerned.

* * * *

"Where the fuck are they going?"

Ken crossed his arms as he watched Grey's private boat speed toward the island. He had a feeling he knew where Theo was taking Drew but his training had always taught him to never guess. Therefore, he followed them to the private dock. It was unfortunate that Linde had wanted to join him.

Unfortunate. He snorted. Who the hell was he kidding? Linde was a fucking pain in the ass and the sooner he got his kill the sooner Ken could disappear.

"Well?" Linde demanded, his accent becoming thicker with each word. "Where the fuck are they going?"

"North-east." He pointed out the obvious then climbed into Linde's car.

The other door opened and Linde, red-faced, joined him. "What kind of answer was that? Do you know where they are going or not?"

Ken swiped the rain from his face then jammed his hands into his pockets trying to warm his fingers. Fuck, he hated all this rain. What he would give to be back home, in the hot dry sun.

Linde shifted in his seat and proceeded to reach inside his jacket. Ken instinctively gripped the handle of his sub-compact pistol in his right pocket and sat watching Linde. The man pulled out his cigarette and lighter. He should have known that was what Linde would do, but when dealing with men like Hendrik Linde, his natural instinct was always on high alert. For that reason, his grip remained firm on his Ruger pistol.

"Grey has a small cabin on Opitsat. That's where he's taking her."

Linde lit his cigarette and blew the smoke out in a frustrated puff. "I thought that land belonged to the Nootka tribe?"

"*Nuu-Chah-Nulth,*" Ken corrected. "It does."

"Then how can he have a cabin there?" Linde replaced the smokes inside his coat. "Aren't their lands sacred to them?"

Ken nodded. "He has some connection with them. My guess would be they know about the wolf."

"So they're protecting him?"

He stared out of the window. "Grey doesn't need protection." He could see the waves smashing against the private dock and knew in the distance was Opitsat. Theo could run free there, and wouldn't have to worry about running across normal humans. Over there Theo was safe, but he was also an easier target. Over there Ken wouldn't have to hold back. He could help Linde get his precious trophy, without anyone being any the wiser.

That was if Theo *could* be killed.

"That might be true." There was something in Linde's smug tone that demanded that Ken turn his head. Linde met his stare with a wicked grin. "But his woman does."

Ken raised his eyebrow, a combination of amusement and anger swirling in his chest. "You plan on using her to get to Grey?"

"Of course. And when Grey is dead I think I'll keep her." Linde stared into space, the grin on his face growing wide. He grabbed at his swelling crotch and shifted in his seat when he finally noticed Ken still watching him. "What? You can't tell me you don't want to fuck that ass?" He took a drag on his smoke and exhaled it. "Get me my kill sooner and I'll throw in some one-on-one time with the vet."

Ken studied Linde as the older man adjusted the now full bulge in his pants. He didn't know whether to be sick, admire his honesty or slam his fist into his face.

Ken slowly nodded, keeping his feelings hidden, and chose his words carefully. "Well then, I want my pay transferred tonight because by this time tomorrow you'll have your kill and I'll have the vet." Ken relaxed his grip on his gun and rested his elbow on the side door as he glanced out the window. "Can you get a hold of a boat?"

Chapter Nineteen

Less than an hour later, Drew stood in the middle of Theo's cabin on Opitsat. She held her small overnight bag with both hands and scanned the one-room cabin.

"Theo, this is really nice."

"Thank you. Why don't you put your bag down and take off your coat?"

She nodded and placed her bag at the end of his bed, then hung her wet raincoat on the hook next to the bathroom.

She walked around the small space while he started a fire. The cabin wasn't a closet but it was comfortable and it offered everything he needed to survive... At least as a human. He glanced over his shoulder and watched as she inspected the old pictures on the walls and his collection of books piled on two bookcases. Would she notice the people in the pictures or how old the books were?

"I didn't know you collected antique books." She cocked her head to the side and read the titles on the different colored spines. She stopped and frowned, then gingerly pulled a tattered brown book free. She gasped. "This is *Peter Pan*." She opened the cover and gasped a second time. "It's a first edition."

"Yes." He stood and placed the metal grate in front of the fire. "You like to read the classics?"

She nodded slowly. "Theo, it's signed by J.M. Barrie."

He crossed to her and looked down at the book. "Yes, it is."

"Wow." With her mouth still hanging open, she asked, "How much did this cost? Wait... I don't think I want to know." She closed the cover and ran her hand lovingly over the worn leather. "This is one of my favorite books."

She believed he was a collector. He sighed inwardly. He should probably tell her the truth—that his stepmother had given him the book as a gift and that if Drew had turned the page she would have seen the message his stepmother had written to him.

"It's one of mine too." He took the book and slid it back into place on the shelf. He wasn't ready to share with her the full truth about his life. He wanted this night first, just the two of them alone, before their lives changed forever. "How about something to eat?"

* * * *

Drew sat cross-legged at the small table. Dinner had been a combination of salad and meat and cheese with crackers—light but tasty. As they sat and talked Drew found herself becoming more and more relaxed. The stress and worries about them spending time socially together drifted away and she realized that she was reacting to Theo. He was calm and so she followed suit.

She looked around again as she toyed with her glass of water while Theo finished cleaning up dinner. She stared at his broad shoulders and smiled, remembering how she had teased him about not being a proper host and offering her a glass of wine instead. As he had placed the glass of water in front of her he'd bent close. "No wine. I don't want anything dulling your senses tonight."

Even now, an hour later, her faced heated at the memory and a fresh rush of arousal caused her insides to ache desperately.

Theo stopped in mid-motion and slowly faced her. He lifted his head slightly and, as strange as it seemed, it was as though he was sniffing the air between them. It was like... He knew what she was thinking and how her body was reacting.

He placed the plate he was holding down onto the small counter then slowly moved next to her. He lifted her chin with the crook of his finger and stroked her lips with the pad of his thumb. She met his stare. The heat of desire transformed his face as he took another deep breath.

Her stomach flipped and she blinked up at him, struggling to voice her sudden feelings. "Theo." His name came out in an achy whisper.

"Yes." He stared at her mouth.

"I..." she began then blurted out, "Let's have sex."

He chuckled lightly as he lowered himself onto his knees in front of her chair. "I was thinking the very same thing." He tugged her legs free, parting them, then pushed between. He stroked her outer thighs then gripped behind and dragged her to the edge of her seat, sealing their bodies tight. Her arms automatically curled around his neck. His face, even close to hers, seemed somewhat sinister, thanks to the dimly lit room, and the flickering of the fire caused his eyes to flash from gray to a liquid silver.

Her stomach flipped again. There was an underlying darkness to Theo, one that could consume him at any moment. But she wasn't scared or even nervous. She liked the idea of it, was turned on and excited by it. She circled her legs around his waist, and as in her office, the intimate contact brought her swollen clit against the heat of his hard body. The muscles in her abdomen clenched tight as he rocked his hips. She sighed, closing her eyes, loving the feel of him, the smell of him. She wanted him, right here, right now, dark look and silver eyes. She wanted all of him and she wanted to give him every part of her. She parted her lips in silent invitation and sighed when he slipped his tongue inside.

His lips were hard against hers while their tongues tangled in a fierce storm of moist flesh. The day's worth of stubble on his chin and upper lip scraped her face but she loved it. She tightened the hold on his neck as his kisses became hotter. He ran his hands up under her shirt, the rough pads of his fingers and palms sending shivers over her skin. Then with the slightest of pauses, he grasped her tight against his chest and lifted her off the chair.

He walked to the bed and released her feet. "Take your clothes off."

He stepped away as he fisted his shirt between his shoulders blades and pulled it over his head. He had his jeans unzipped and opened before he issued her another command. "Drew," he growled. "Clothes off, now!"

She nodded and began tugging off her clothes. He reached for the small bag he had brought with him. She assumed he was getting condoms but he pulled stainless steel handcuffs from a black nylon holding case instead.

Handcuffs!

She dropped her jeans to the floor in surprise. "What's going on?"

He gave her a naughty grin. "Something kinky, I hope."

Yah, totally kinky! But she had never thought it would actually happen.

He closed the minute gap between them, his bare chest pressed against her bra-covered breasts. "Dr O'Bannion…" He brushed his mouth over the shell of her ear as he gripped her arm. "You're under arrest." Then he snapped the cold steel around her wrist.

There was a glint in his eye even though his face was expressionless.

Her heart pounded with excitement at the idea of him cuffing her then fucking her silly but she kept her cool and asked, "What for, Officer?"

His gaze scanned the length of her, stopping on the lace-trimmed bra and matching panties. "For wearing too many clothes."

It was a corny line and she fought to contain her smile.

"But these are my lucky panties, Officer." She pouted as he gently cuffed her bandaged wrist. "They've gotten me out of some sticky situations."

"Is that right?" He reached between her legs.

She sucked in a breath when he slid his fingers along the damp material. "If I don't wear them I won't get lucky."

He gave her a wicked grin. "Luck has nothing to do with this." He pressed deeper into her folds and rubbed her damp bud.

A carnal urgency swept through her body. She tilted her head back as he pulled her close. He towered over her, his dark stare drilling straight into hers. "This is about want and need. You want me to do this." He slid his knuckles up and down in quick succession then stopped. "Don't you?"

She rocked her hips, hoping to get him to move again. "Yes." She nodded. "Please."

He continued his torment. "I need to do this to you. I need to feel you come. I need you to scream my name. And I need to know that I was the man who made you feel this." He lowered his face close to hers, his breath hot and sweet on her face. "Nobody else, just me."

He abruptly pulled away and, turning her, helped her to walk the two steps to the bed. Her legs were shaky, her body cool without his hand to keep her warm yet her skin was hot... Burning. He trailed his fingers up her back until he stopped at the base of her neck. He massaged gently then his grip tightened and she thought he was about to force her to bend forward. She wanted him to do that, she wanted to feel him pressed up against her ass, so she proceeded to on her own.

"Are you going to frisk me?" She pushed up onto her toes, lifting her ass.

She heard his low groan as he tugged on the thin material of her panties and glided his finger along the strip tucked between her cheeks. Her core contracted along with the flood of excitement that filled her lucky thong.

She automatically opened her legs wider. "Fuck yes!" she breathed out raising her ass higher for him, practically begging him to touch her.

He did.

He continued following the lace until he was buried in her folds and his knuckles tormented her inflamed bud. If he hadn't she might have screamed her head off. Who was she kidding? Screaming might still be a possibility.

"Is this how you frisk everyone you arrest?" she managed to ask through her panting.

Theo slid his fingers along her flesh, sending shivers up the length of her spine. "Only blonde veterinarians."

"And how many have you arrested?" She didn't know what had possessed her to ask that but she realized that she wanted to be the only one. Which was unfair—Theo had had a life before he'd met her. He couldn't erase his past. Still she really hoped she was the only one.

As though he knew what she was thinking, Theo bent forward, his chest pressing against her back. His heat warmed her as his breath tickled her neck. "You are the only blonde veterinarian I've arrested." He pulled his fingers free and fisted the strip of lace between her behind. "And the only one I've wanted to tear all her clothes off." In a swift jerk the thong was ripped free.

She gasped and laughed at the same time and gripped the quilt on his bed, pushing her ass against him once again.

Theo pressed his mouth to her neck. "You enjoyed that, didn't you?"

She giggled, then lied, "No. It was awful."

"Mm-hmm." He roughly parted her thighs and cupped her wet sex. "Your body tells another story." He slid two fingers through her lips, pinching her clit as he went.

Another gasp escaped her but this time it was in pleasure instead of shock.

Theo teased her for the longest time. He kissed her shoulder as he petted her body. She wanted him inside her. She wanted his cock to stretch her so she would feel that delicious pleasure mixed with pain. She almost had a taste of it when he briefly slipped two fingers inside her but he quickly pulled them out.

"Get up on the bed," he grunted.

Her body was hot, wet and achy. She didn't want him to tease her anymore.

"No." She shook her head. "We're done with this, you need to fuck me."

He gave her bottom a light slap. She moaned when she probably should have yelped. She just couldn't help it.

"Get up on the bed and turn onto your back."

"No." She fought him again. Was she hoping for another paddle on her backside? Absolutely.

Theo growled and lifted her off her feet and tossed her easily onto the bed. She landed on her side and was quickly flipped onto her back. Before she could register his movement Theo loomed above her. He gently pulled her hands away from his chest and positioned them above her head.

He stared down at her, his lips curled in a harsh smile. "This is not done. I'm not done. I want to feel your breath on my face. I want the sweet taste of your mouth. I want the heat from your body to soak into mine. You will gasp in pleasure and you will be dripping wet by the time I am done with you. And I will feel your pussy squeeze tight around my cock when I make you come." His mouth was now only a breath away from hers. "So, no, we are far from being done." Then he kissed her.

His lips were forceful, the hard pressure bruising hers. Releasing her, he cupped the side of her face. Then using his thumb, he tugged gently on her chin. The slight pressure forced her mouth to open. It wasn't necessary. She would have done it on her own. How could she not actively participate in the most romantic kiss of her life?

She felt goose bumps tickle their way up her arms. The physical reaction wasn't just from his kiss but from his declaration. Nobody—*ever*—had said anything like that to her before. But what had caused the giddy swirling in her stomach was when he'd said he wanted to feel her breath on his face. Nobody said that unless feelings ran deep. Her head spun and she smiled like an idiot against his mouth.

Theo had deep feelings for her. *Weeeeeee!* The joyous sound echoed around her head. It was silly and childish but at least she didn't say it out loud. She could be wrong, she didn't know if it was love, but there was something good.

He kissed his way to the side of her mouth and along her jaw. He flicked her earlobe with the tip of his tongue then sucked it between his teeth.

A shiver ran through her and impulse had her reaching for him but he stopped her and pinned her arms in place. She suddenly became frustrated with her need to touch him. She flexed her arms with the intent of breaking free but he easily kept her still.

"I said I wasn't done." He nipped the base of her throat. "Now keep still."

He made his point this time by cupping a single breast and sucking her nipple through the lightly padded material. The heat and suction sparked a sizzle through her bloodstream and ignited the throbbing between her legs. Her hips arched up on their own when he repeated the torment. He growled low as he nuzzled at the tender skin between her breasts. He slid his hands under her back, unhooking the clasps of her bra, then the lace and silk padding were impatiently shoved up her arms where they were forced to stop at her bound wrists.

He found her breasts once again and kneaded the flushed skin. His mouth joined in on the torment by sucking a single nipple so hard she fisted the quilt and cried out.

He mumbled something against the tender skin but she couldn't understand him, she only felt. She felt the warmth of his body and the rough texture of his whiskers. She felt the weight of the cool steel against her wrists then focused on how his chest hair tickled her stomach and breasts and loved how his warm breath made her nipple moist. She felt everything and she didn't know if this was because she wasn't participating in the foreplay or because it was Theo's touch.

A sigh escaped as Theo kissed a wet trail down to her belly button and gently tugged on her belly button ring with his teeth. Either way, the multitude of sensations were heavenly and erotic and she wondered, very briefly, why they hadn't done this before.

Theo had never craved anyone the way he craved Drew. It was a deep craving that sat heavy in his chest, painfully close to his heart. The new-found feelings didn't stop him—in fact they turned him on, made him want more of her. He kissed the top of the thin strip of hair that directed him to her wet sex. He forced her legs to open wider and nipped at the inside of her thigh when she didn't comply fast enough. Her gasp made him smile and he eased the pain with a slow lick and a kiss.

Her damp scent made him dizzy. No other woman had ever had that effect on him. And there had been many women over the years. Most of his sexual interludes had been one-night stands. A quick in and out, so that he could sate his human needs. The needs the wolf couldn't understand. With Drew it was different—the wolf was silent when he was making love to her, as though it was at peace. He searched for the wolf now as he kissed the inside of Drew's other thigh. The animal was tucked away in the shadows of his mind, aware of what Theo and Drew were doing yet not interfering. Drew was the one. She was his mate, the one woman on the planet that he would die to protect and the only woman he would ever love.

He blew cool air on her slick folds and smiled when she rolled her hips impatiently. He glanced up and saw the desperate need on her face. She needed to be touched by him. Not by Kevin or anyone else, just him. He could smell her desire, see it gathering in her folds but he asked her the question anyway, "Do you want me to touch you, Drew?" She probably thought this was all part of his 'cop and naughty prisoner' game, but the truth was that he needed to know so his jealous side would be appeased.

"Yes." She breathed out. "Please."

"How do you want to be touched?" He scraped his chin lightly over her inner thigh, and watched as she shivered.

"Kiss me. Suck me. Fuck me. Anyway, I don't care. Just do it." Her demand ended on a yell.

He nodded and as he looked her dead in the eye he roughly closed his mouth on her sex and sucked on her clit. Her hips jerked against him and he had to hold her still as he feasted on her. He couldn't get enough and knew he was being quite rough yet he couldn't seem to stop. He loved how her body was highly sensitive and how she tasted like honey-sweetened cream. He flicked his tongue against her several times before she sucked in a mouthful of air and biting her lower lip in the process.

Theo rode her orgasm until it was through and she sighed dreamily. He quickly removed his jeans and boxers and grabbed the condom he had left on the top of his bag, tossing it onto his old bedside table.

He stretched out beside her, cupped her breast and kissed her collarbone.

"You're doing it again."

"What's that?" he asked, brushing his lips over the tip of her rosy nipple.

"Not letting me play."

He laughed against her breast and sucked hard on the taut bead. "You want to play, do you?"

"Yes," she moaned and rolled her body toward him. He slid his hand between her damp legs, cupping her slick lips, then nestled her clit between his fingers. He stroked once, twice. She tried to touch his face but he stopped her.

"No. Keep them up or no playtime." He gave her the warning against her parted lips as he increased the torment. Soon her hips rocked along with the rhythm of his ministrations, and just when she was about to come for a second time he pulled away and moved down her body, so that his head was between her quivering legs. Then, grabbing her thighs, he proceeded to roll onto his back. She had no choice but to follow his lead and ended up straddling his face.

The second he flipped the opposite way he knew what she would do, had counted on it in fact, yet he encouraged her anyway.

"Playtime is here, you'd better take advantage of it." A scant second later his cock was surrounded by the moist heat of her mouth.

His groan was loud and feral and he couldn't have stopped it if he had tried. Christ, she was sucking him like a wild woman—it was all he could do not to slam into her.

He focused on her body and fed on her again, delving his tongue deep, while she tried to fist his cock and suck him at the same time. It was awkward for her, he was sure, but it felt so fucking good to him.

He slid his tongue into her creamy depths and felt her inner muscles tighten and her thighs squeeze his head. She pulled away and cried out as the next orgasm overtook her.

She collapsed over to the side, her arms automatically falling above her head. Theo righted himself and lay down next to her, pulling her close. She was still breathing hard, her eyes were shut and her lips were swollen. He lapped at the bead of sweat sliding down between her flushed breasts.

She rolled onto her side away from him and sighed. "I need a break."

He playfully bit at her shoulder. "No break."

"Boy. I must have really been a bad girl to deserve all this torment." She chuckled.

"Yes you were." He rocked his hips so that his cock slid up and down against the crevice of her behind.

He repeated the movement but pushed a little deeper into her folds. He wanted to feel her wet desire coat his cock.

"Theo?" Drew asked in a husky voice.

"Mmm."

"Are you ever going to fuck me?"

"Yes," he mumbled against her neck.

He sat up and grabbed the condom. He tore open the package then covered himself. He lay back down behind Drew then lifted her top leg onto his. He guided his cock into her tight sheath and sighed from the sheer pleasure of it.

She rolled her hips and slid along his length.

"Fuck, Drew," he growled and pumped into her in quick shallow thrusts. It wasn't as deep as he wanted but damn, she felt good, so fucking good.

Drew struggled to pull her arms down and before he could scold her he watched as she slipped her fingers between her lips and circled her pink bud. He pushed up and watched her toy with herself as he entered her from behind. The sight was so incredibly sexy.

It suddenly wasn't enough. He wasn't satisfied to watch and get this little taste. He wanted deep, he wanted tight, he wanted it all.

Without giving her any warning, Theo flung Drew onto her back and spread her legs wide apart. She flung her cuffed hands above her head and gripped the quilt. Theo pinned her down covering her smaller body with his own. She was so different from him. So soft and smooth, and she smelled lusty-sweet.

Drew. He whispered the name in his head as he lowered himself over her. Her moist desire filled his nose and he slammed deep. He was rough when he took her, moving too hard, too fast. But he would never hurt her because she belonged to him. She was *his* Drew.

The wolf lifted its head and huffed, *"Mate."*

"*Mate,*" Theo agreed, wondering how this woman had been able to weave her way into his heart so quickly.

An indignant snort came from the dark corner of his mind where the wolf was curled up.

"*Mate no weave into heart. Mate always there. I... You just need to find her... Them.*"

Theo hated to admit it but the bloody animal was right. Drew was undeniably his mate. Honestly, it felt as though she had always been so, just lost to him until now.

Theo received the impression of an eye roll as the beast wrapped his tail around his body and yawned, settling himself in for a long nap.

Theo pushed onto his forearms, slowing his pace, and looked down into Drew's lust-filled eyes.

"Drew." He cupped the side of her face, ran the pad of his thumb over her bottom lip. He was going to tell her that he loved her but she parted her lips ever so slightly and sucked his thumb and, flicked the tip with her tongue. His words were lost in his groan and he felt his need and the vibration in his chest shoot straight to his cock.

He claimed her mouth in a hard kiss, tangling his tongue with hers, soaking in the sweet heat of her mouth just as he soaked in the heat of her damp body. He took her hard, allowed the need to dominate to take full control. He tilted her head to the side, nibbling on her chin and down to her collarbone. His body pounded into hers, the friction causing unbelievable pleasure.

"Don't stop." It was a demand whispered in heated puffs of air.

He found her breast and latched on, sucking hard. Her breasts and nipples were very sensitive and he loved hearing her cry out when he clamped the rosy bud between his teeth and flicked it with his tongue. He also loved the way she pulled his hair, forcing him to lavish the same attention onto the other breast.

The heat between them burned white hot as he continued to fuck her. She was stretched out, arms above her head, fingers clasping the heavy quilt on his bed. Her breasts jiggled each time he entered her, sweat covering every inch of her soft skin. He watched as he took her, the way her body accommodated his so eagerly. The sight was intoxicating. He licked his thumb and placed it on her swollen button, moving it in slow, lazy circles until she cried out and reached for him.

He went, of course, tangling his arms and hands with hers. She kissed him, a hot open-mouthed kiss that turned into heavy panting. The old bed rocked with their loving. She raised her legs and pulled him in deeper. He groaned, his breath mingled with hers and their sweat-coated bodies slid together. The contact was more intimate than any of the other times they'd been together because neither of them held anything back.

Theo felt the sudden tightening of Drew's body. "Theo," she cried out. "Now?"

He smiled inside. She was waiting for him again.

"Yes, baby. Come with me." He thrust into her with a renewed speed when she exploded into orgasm. Her body quivered and shook, drawing Theo into the same erotic world until he cried out her name.

Chapter Twenty

Lying on her side with Theo spooning behind her, Drew sighed dreamily. She was physically drained, but in a good way. She still couldn't get over how intense it had been making love to Theo. He had said he was going to make her feel everything, she just hadn't thought it was going to be that overwhelming. And she had been overwhelmed. He seemed to have been everywhere touching her, kissing her, making her cry out more than once, and she never did that, ever...with anyone. She moved to scratch the sudden tickle on her nose and realized that her wrists were still cuffed.

She lifted her hands. "Can these come off now, Officer?"

Theo chuckled behind her. "I was wondering how long it would take you to notice they were still on."

"Well, I've been a little distracted the last couple of hours."

He stilled her arms. "As long as I'm the only one distracting you." He unlocked the cuffs then tossed them on the bedside table.

She rubbed at her wrists and looked over her shoulder. "Who else would be?"

The air in the room became heavy when Theo didn't answer.

"Is this because I kissed Kevin?"

He touched her hip and waist but remained silent.

"Would you like to know what I was thinking when Kevin kissed me?"

"No." He squeezed her hip. "It's over."

"I was thinking that he wasn't you. That he didn't make me feel..." She didn't know if she should tell him about the emotions stirring around in her heart.

He curled his arm around her and he pulled her against his chest. She dropped her head onto his pillow and closed her eyes when he kissed the top of her shoulder.

"Are you all right?" he asked softly.

She shook her head.

"I didn't think so. Do you want to tell me why you are not all right?"

"Too scared to," she mumbled into the pillow.

"All right," he began patiently. "Then while you decide whether or not to tell me why you are confused about loving me, I want to tell you the reasons why I brought you over here early."

She slowly lifted her head up from the pillow. "What did you say?"

"Which part?"

"Both." She frowned.

"I know that you love me and that you're confused as to whether you should share your feelings with me. And I want to tell you the reasons why I brought you over to my cabin tonight instead of tomorrow."

"How...?" She swallowed hard. "How do you know that I love you?"

"I can smell it." He tightened his hold on her. "Your confusion, your love. It's surrounding you like a thick blanket."

"What?" she whispered.

He sighed and slid out from under the covers and got off the bed. He walked around the bed and grabbing his jeans, before tugging them on. He crossed to the bed and squatted down in front of her and rested his arms on the quilt.

"I need to tell you about me." He didn't blink as he locked eyes with her. "About who I was before you met me and what I am." He tucked a loose strand of her hair behind her ear. "Only after I tell you that will my reasoning for bringing you here early make any kind of sense. Will you listen?"

She blinked at him, a nervous swirling beginning in her stomach. "Yes."

"I need you to keep an open mind, Drew. Do you think you can do that?"

She blinked again, surprised by his question. A question she had never been asked before. "I think so, yes."

He narrowed his eyes, studying her intently before nodding. "Hold on to the good feelings, baby. It will help push the nervous ones away." With that said he stood and walked to the bookshelves on the other side of the room. He pulled the copy of *Peter Pan* from the shelf then walked to his bag and pulled a large leather book free. He stopped in front of her once again, and after she sat up and covered her breasts with the blanket, he gave her the books then sat at the small table.

"Read the inscription in the front of *Peter Pan* first."

She nodded and opened the old book, flipped through the first few pages until she saw the most elegant handwriting.

She began reading the message.

"April 15th, 1911

Percy,

I know how much you enjoyed seeing the play with your father so many years ago. When I heard that Mr Barrie's play was becoming a book, I requested a copy for you, so that you might read it whenever you want.

Happy Birthday, my darling son.

Mother"

Drew paused and looked up. "Who's Percy?"

"I'm Percy." He rested his elbows on his knees and sighed. "Percival, actually."

She raised a single eyebrow in doubt. "Percival? But you said…"

"Theodore is my middle name. My family called me Percy when I was living at home." He nodded toward the much larger book sitting next to her. "Read the next one out loud." He clasped his hands together. "Start from the beginning."

She nodded and did as he had asked. As she began reading, she had the distinct feeling that she had seen this same handwriting before.

"My full name is Percival Theodore Grey. Yes, Percival or Percy to my family and close friends. Thankfully, I haven't been addressed by my full name since before the war. I was born 15 April 1885 in London, England, to Lord Theodore Grey…"

Once Drew had finished reading the first entry, she frowned at him. "I don't get it."

"Keep reading." His words were curt as his jaw clenched.

She flipped to the next page.

"Read it out loud as well, just like the first one."

She gave him a confused frown, then, licking her lips, began reading the secret he had kept hidden for almost a hundred years, a secret that would most likely have her running from him in terror.

"*20 January 1919. The final moment of my life didn't arrive until well after dark, June 1915. I was resting silently against the base of a large chestnut tree…*"

When she was finished, she met his stare and shook her head. "This doesn't make any sense. What does this old story you're trying to write have to do with why you brought me over here tonight?"

"I'm not a budding author and it's not a story. It's a journal." He casually rested his elbow on the table.

"What?"

"A journal. It's similar to a diary."

"I know what a journal is," she huffed. "What does it have to do with why we're here?"

"Drew," he sighed out. "That is my journal."

"Okay, so you bought an old journal. That doesn't—"

"No." He shook his head. "Listen to me, Drew." He sat forward and ran his hand over his face. "That journal is mine. I wrote the entries into it."

"What?" She shook her head as she snatched up the old book and flipped it open to the first entry. "This date says January the twentieth, 1919." She flipped the journal around so that he could see what she was pointing to and tapped the top of the page. "See? Right there. And look how old this thing is." She laid it on her lap and smoothed out the worn pages.

He stood and crossed the room to her. "It's not in too bad a shape considering how many times I've thrown it across the room." He stopped next to the bed and held out his hand. "I commissioned Kelmscott Press to make this for me." She passed the leather-bound book to him. "My father was good friends with the owner at the time, but it still cost me a pretty penny." He stroked the front cover and down the spine, where he traced the letters embossed into the fine leather. She hadn't noticed them before but now she pushed up so that she could see the clear outline of the letters *P.T.G.*

Initials. They were Theo's initials. She sat clutching the quilt to her breasts.

"This is Moroccan leather. See the grain?" He bent, pointing out the delicate grain of the leather. "That's called a bird's-eye pattern. It's brought out by hand tanning the leather. I specifically asked for Moroccan leather. Would you like to know why?" He looked down at her, shadows covering one side of his face.

She nodded before she could stop herself.

"I wanted Moroccan leather for two reasons. One, because of the deep red coloring and two, because of its strength. I needed it to last a long time." He handed the journal back to her. "I have another two tucked away for when this one is full."

He walked into the center of the room. "Read the date of the last entry."

"The last entry?" She deepened her frown. "I don't understand." A nervous fear twisted her belly into knots. How could this old book belong to Theo? And what did he mean when he said he needed it to last a long time? How long was...long?

Her mind swirled in confusion as she looked at him. She had said she would keep an open mind, but these thing he was saying to her... They didn't make any sense.

"It's okay, Drew." He gave her an encouraging smile. "Go on, read it out loud." He slid his jeans off and stood naked before her.

A light rosy hue colored her face as she stared at him. He loved that flush of desire that covered her face and breasts as her eyes trailed over his body. He could feel himself begin to lengthen but he fought the desire and nodded again toward the book. He needed to do this, to tell her the truth. Consequences be damned, he and his wolf had lived too long alone and Drew deserved to know the truth.

Swallowing hard, Drew looked down and began flipping through the pages until she reached the last entry. She read it to herself and shook her head. "No. This can't be right."

"Read it."

She shook her head again. "It's dated July eighteenth. Three days ago. The same day Ruby was shot."

"Night, actually. I wrote that when I came home from work. Keep reading." He pushed again as the wolf flexed beneath his skin.

"Show Drew... Mate."

The beast knew what he wanted to do, what he was about to do, there was no need for him to ask.

"Yes. Drew loves me. I don't want to hide anything from her. She deserves to know you."

She cleared her throat and began reading aloud. *"Heading over to Drew's again tonight. It will be a good opportunity to give the wolf a run."* Her cheeks flushed as she continued. *"Drew... Jesus, I can't seem to get enough of her. When the wolf said she was our mate I thought he was losing his mind, but now... I know he picked up what I was scared to. Wanting Drew is scary, but I wouldn't change it, and I've stopped fighting it. I've fallen in love with her. What now? Do I tell her about the wolf? Show her the wolf? Jesus, that scares me more than falling in love with her. What if she runs? I don't think I can live without her now but I don't want her scared of me either. Fuck, I hate not knowing what to do."*

She glanced up at him, then back to the journal, her eyes huge. She flipped through the pages, opening up on random entries and scanning the pages, then repeated the process until she was looking down at the first entry again.

"The handwriting is all the same. It never changes," she whispered, still scanning the entry.

"No. My handwriting has never changed," he confirmed gently. "Look at me."

"What wolf?" She raised her eyes to meet his and asked, "Do you own a wolf?"

"No, sweetheart."

"Then tell me what you meant by 'show her the wolf'."

"Explaining about the wolf would only make you confused and angry with me. Showing you is the simplest way and I give you my word that you are completely safe. He would never harm you, and I would never allow him to harm you."

"What are you talking about?" She pulled the quilt tight around her. "Are you going to let a wolf in here?"

"No. I'm going to set him free so you two can properly meet."

Theo let the wolf take control before Drew asked any more questions. His body began to contort as the wolf fought to free himself.

Drew's confusion and fear filled the room. "What…? I don't understand…"

His body jerked to the ground, the conversion now well underway.

Drew screamed and jumped off the bed and rushed over to him, trying to hold him still. "Theo! Oh my

God. Theo, what's happening?" Her touch was warm on his skin. That changed the second that thick coarse black hair sprouted out of every pore, covering his body. She gasped and snatched her hands away.

He rocked forward, so he was on all fours. She squealed when his arms and legs transformed into the legs of the wolf. The last thing he saw through his own eyes was Drew scurrying back against the bed, a horrified expression transforming her lovely face, just as he had feared it would.

The familiar pulling and tugging of skin and bone continued as the swap took place and finally the wolf's head thrust up and out through his chest, the conversion now complete. When Theo saw Drew next, it was through the eyes of the wolf.

He stood in the center of the room and pulled in her fear. It was so thick that it coated Drew in a heavy invisible layer. He felt like a real bastard for revealing the beast this way but what other choice was there? She needed to know.

His heart ached as she tucked her naked body into the corner next to his bed. She looked so small and frightened, her eyes glistening with unshed tears as she sat on the floor trembling. She was so scared—he hated doing this, he wanted nothing more than to wrap his arms around her and tell her she was safe. But this was the way it had to be, she needed to see the wolf.

Drew slowly pulled her knees up to her chest and wrapped her arms around them. She couldn't believe what she had just seen. Once second Theo had been standing in front of her, tall and proud in his glorious birthday suit, and the next a wolf was there. And not just any wolf—the black wolf from the beach.

"Oh my fucking God," she whispered. "I've lost my mind."

She couldn't control her language any more than she could control her shaking. She stared at the creature sitting on its hind legs. It watched her closely, unmoving. It didn't even blink its silver eyes.

Silver eyes. It had silver eyes, just like —

"Oh my God!" She placed her hand to her forehead. "No. That's impossible. Shit like that doesn't happen. I'm just having a run of the mill hallucination. No big deal." Her lungs felt as though they were being squeezed. Oh God, she was going crazy.

"No! This is Theo's fault." She needed to find some sort of reasoning to help her adjust. "He must have been too rough and now I have a concussion." She struggled to see in the cabin, the glow of the fire her only light. "Can you get a concussion from sex?" she mumbled.

The wolf cocked its head as though it understood what she had said.

"No way. You did that on the beach too. But you can't understand me, there is no way."

As though the animal could feel her panic, it stood and closed the distance. Was it trying to offer her some sort of comfort?

She gasped and squeezed tighter into the wall, turning her head away. No eye contact. *Yeah that might help. Ha!* God, she was a dumbass. The thing was huge. Gluing herself next to a wall and not looking it in the eye wouldn't save her if it decided it wanted her for a snack. She was royally fucked.

She stiffened when she felt the brush of thick fur along her arm and leg. When the touch remained, she slowly turned her head, not a lot, just enough to see it was sitting right next to her. It lowered its massive head and rested it on her bent knee—its very large mouth, full of sharp teeth, was inches from her face.

She held her breath for a long time, and when she finally let it out, the beast apparently took it as a good sign and proceeded to give her cheek a lick.

"Tasting the goods before you commit." She kept her voice low. "Fantastic!" She turned her face a little and looked into beautiful silver eyes. Thoughtful eyes. Old eyes. Theo's eyes.

Theo.

The urge to cry out bubbled up in her chest. No concussion, no hallucinations. It had happened. She had seen Theo transform into a wolf. And not just any wolf—this was the same stunning creature that had protected her from the pack of gray wolves and had run up and down the sand with Ruby. Yet it was also Theo. Theo and a wolf. Theo was a wolf.

Theo was a werewolf!

"Holy shit! You're real." She turned her head fully to get a better look. "Werewolves are real," she whispered in awe.

The creature gave her a snort that sounded a bit on the annoyed side.

She sucked in a breath. "Too loud? Sorry. But... How can this be?" She felt the confusion and tears build once again as she whispered her questions to the wolf. "How can you be...? How?"

The wolf blew out a long puff of air as its muscles flexed and its ears flattened out to the sides. An almost concerned expression appeared on the fur-covered face. It was as though the beast... Or was it Theo? Jesus. She didn't know what or who was which. But it appeared as though it was going through some kind of internal conflict. After another minute of silence, it nosed her arm up and slid its head underneath so she would have to pet him.

A bit uncertain at first, Drew finally stroked the dark fur. The texture felt different somehow — thicker, softer than the time she had touched it on the beach. The wolf leaned into her and expelled a contented sigh.

Drew smiled. She had heard that sound many times — it was the same noise Ruby would make when she was receiving a butt rub.

After a while of sitting in silence and petting a wild animal, Drew realized that this giant werewolf thing was also Theo or was that the other way around? "This is too much. My brain is beginning to hurt." *Ah man*, would she ever get used to this? She shook her head, trying to rattle some sense into it. It didn't help that she was still so confused and freaked out and scared and a lot of other things. But there was one thing she did know — she truly believed Theo when he had said the wolf would never hurt her because it hadn't, and there had been plenty of times when it could have.

What bothered her was Theo. How was she going to be able to love a man who turned into a wolf? What would her life be like with a werewolf? What was she going to do? She loved Theo. She had even put her faith in him without realizing it, so she knew she would never be able to walk away from him. Yet, she had no idea why. That really scared her.

She dug her fingers deeper into the inky fur and massaged the muscles hiding beneath. Holy hell, Theo was really inside this animal. Was he able to see her or to hear her? Would he understand what she was saying if she talked to him?

She had no idea of the answers to any of her questions, but that didn't stop her from asking. She leaned closer, could smell smelly-wolf breath. "Are you in there, Theo?" A large ear honed in on her voice. "Can you hear me?" The beast angled its head the smallest amount so that its soul-filled eyes locked onto her. "Can you see me?"

No answer. Not that she had really expected one. Yet she had a feeling.

"I don't know what to do with this, Theo. I don't know how to handle something like this. You're like a Grimm character come to life." She pulled her arm away and wrapped it around her bent legs.

The wolf stood and padded back into the center of the room, its long nails clicking on the wood floor. It stopped, then froze in place. Its ears suddenly perked up and it cocked its head, looking at the front door. Drew followed its gaze and listened. She didn't hear anything but then again she didn't have the same acute hearing as a wolf. She studied the animal as it trotted to the window and hopped up, placing its two front feet on the ledge. Did Theo have that same hearing as the wolf while he was in human form? What other traits—if any—did he have? Smell? Sight? Fleas? *Eeew!* She wrinkled her nose. *Where the hell had that come from?*

The wolf let out a low whine, the fur went up on its neck and shoulders yet the long black tail swung back and forth. Now that was interesting. It... *Argh!* She had to stop thinking about him as an 'it'. He was a he, not an 'it'.

He was excited about something, but in an aggressive way.

Drew pushed up onto her knees and stood. She tugged the quilt off the bed, wrapped it around her shoulders and walked to the window. She squinted into the dark. She didn't see anything until she caught movement to the right of the cabin, just inside the tree line. A gray wolf stepped from a group of Rocky Mountain junipers and stared at the cabin.

"Hey! That's the female I fixed up." She could see the shaved area around her neck. "Wow! She looks really good." Drew gasped. "I guess Theo was right in bringing…" She stopped when she realized that the wolf was staring at her. She couldn't meet his gaze knowing that Theo might be in there staring at her. "You were right to bring her here." The animal didn't make a sound but she could see that his attention was back on the wolf outside the cabin.

Drew focused her attention on the gray wolf too and watched her lower her body into the thick ferns at her feet. Her beautiful yellow eyes were now fixed on the left side of the cabin. "What's she doing?" Drew looked in the same direction but couldn't see anything.

A low rumble came from the black beast next to her. Drew jumped and moved to the far side of the window. She looked from the wolf standing next to her then to the wolf outside. Something bad was happening, and just as she had thought she should probably throw on some clothes, the gray wolf bolted into the trees at the same time that a dark figure appeared from the forest.

Chapter Twenty-One

"Kill," the wolf demanded again.

Theo watched through the wolf as Linde stepped from the forest. He growled at the same time as the wolf.

Linde was here earlier than he'd expected. *Damn it!* He had been hoping to have time to tell Drew what was going on and get her safely to the Reserve. Now she was caught in the middle and that was the very thing he had been trying to avoid.

"Kill!" the wolf snapped along with a bark.

"No. We can't leave Drew unprotected. If we go after Linde the other shooter will get a chance to get at Drew." The wolf continued to growl.

"What the hell is that nut-job doing here?" She inhaled a short breath. "Is that a gun? Oh my God."

The wolf hopped down from the window ledge and bit at the quilt hanging around Drew's shoulders. She gasped but stopped when the beast tugged her away from the glass. "Stay away from the window, got it. In fact I'll do one better." She rushed to the bed, dropped the blanket and began pulling on her clothes. "Oh fuck, oh fuck, oh fuck." She shook as she tugged up her panties. She was terrified and rightly so. Linde was a nut-job, and Theo had no doubt that if he was able to kill him and the wolf, Linde would do bad things to Drew.

Theo was torn. He wanted to swap back and go to Drew. She was scared and confused at what he had just dumped on her. He wanted to hold her tight, explain about his life with the wolf, how he had come to be this way, how the wolf had saved him, but with Linde outside the cabin and with a rifle no less, allowing the wolf to remain made more sense.

"Just Drew need my Theo now."

Theo tried to stop it but the wolf had already forced the conversion to begin.

Drew sucked in a breath that mixed with the squeak of bed springs. He saw her sit down on the edge of the bed and watch him change. The dark fur shed from his body, piling on the floor as the animal's four legs snapped into human form and his shoulders and head popped back into place.

He stood to his full height and held up his hands.

"I'm sorry I didn't tell you before and I'm sorry I can't explain it to you now. But I will." He crossed to her very slowly. She didn't flinch from him when he reached for her. He had honestly thought she would. He grabbed her upper arms and pulled her up, looking into her eyes. "I need you to finish getting dressed." He kissed her cheek lightly. "Can you do that for me, Drew?"

She nodded, then reached for her long-sleeved T-shirt. He grabbed his jeans and quickly tugged them on. There was a light patter on the roof and Theo recognized the sound of water hitting the wooden shingles.

"Please tell me that's only rain?" Drew asked quietly.

"It's only rain."

"Oh! Good." She expelled a shaky breath and looked up at him. "Is Linde here for you?" She pulled her shirt over her head. "Does he know about you?"

"Yes."

She stopped moving. "Does he want to kill you?"

Crack!

The cabin door splintered as the handle was blown apart. Slivers of wood flew across the room as Theo pulled Drew to the floor. The door swung wide, bouncing off the wall, and flew shut hitting the doorjamb with another bang. The momentum slowed and the damaged door creaked open then came to a stop. The small gap and large hole where the handle had once been did nothing to show the location of the intruders.

"Yes," Theo whispered against her ear. "Linde likes to hunt big game... Illegally in his spare time."

"Spare time?"

"Here, wolfy, wolfy," Linde sang. It sounded as though he was standing just outside the front door. No. Theo hadn't heard anyone climb the stairs that led onto the front deck and the man was too much of a coward for that. But he was close.

"Come out, come out, wolf boy, and I'll give you a fat, juicy steak." As soon as the words were said, the odor of raw meat hit him.

Theo chuckled. "Son of a bitch."

Drew, who was still pinned down next to him, gave him a questioning glare. "What?"

"He really does have a steak."

"Oh my God!" she said quietly. Then she frowned. "Does that bother you? Do you eat raw meat?"

Theo rolled his eyes. "No, Drew, I don't eat raw meat."

"Oh." She sighed in relief. "That's good."

With a smirk, Theo pushed up onto his knees and said, "The wolf does, though."

Keeping low, he moved quickly to the window, hearing Drew's shocked gasp as he went. When he reached the wall, he crawled to the door, positioned his face close to the gap and drew in a deep breath.

Sweat and excitement. Fear and deodorant. Cigarettes and— Yup! That was steak all right. His stomach grumbled. Drew's eyes widened in panic and the wolf rolled beneath his skin, causing his muscles to tighten. He gave Drew a dispassionate shrug, hoping it would calm her fears. Then he addressed the wolf.

"Damn it! Would you stop, we are not eating that meat. It's laced with something. Can't you smell it?"

"Smells... Other. Other smell. Friendly smell. Not right for here."

He was right, there was another scent besides that of Linde and the meat. It was layered with smells from the forest around Tofino, not here on the island. The other odor was one he had smelled many times, but had not been expecting.

"Fuck me." Anger had him pushing to his feet and swinging the door open.

"Ah, there's a good dog." Linde retreated slowly, pointing his rifle at the center of Theo's chest. There was a chunk of meat tied to his belt.

Theo laughed as he slowly crossed the deck and descended the wooden steps. "You are a fool." He scanned the surrounding woods as he addressed the older man. He tried to pinpoint where the other scent was coming from but was having a hard time. It was as though something was blocking the scent... But not.

"Am I, Officer Grey? Really?" Humor laced his words. "I'm the one holding the rifle. Your life belongs to me now and I will do what I want with it."

Theo stopped midway down the steps and grinned. "You have no idea what I am."

Linde stood glaring at him. He was clearly stunned that Theo would have the nerve to not only laugh in his face but that he wasn't afraid of him and this man thrived on the fear of others. He needed it — depended on it. If it wasn't there he wouldn't be able to live the life he did.

"You are a werewolf."

Theo burst out laughing. "I am many things but I am not a werewolf."

Theo's laughter continued until, red-faced, Linde shouted at him, "Shut the fuck up!" He pushed forward with his gun and fired, hitting Theo in the upper chest, knocking him to the ground.

"No!" Drew screamed. "No, please stop." Drew burst from the cabin in only her shirt and panties. She rushed down the stairs and stopped next to him. "Theo," she cried. She flattened her hand on his chest in order to stop the bleeding. "You fucking nut-job," she called over her shoulder. "Look what you did."

Honestly, the pain wasn't all that bad. He had dealt with worse or maybe he was getting used to being shot — which wasn't a pleasant thought.

His body was already responding quickly to the foreign object — thanks to the wolf — and expelled it from his chest.

Tears were streaming down Drew's face as he cupped her cheek. "Hey, no tears. I'm okay." He pushed up to the sitting position and urged, "Go back inside."

"Theo, no! Sit still." She kept pressure on his wound.

He pulled her hand away. "Take a good look, Drew," he said, staring at Linde. Theo loved that mix of shock and fear on the bastard's face. "The blood has already stopped."

She blinked several times then gasped as the bullet breached the opening of the hole and tumbled down his chest, landing with a gentle thud on the ground. She gasped a second time when the tear in his skin began sealing shut. "This can't... How...?" She frowned as she picked up the bullet and cupped it in her hand, staring down at it. "You really are okay?"

"Yes." He focused on Linde and asked, "Your idea of a test?"

The bastard gave him an impassionate shrug, trying to mask his surprise but it was already too late, Theo had picked it up. "Your little comment today about time piqued my interest."

"Shooting me will confirm your suspicions," Theo agreed. "It will also prove..." Theo watched as the owner of the other scent, stepped from the forest. "That you can't kill me." He stood, looking Kevin Beauchamp straight in the eye. "Or the wolf."

Drew followed his gaze and called out a warning, "Kevin, be careful, he has a gun!"

Kevin gave her a tender smile. "I know, Drew." He walked from the shadows, exposing the rifle he had cradled in his arms. His clothing was covered from top to bottom in dried mud and dirt, pine needles and leaves.

"So that's how you hid." Theo nodded to his clothing. He could smell the Tofino forest on Kevin from where he stood.

"Local vegetation works the best."

Theo shrugged. "I wouldn't have known you were out there if you hadn't used G-Tac. It's a good gun cleaner but it's the same one I use at work."

"Huh. I'll make note of that."

"What's G-Tac?" Drew looked from one man to the other. "What's going on here?"

Silence.

Nobody moved. Nobody made a sound.

The wolf coiled like a snake, just under his skin ready to strike. If either man made a move in Drew's direction, they were dead. Theo knew this with complete certainty, because both he and the wolf agreed upon this.

Drew's fear and agitation got the better of her. "God damn it! Kevin, what the hell are you doing here?"

Kevin sighed and relaxed his hold on his gun. "My name is not Kevin, it's Ken. I hunt big game for him." He nodded toward Linde.

"Hunt big game?" Drew snapped. "This isn't Africa. This is Can-na-da. There's no big game here."

"There is game everywhere. You just have to know where and how to look for it."

"Working for Parks and Wildlife would help with that," Theo pointed out.

"That..." Ken agreed. "And spending time in the Marines helped a bit too."

Theo nodded. "Sniper trained, I assume."

"One of the best."

"You're a sniper!" Drew gawked then marched toward him. Theo followed and grabbed her about the waist. "You shot at me on the beach. You killed Ruby. You motherfuc—"

"Wait." Ken shifted slightly so the barrel of his gun pointed away from Drew. He held up his free hand. "I did not shoot at you and I did not kill Ruby. I would never do that to you, Drew."

"Oh that's so nice of you. Then who did?"

There was a pause as they all looked to Linde. Theo's stomach lurched when he saw Linde ogling Drew's chest. He inhaled the man's desire for her and noticed the bulge in his pants. Theo pushed Drew behind him, blocking her from Linde's view.

Linde smiled and nodded. "Not my best shooting. But practice makes perfect, I always say."

Drew tried to bolt around him and make a move for Linde. If Theo hadn't grabbed her she probably would have gotten in a few good hits before Linde could have shot her.

"Let her go. I'd like wrestling with her." Linde grinned and licked his lips as he stared at her nipples poking against her shirt.

"You are fucking twisted," Drew called out. Then she glared at Ken. "I thought you were a good guy, you were so convincing when those wolves were shot. But I bet you were the one who shot them? Weren't you?"

He shrugged. "I have to keep up my skill and I was tracking a wolf." He looked at Theo. "It only made sense."

"How could you do that? They were innocent creatures. I thought you were a friend. You helped me when Ruby was shot and you kissed me. Argh! What was I thinking?"

The expression on Ken's face changed to serious in a heartbeat. "I did want to help you after Ruby was shot, it should never have happened. And this stuff with Linde has nothing to do with how I feel about you. " The muscles in Theo's shoulders tightened in anticipation and jealousy. "But I want you, Drew, we'd be good together."

"Good together! Are you on *crack*? How could you do all of this? How could you work for this" — Drew pointed at Linde — "piece of trash?"

Ken chuckled. "Mr Trash pays me a lot of money to track his game. I, like everyone, have bills to pay. Although I have to say, I didn't think this job would be as difficult or as interesting as it has been."

"I bet." Theo kept an eye on Ken and his rifle. Then he noticed a shadow creeping along the inside of the tree line.

He caught the scent at the same second as the wolf. Theo tried to hide his smirk as the wolf growled in satisfaction.

"You got a job with Parks and Wildlife so you could kill animals for this piece of shit?" Drew shivered in disgust. Light drizzle probably didn't help either. Drew was hurt by this new-found knowledge — it was evident in her words. Theo pulled her closer into his side hoping his heat would help stop her shivering.

"I don't kill them. I track them, so he can kill them."

"Oh well… Then that's okay."

"Drew, I'm sorry you got pulled into the middle of this," he admitted, with more feeling than Theo was expecting. Theo didn't detect anything that would hint that Ken was lying. Unlike Linde's desire for control and destruction, Ken was simply following orders like a good soldier. He was here for the money. Plain and simple. And the feelings Ken had developed for Drew had not been part of his plan. It was those feelings Theo was picking up that might be the only thing that kept him from killing Ken.

The shadow in the trees steadily crept toward the cabin, closer to Linde.

"That's all very sweet," Linde began with a snort. "But how in the hell are we going to kill him? I shot him in the chest and he just got back up."

Ken braced his legs apart and rubbed his chin. Then quickly raised his gun and fired. The bullet hit Theo in the center of his heart.

Drew screamed and tried to keep him from falling, but it was no good, he was just too heavy, and he pulled her down as he crashed onto the dirt.

Chapter Twenty-Two

Drew screamed again. She couldn't help it, she didn't want to help it. Kevin had just shot Theo in the heart. Dark red blood poured out of the hole in his chest and it didn't appear to be slowing. Kevin's aim had been flawless.

"Whoo-hoo!" Linde called out. "That did it. What did you use, hollow point?"

"He's a werewolf," Ken pointed out. "I used silver."

Silver.

In his journal, Theo had said he wasn't a werewolf. He had just said the very same thing to Linde. *The soul of the wolf rested next to his own*. He had two souls inside him. A werewolf was a single being... Wasn't it? And if he wasn't a werewolf then silver couldn't kill him. Right?

She tried to help Theo by putting pressure on the wound but she was jerked away and forced to stand. The death grip on her arm stung and increased when she tried to pull away. She clawed at Kevin or Ken's hand and face, anything to get away from this killer and back to Theo, but his grip was unrelenting. "Let me go."

The blow to her cheek made her world spin and the eye that had taken the blow felt like it was about to explode. Then things went dark for a moment and her legs gave out on her.

"What the fuck are you doing?" Ken demanded in a harsh voice. She was half carried, half dragged to the steps and was helped to sit.

"I like her fight as much as you do, but if I don't teach her who's boss now, she'll become problematic in the future and then I'll have to have her killed. And I have no intention of that happening for a very long time." A hand stroked her head then tilted her face up. The light rain was cool on her throbbing cheek.

When she opened her eyes Ken was examining her. "Are you okay?"

"Fuck you." Her head spun when she jerked it away. "You killed Theo."

He shrugged and sighed at the same time. "We'll see."

Linde laughed. "See the attitude? We need to teach her her place." He gripped his crotch, adjusting the bulge. "I can charge top dollar for a pretty blonde submissive."

As Ken straightened Drew took advantage and lunged forward, trying to get closer to Theo's still form. She needed to be near him, needed to help him. She didn't care about anything else, not Kevin or Ken or whoever the hell he was, not Linde, not even the wolf. She just needed Theo. She wanted to see the wound, had to know if he was healing like the last time. He had healed so quickly when Linde shot him, was it happening again? It *had* to happen again, she had to have Theo in her life.

Both men caught her this time but it was Ken that snapped out a command, "Enough. Drew, stop fighting."

Linde pressed his body against hers. Her stomach heaved when she felt his hard-on rub against her hip. "I'll take her inside and calm her down, you get me my trophy."

"I don't think so." Ken's voice dropped low and was laced with a warning. "You paid me to track your prey. I did that. Now you finish him off and I'll take care of Drew. Remember our deal."

Linde released her arm and thankfully moved away from her. "You just remember who you are working for."

Ken faced Linde. "I know exactly who I've been working for — human trafficker, drug smuggler, arms dealer, a lowlife trying hard to blend in with the upper crust of society. Does that about sum it up?"

Drew looked from Ken to Linde's red face. "Human trafficking," Drew said softly. Drugs and guns. A sudden tremor shook her body. Oh boy, she was in some deep shit. What was she going to do? She tried to see Theo but Ken's large body was blocking her view.

"My businesses are none of your concern. Your job is to get me my kill. But seeing how Officer Grey is anything but a normal kill, would you mind explaining how you would have me do that?" Linde bit out through clenched teeth.

"Do what you normally do — cut the head off."

"Nooo!" Drew screamed. She fought Ken but was unable to free herself.

Linde stepped forward and laughed in her face as Ken struggled to keep hold of her. Linde grabbed her chin and smashed his mouth down on hers. The smell of desire and cigarettes and sweat made her gag and she hoped she had eaten enough to throw it up all over him.

Ken jerked her away. "Don't touch her again."

"Shit." Linde licked his lips. "She tastes good." And he reached for her a second time. "Don't worry," Linde soothed. "You still get to have her first. But fuck her now." He stroked his groin again. "I don't think I can wait to get back to the mainland to have my turn."

Ken shook his head. "Deal's off." He released her then protectively circled his arm around her waist pulling her close.

Linde eyed him. "You fell for the vet?" Then he laughed. "I don't blame you. She will be the perfect little fuck toy. But..." he continued with a smug grin. "If I don't get her, you don't get your bonus."

"Get me?" she blurted out.

"Yes." He licked at his lips as he stared at her chest.

"You don't get to have me." She struggled to pull away from Ken's hold. "You disgusting pig."

He ignored her statement. "I love that mouth of yours. I plan on keeping it very busy."

"Ha!" she barked. "Go ahead, stick something in my mouth, and we'll see how long it stays attached to your body."

Ken chuckled. She was relieved that Ken wanted to keep this pig away from her but at the same time she was furious that he had shot Theo and fought to free herself. His hold only tightened.

"You seem to think you have a choice. How very naïve of you, Dr O' Bannion." The older man shook his head. "Ken and I had a deal. He gets to play with you first, then it's my turn. Although, I doubt he'll have as much fun with you as I will." He reached out to touch her face but Ken shoved her behind his back before she could feel Linde's slimy touch.

"I said don't fucking touch her." Then, very slowly, he raised his rifle and aimed it at Linde.

"What are you doing?" Linde retreated.

"Do you really think I would let you touch her, you sick fuck? I couldn't care less about your bonus. I'm not letting you near her." Ken took a threatening step closer.

Was Ken going to shoot Linde? She wasn't big on violence, but the world would not miss this sickening excuse for a human being. Although, how he would die was up in the air now, because the pretty gray wolf she had seen earlier was back and by the look on her face she was about to get her long overdue dinner for one.

Ken stopped in mid-stride. "Don't move." He spoke low. Drew found that a bit odd at first then realized that Ken hadn't given any type of warning about the animal creeping up behind Linde on purpose.

Linde curled his lips into a cruel smile and raised his hands. "You won't shoot me. I pay you too well."

"Not everything revolves around money."

Linde snorted. "Of course it—" He caught movement to his left. "It's not dead." His voice was higher than normal. "The silver didn't work."

The area surrounding them suddenly vibrated with a deep, menacing growl.

Ken spun to face the noise. He pulled her close, keeping his larger body in front of her.

Theo's wolf braced his legs apart as he lowered his giant head. His sharp teeth were very white next to the black of his muzzle. The magnificent ebony fur rose along his neck and back as his silver eyes glowed an eerie silvery-white similar to steel covered in a heavy frost.

My God, what a beautiful sight.

She had never been so happy to see a wolf in her life. Given that she knew Theo was somewhere inside, which probably helped with her fears, even so, she would take a wild animal over these two nut-jobs any day of the week.

Theo's wolf looked at the female. He growled and stomped a front paw while snapping his large muzzle.

That's when the gray wolf attacked Linde from behind, catching him completely unaware. She jumped on his back, digging her claws into his shoulder, and clamped her long teeth around his neck. Blood squirted into the air as Linde screamed. He swung his gun over his shoulder, trying to hit the creature. A shot rang out and Drew ducked, covering her head.

As Linde fought with the gray, Theo's wolf stalked Ken. He stepped back, forcing her to do the same, and stumbled on the wooden steps that were slick from the steady drizzle. He took her with him and she landed hard against his chest, the barrel of his rifle jamming into her side.

"Call him off, Drew," Ken demanded as he struggled to sit up. "He'll listen to you."

The wolf slowly crept forward, glowing eyes locking onto his target.

"No!" She fought against him. "I won't. Even if he would listen to me, which I don't think he would at this point, you shot him. How could you do that?"

"I was trying to protect you."

"From who? Theo or Linde?"

"Both." He gave her an intense look. "I can take care of you, Drew. I have enough money for us to buy our own tropical island and disappear."

"But I don't want to disappear." Her voice dropped. "I want Theo," she confirmed. "I told you that."

He watched the wolf as he asked the next question. "And how's that going to work? Look at him, Drew. He's a werewolf. You can't love a werewolf."

"I do love him," she cried. "And he's not a werewolf!"

With a frustrated curse, Ken pushed Drew up and away from him. "Fine. Suit yourself," he called over the growling.

She landed on her feet but slipped on the wet grass and fell onto her knees. When she raised her head, Theo's wolf was directly in front of her, his black, shiny nose less than an inch from hers. The silvery eyes blinked once and the nose twitched slightly but other than that, it barely registered her.

It moved around her and continued on its path, a path that ended with Ken.

Drew struggled to stand and gripped her toes into the grass to keep from slipping again. She looked between the two scenes.

Ken stumbled up the cabin steps away from Theo and his wolf, and Linde, now on his knees, was still trying to fight off the gray by hitting it with his gun.

She could barely move—she was transfixed by the two battles happening right in front of her.

Linde took another swing at the wolf but the female hung on tight. His face was draining of all color, his skin almost gray. His eyes were wide as blood ran down his neck and soaked into his shirt. God there was blood everywhere. It covered his hands and arms, his chest and stomach and a bright pool of it spread over the ground where Linde knelt seeping into his pants.

She gagged when a gurgling sound came from his direction.

Then, in a last ditch effort, he brought his gun up for one last swing.

It went off again and a sharp pain stabbed Drew in her middle.

She sucked in her breath and blinked. Then she looked down and found her shirt soaked with blood.

It was kind of funny, really. Her vision blurred a bit and she did waver as she stood but that was all. No dramatic gestures like she'd seen in the movies. She just stood there staring at the blood on her shirt.

She looked up in time to see Theo's wolf watching her then with a harrowing roar it charged Linde. He hit the man square in the chest, knocking him to the ground. He clamped his muzzle around the dying man's throat, shaking his head ferociously, tearing at what was left of Linde's throat, every bit the wild animal.

"Drew," Ken whispered, looking at her side. "Fuck, Drew. I never meant for this to happen. Come with me, please. I can help you."

She laughed softly. "Sure you didn't. Right after you got your turn with me." She pressed her hand over the wound and cried out.

The wolves stopped their attack when they heard her cry and slowly turned to face her and Ken. Blood dripped from their snarling lips and strips of torn clothing hung from their teeth.

"I'm serious, Drew. I was never going to let Linde hurt you. I'm not part of the man's life other than tracking prey for him. That's it. I can love you, Drew, the way you deserve to be loved." He dropped his arm when the wolves closed in on their new prey. "Drew," he pleaded one more time, then called out in the wolves' direction. "I would never hurt her."

She looked over her shoulder as he withdrew into the surrounding forest. "No, you just kill innocent animals for money and you shot the man that I love. You are no better than Linde." She turned her back on him, saddened by the man that he really was. "If I were you, I would run far and fast."

When there was no response, she glanced over her shoulder. Ken was gone.

Chapter Twenty-Three

Theo watched through the wolf as Drew swayed slightly. She looked at Linde and wrinkled her nose at the gruesome sight. Then she suddenly lost the use of her legs and fell hard to the ground.

Damn it. He should have swapped sooner. He knew she was hurt, could smell the blood, her fear. But the wolf was so jacked up it was hard trying to rein him in. Even now, the damn animal fought him. It wanted to hunt Ken, to kill him for what had happened to Drew.

He tried to force the conversion to begin, but the wolf fought him again.

"God damn it. Stop! Drew needs us. Our mate needs us. She is hurt, maybe dying. We are nothing without her."

The wolf whined and swung his head to look at the female wolf standing behind him. *"Mate. Hurt."* The beast sniffed at the air, then stepped closer to Drew. *"Just Drew hurt. Mate, no hurt."*

Theo didn't have time to figure out what the hell that meant and tried forcing the change once again.

Theo was pulling Drew close to his chest less than a minute later.

He began lifting her shirt but she clamped her hands over the wound and cried out.

"Easy, baby. I just want to have a look."

"No. If I..." She took a ragged breath. Her face turned white. "Don't... Keep pressure on it... More blood loss."

She was covered in blood. The front of her, the back of her, there was even a small pool that had gathered on the ground.

He ignored her plea and lifted her hand away. The bullet hole wasn't all that big but he knew the exit wound would be and for the life of him he couldn't bring himself to look at it. The memory of her being hit by the bullet was bad enough. Hearing the fear in her voice, smelling the coppery scent of blood surrounding her was killing him slowly and in the most painful way, because she was dying.

He would not let her go, not now that he had found her.

"Found them," his wolf added.

The gray wolf that had fought beside him, the animal that Drew had saved weeks before, stepped closer, sniffing the air. She lowered onto her stomach and whined. His wolf whined back as though trying to communicate with the female.

"Mate," the wolf sighed.

Theo quickly studied the female wolf as she stared at him. She whined again, inching closer to his side.

"What is...?" Theo hesitated, then asked the question, even though he thought he knew the answer. *"The gray is your mate?"*

"Mate," the beast agreed.

"But how? I thought Drew was our mate?"

"Drew Theo's mate. Gray—wolf's mate."

"Holy shit." He swiped at his face. Drew was hurt, dying. He didn't have time for this crap now. Drew needed help. He had to get her to a hosp—

He stopped and glanced down at the animal now nudging at his thigh. Theo could clearly see intelligence and understanding in those startling yellow eyes.

Theo froze. "Holy shit." Then he looked from the wolf to Drew and back to the wolf. "I must be crazy to even think it."

"Theo," Drew whispered cupping his cheek. "Are you okay?"

He smiled and held her tight. "Yes and you will be too." He lowered her carefully to the ground. "I'll be right back. Got to get my boat keys and phone." He pointed to the gray female. "You stay and watch her."

The female, understood, inching closer and licking Drew's cheek. This would work, it had to work. He didn't have any other options. Tofino and the medical clinic were too far. She would never survive the trip.

He took the steps two at a time and flung the door open, then searched for his keys and cell. Once he had found them, he scrambled through his bag looking for a pair of track pants while he called Tom and filled him in on what had happened.

"Beauchamp, that dirty son of a bitch!" Tom yelled into the phone. "You okay?"

"I am, but Drew was shot." He tugged on the pants.

"What! Oh my God!" Tom called out again.

He headed out of the door and cleared the steps and the distance to Drew in one jump, landing next to her. That was new. He shook off the unusual feat as a spike of adrenaline.

"I need you to wake the elders. I need their help."

"What for? You'd be better off taking her to the clinic."

"That's not possible."

"She's that bad, eh? Shit. I'm sorry, Theo." He could hear the sympathy in Tom's voice. It was the one thing he didn't want to hear.

"Tom!" Theo snapped. "Go wake the elders and meet us at the main house."

"Why? What for...?" He realized what Theo wanted. "Are you sure you want to do that?"

"Of course. The alternative is...unacceptable. Do this for me, Tom."

"But you need a wol—"

"I have one. We'll be there in five."

"It must be willing, Theo. Any wolf won't do."

"Just do what I asked, Tom. Please."

Theo shut off his phone and looked down at Drew. She was so pale—even her normally plump lips were drained of color and pulled tight in pain.

He lifted her carefully into his arms.

"It's about time you decided to take me to the hospital."

He kissed her head and smiled. "Sorry about that."

"Is Tom going to help us?" she asked, closing her eyes.

"Yes, baby. Tom is going to help us."

He looked over his shoulder to the gray following close behind. "Come on then." He began a slow jog to his small dock where his boat was waiting.

They made it to his boat minutes later. He climbed on board, careful not to jar Drew, and laid her down on the bench seat at the back of the boat. "Hang on, baby." He smoothed the hair from her face.

His stomach dipped when she didn't respond. "Drew." He used a harder tone. "Answer me."

Her eyelids fluttered open and she blinked up at him but still didn't answer him. He cradled her face between his palms. "Say something, Drew. Please."

She opened her mouth and licked her lips. "What do you want me to say?" Even with a bullet wound, she still had the ability to lace her questions with sarcasm.

He smiled and kissed her softly. "That's my girl."

He quickly untied the lines anchoring the boat and moved to the steering wheel. As he fired up the engine, the female paced nervously at the end of the small dock.

"You have two choices," Theo called out, throwing the boat into reverse. "Come with us or meet us there. What's it going to be?"

His wolf paced in his head, the movement a mirror image of that of the gray. His attention was so focused on the female it was as if he was willing her to join them. Theo didn't hear the wolf say anything, but impressions filled his mind and Theo could have sworn he was trying to link with her on a psychic level.

Impatient, Theo began turning the boat in the direction of the Reservation and was about to hit the throttle when the gray walked out onto the swaying dock, cautious about where she was walking, she dug her long nails into the wood to help steady her, and she whined about it the whole time.

Theo sighed and pushed the throttle forward. His wolf began to clench his muscles tight in order to slow his movement. A low growl told Theo the beast was not happy about leaving the female behind.

Theo looked over his shoulder and barked out an order. "Move it."

She perked up her ears and suddenly bolted for the end of the dock and jumped into the boat. She slid into the side with a huff and settled herself next to Drew.

Looking up into the night sky, Drew saw nothing but dark clouds. Water hit her face and body and she was sure it was coming from the waves. God, she felt awful, sick and cold...freezing. Her body shook violently. Except for her arm and shoulder on her right side—they were surprisingly warm. She looked down and saw the gray female sitting next to her. Her ears were back and her nose was up, sniffing the air. She then focused on Theo's tall form. His one knee was bent and resting on the white driver's seat as he maneuvered the boat through the water.

Theo. God, she loved him. So much it scared her. Except now, it scared her for a different reason. She was going to lose him. She was dying. She knew it, could feel the blood covering her body, the stickiness gluing her fingers together. Knew the damage to her body could not be fixed at the small clinic in Tofino. To be honest, she was surprised that she was still alive. Was Theo helping with that? Or maybe the wolf? Did they possess that ability too?

It didn't matter. She closed her eyes when tears streamed down her cheeks. She knew it would be too late.

* * * *

Theo was in the process of laying her down on the ground when she opened her eyes next. No, not the ground. It was something soft, warm and it cradled her body with surprising comfort. Drops of rain hit her face and ran down the sides. They were still outside.

Theo gave her a nervous smile. "Hey. You had me worried." He brushed a kiss on her forehead. "It won't be long now. Just hang on a little longer." Theo looked across her and asked a question, "Are you sure we should do it here? The rain is picking up and she's already so cold."

A weathered old man appeared in her line of sight, just behind Theo. He placed his wrinkled hand upon Theo's shoulder. "It is better done outside. We must be one with nature when the dance is performed. We must be one with the wolf."

Tom came into view next and lifted her arm, his fingers resting gently on her wrist. "Her pulse is weak." He mirrored Theo's concerned frown. "I can't believe she has held on this long." He addressed her, giving her a gentle smile, "You are one tough broad."

"It is her strength and will to live that have attracted the wolf." She couldn't see who spoke this time but knew it was a woman. Her voice was confident but in a soothing way. "The bond is already strong between them. Look, even now the wolf wants to be with Drew, yet is nervous of us." Theo and Tom both looked in the same direction. She tried to turn her head to see what the hell they were talking about, but her muscles refused to obey.

Tom nodded approvingly. "She will be worthy of the wolf."

There was a collective murmur of agreement.

What wolf were they talking about? Theo's wolf? Better yet, why was she still alive?

"Theo." Her throat was dry and scratchy and she had to blink several times when the rain blinded her already fuzzy vision. "What's...going on...?"

"Shhh," he soothed. "It's okay."

An older woman tapped Tom on the shoulder and shooed him out of the way. She knelt next to her and grasped her hand. Drew stared at the woman, and guessed she was in her fifties or sixties. She had beautiful tanned skin and dark hair streaked with white. Her dark coffee-colored eyes were gentle, but full of wisdom and secrets.

"We are going to help you, Drew." She brushed her hand up her forehead and over her head in a long slow stroke. Her touch was warm and inviting. Drew closed her eyes when she repeated the action. "That's it. Close your eyes and breathe deep. Pull the crisp air into your body." There was another gentle stroke to her forehead. "Feel the heat of your mate next to you. Feel his love seep into your body and surround your heart."

On cue, Theo squeezed her hand tangling their fingers together. "I'm here, baby. Right next to you." He kissed the corner of her mouth and whispered against her lips. "I love you, Drew, so much. I want you next to me always." A sudden flush of heat flooded her body and her heart sped up.

A low sound echoed in her head. It was almost like music, as if people were singing. She didn't understand any of the words, the voices were too low to make any sense, but it sounded beautiful. She sighed when the woman urged her to be one with nature, to accept the gift that was being offered to her. Drew really had no idea what the woman was talking about, but she sure as hell wouldn't turn down a free gift.

Her body warmed as the voices in the background increased in volume. There was a lovely musical effect and the words were becoming clear. Something about the wolf saving her body and soul and how they would be tied together forever. She wasn't sure what it all meant, she didn't really care. All that mattered was that Theo was with her and that she didn't feel any more pain.

Theo blinked away the stinging in his eyes.

God. Please let this work. Please save her. Only the wolf heard his plea and agreed.

He stared down into Drew's pale face and repeated the plea.

He couldn't lose her. He wanted her in his life, more than he had ever wanted or needed anything. He didn't care what he had to do, Drew had to stay alive. It scared him to think what life would be like without her — she was his mate and his anchor to this world, to sanity.

The circle of people that surrounded them was small, the wolf dance only known by the elders of the tribe. Their voices grew in strength as they continued. He recognized the words from when Jon had sung them to him all those years ago while he sat dying in a Belgian forest. At the time, he hadn't noticed the effect, but now with so many others performing the dance, the influence was overwhelming and very powerful.

The gray female, who hadn't stopped pacing since they had arrived, circled the group several times. When she finally got up the courage to walk between the dancers, their sudden movement startled her and she flinched. She let out a couple of frustrated barks and finally darted between a man wearing a large headdress and a woman covered in brown fur, and crept closer to Drew. She sniffed the woman who knelt next to Drew and stepped warily behind her.

Then, crouching down on all fours, she lowered her face right next to the wound on Drew's side.

Theo didn't like the idea of the animal being so close to Drew when she was hurt. The smell of her blood was strong and surrounded them in a coppery halo. Yet even after Tom had explained what would happen, Theo had tensed up so tight it felt like his bones were about to snap from the strain. He knew Drew couldn't afford the wolf to bolt—she wouldn't survive without the female and he just hated the idea of what was to come. He gripped her hand tight and whispered to her. Told her how much she meant to him and that he loved her, all the while terror filled every cell of his body.

The woman who sat across from him rose and moved to join the others. The collective voices of the group rose to a fevered pitch. Their bodies moved in unison as the rain fell and the wind picked up. The wolf whimpered and growled as it inched closer to Drew. Theo locked eyes with the female and held his breath when her yellow eyes began glowing. Then in one swift movement, she clamped her jaws around Drew's side. The scream that echoed through the forest was so loud and so unnatural that even nature itself gasped in shock.

Chapter Twenty-Four

"Drew." Theo's deep voice was comforting. Like a warm blanket on a cold day. It wrapped around her, warming her from the inside out.

"Drew. It's time to wake up." His voice became hard. "Drew, baby, open your eyes and look at me. Now!"

She wrinkled her nose at the demand. "All right, you don't have to get bitchy. That's my job in the morning."

She opened her eyes only to snap them shut. "It's bright in here." She covered her eyes and made a second attempt. She expected to find herself in Theo's cabin but she wasn't, she was lying in her own bed, in her own room. Squinting, she sat up and looked around. "How did I get here? I thought..." That's when the memories—sharp and crystal clear—suddenly filled her mind.

She yanked up her shirt and examined her body. Nothing. No blood, no hole, no pain. Not even a scar. She touched her side and slid her hand around to her lower back. Still nothing.

She met Theo's worried gaze. He'd looked like that the last time she had seen him. She remembered. It was night and it had been raining and people were singing close by.

She placed a shaky hand on her forehead. "What happened, Theo? I'm sane enough to know it all happened, so don't try to tell me otherwise."

He sat on the bed in front of her, and, shifting his weight, he turned to face her fully. "I would never lie to you." He sighed. "And yes, it happened."

"Linde shot me. Right here." She placed a hand on the area where the bullet hole had been.

"Yes."

"But you…" She shook her head. "I mean, your wolf and the gray female ripped him apart."

"Yes. He wasn't a good person, Drew. He would have done terrible things to you."

"I know." She nodded. A disturbing image of blood and pieces of skin scattered on the ground flashed before her eyes. "You heard."

"Yes. A shot to the heart takes a bit longer to heal. I couldn't move but I was still able to hear what was going on around me."

"The wolf healed you. Just like the first time."

It was his turn to nod. "The wolf has been healing my wounds…our wounds since he first joined with me."

"He joined with you in 1915?" She didn't know why she asked, she had read his journal, had seen the living proof. Geez, it was sitting right in front of her.

"Yes."

They were silent for a few minutes. She replayed the scene of Theo being shot in her head and him standing up seconds after. It was amazing and freaky at the same time. How could the wolf do it? What abilities would it have to possess in order to pull off such a miracle?

She wished she'd had that last night. She could have done without all that pai— She met his silver gaze. "How come I'm not dead? I should be dead."

"But you are not dead." His voice became firm as though he thought she would argue. "You are alive and *whole*."

Whole?

"Oh my God." She jumped off the bed and pointed at him. "What did you do?"

"I did what was necessary to save your life." He swung his leg to the floor and watched her frantic movement.

"Which was what?" she demanded in a high voice. She shook her hands as though she had touched something gross. She stopped when she heard his sigh and realized what he had done but still needed to hear. "Tell me!"

"The gray female joined with you."

She was about to scream at him when he held up his hands to silence her. "By doing so, she healed your wound and saved your life."

She gasped. No. She couldn't, wouldn't accept that. She stomped toward him and pushed at his shoulders. "Take it back, take it back. Undo what you did."

He let her push at him once more before grabbing her arms. He gave her a little shake. "No! I won't take it back. I wouldn't even if I could." He stood still, holding her arms. "You were going to die. Die, Drew! How could you ask me to take it back? Doing that would be like killing you myself."

She stared at him. His handsome face showed the strain of the events of the night before plus something else, something deep and consuming. "I love you,

Drew." He pulled her close and looked her directly in the eye. "I can't live in this world without you. You are my mate. The wolf sensed it the first night we met. I thought he was wrong, and I've tried fighting it. I know the dangers it would put you in, but I can't stop it. I don't want to stop it, even though I'm drawn to you in a way that is…alarming at times."

She felt her eyes grow wide and her heart squeeze.

"This feeling"—he tapped the center of his chest—"isn't just sexual. I love being with you. I love the sound of your voice, your laugh, your sense of humor. You are honest, insecure and unpredictable." He touched the pink highlight hanging down the side of her face. "I need unpredictable. My life has been regimented since the wolf and I joined. I've been doing what I needed to do so we could survive in a world that would never understand what we are." He cupped her cheek, ran his finger under her eye and wiped the tear away. "I feel at peace when I'm with you. I haven't felt that way since I was a boy in London. I have that feeling only when I'm with you."

She pulled away, shaking her head. His hands dropped and curled into fists. "It's too much, Theo." More tears formed in her eyes. "I only found out about you last night and now I'm a werewolf."

He silenced her. "First off, it's been two days since Linde shot you. I brought you home because I thought you would feel more comfortable when you learned the truth."

"Two days?"

He nodded. "You were still out of it and I knew you would be very tired, you needed to sleep and heal. Second you are *not* a werewolf. I thought you knew that. A werewolf is part man and part wolf. It does not develop fully into a wolf, it retains human attributes.

You have the soul of a wolf inside you. It rests next to your own soul. When you are ready to swap, you will become fully wolf. And you *cannot* stop halfway during the conversion, it is impossible."

"This was all in your book."

"Yes it is," he agreed. "I brought it with me. I think you should spend some time reading it." He shrugged. "Maybe it will help in some way."

She nodded. "I need to be alone. To think this through." She pressed her lips together when he nodded. He stared at her briefly then stepped close. His heat engulfed her as he brushed his lips against her head. "I love you, more than anything, and I will do anything to make this easier on you. Just remember that when you start cursing my name."

He pulled away from her, taking his heat with him, and walked around the bed, heading for the door. He stopped by an open backpack sitting on the floor and pulled his old leather journal free. He tossed it on the bed.

"I'll be downstairs if you need anything." He left, closing the door behind him.

Her heart ached for him and not because he looked so hurt and dejected, but because of all those wonderful things he had just said to her. And what had she done? She'd stood there acting like a bitch. But damn it! He had turned her into a...wolf... Well, not right this minute, but she would become one...at some point. She would have hair growing out of her in places she spent a small fortune getting waxed. The idea of hair growing out of her anywhere other than the top of her head was just wrong.

There were a hundred other things that she wouldn't be able to adjust to. Like changing into the wolf. When Theo changed it looked very painful, she didn't know if she had the strength to go through that. And what about eating? She flopped onto the bed and stared at the ceiling. She was on her way to becoming a serious vegetarian. Sure, she'd had a few relapses, she was only human and bacon smelled sooo good. But it was a goal of hers to lead a healthy life style — how in God's name was she going to do that if this damn wolf inside her decides to munch on a squirrel, or some fresh roadkill?

Her stomach heaved at the idea of swallowing rotten meat.

"I can't do this." She covered her face when her lips began to quiver. "I can't. I just can't."

"Yes you can." She heard the words over her soft crying and didn't know if she had thought them or she had heard them. Yet the deep voice was damn familiar.

Theo?

Argh! She was still mad at him, but she wasn't. She pressed her palms into her eyes. Yet, he had killed the man who was going to hurt her. He had protected her from a monster then done everything in his power to save her life. Yeah, by turning her into a meat eater!

Sighing, his words replayed in her head all on their own.

'I love you. I can't live in this world without you. You are my mate.'

Her chest constricted. She closed her eyes, trying to remember what had happened after Linde had shot her. Just bits and pieces floated in her mind. The wind whipped at her as she lay in his boat, Theo placing her on a soft bed out in the forest. There was singing, and a woman with the gentlest brown eyes had talked to her as Theo whispered and kissed the side of her mouth. She stopped and focused on his words.

'I'm here, baby. Right next to you.' Her breath caught in her throat at the way he had whispered the words. His voice had been thick with emotion. She remembered, now.

'I love you, Drew, so much. I want you next to me always.'

Next to him always. Well, that wouldn't be a problem now. Not that it would have been before. She loved him, very much. Loved everything about him and that included the wolf and... He loved her back.

Theo loved her.

She placed her hand on her heart as it thumped heavily, and wings brushed the inside of her stomach.

"Argh!" Tears stung her eyes. "He couldn't tell me that before I became a walking flea motel?"

She caught the sound of a deep chuckle but wasn't sure where it had come from. Her mind again? Probably, she felt a little crazy right now.

What was she going to do? She was joined with a wolf. A wolf! Sweet Jesus!

How in the hell was she going to live with this? What was her life going to be like?

She covered her face and imagined herself as the wolf running through the forest. Taking in every scent, every sound. A squirrel running in front of her and her giving chase.

She snapped her eyes open. "No way. I will not chase squirrels." She rolled over and punched her pillows a few times in an attempt to adjust them then sat back in a huff. She stared at Theo's journal for a long time, debating with herself if she even wanted to know what she was in for. Finally, with a long sigh, she reached for it. She settled it on her crossed legs and opened it to the first page.

* * * *

Three hours later, she closed the heavy book and placed it next to her.

Theo's life had been incredible and long and scary and...very, very lonely. He had survived two wars and during that time he had witnessed some of the most gruesome acts a human being was capable of committing. Yet, in spite of all that horror, he still fought.

He had gone home to his family after the First World War a different man. His fiancée had married a childhood friend, with a little one on the way. Over the years, he'd watched his younger sisters marry and have children and he had watched his parents grow old. All the while, he had remained the same. He had stayed in England longer than he should have, but he'd wanted to make sure his family would be safe and secure. He'd left in the middle of the night without a word, never sharing his secret with them, and he'd watched from afar as his family died.

He'd come to Canada searching for answers and had made his way across the country. He had lived in every single province and had had many jobs along the way. He had worked for a family who owned a small bakery in Ontario, had fished for cod off the coast of Newfoundland, had been a logger in northern Saskatchewan and a ranch hand in southern Alberta. Out of all the jobs he'd had—and there had been many—he had kept going back to policing. He had a protective side to him and she didn't believe the wolf had any influence over that quality. That trait was all Theo.

In 1939, Germany had invaded Poland and the Second World War had begun and Theo had once again been a soldier battling in Europe. Hell, he had landed on Juno beach with the 3rd Canadian Infantry Division on D-Day. Which meant—if her math was correct—he would have been fifty-nine at the time.

Once back from the war Theo had taken up where he had left off, moving farther and farther west. During his travels, both he and the wolf had been hunted for the wolf's prize fur. They had escaped every time no worse for wear, the hunters unaware of what they had actually been hunting.

It was amazing when she thought about it. Theo had witnessed every major event of the twentieth century. The start of the First World War, the stock market crash of 1929, and the 1969 moon landing. Theo wasn't the disco type and she doubted that he ever did the hustle but she could 'totally' see him wearing a 'Member's Only' jacket and cruising through the '80s.

Her head spun. My God! Theo had already lived two lives and she wasn't even half way through one.

"Oh God. What am I going to do?" she asked the empty room.

"Let me love you."

She gasped and sat up, looking around expecting to see Theo standing close by, except the door to her room was still closed, just as he'd left it.

The sudden image of Theo's black wolf appeared in her mind, followed by a deep longing sigh.

She paused. Okay, she had heard Theo's voice clearly. It was not her mind playing tricks. But that sigh and the image... That had to be her wolf... It had to be. The image of Theo's wolf wasn't hers, she hadn't conjured it up, yet she could still see it hovering behind her eyes. That longing feeling wasn't hers either, still she could feel it deep inside.

Lord, this was bizarre.

She flopped on the bed, and in a normal speaking level asked, "Can you hear me?" She held her breath.

"Yes. Just as you can hear me."

She exhaled. "Whoa!" Then she swallowed. "Where are you?"

"Just watching the news while I wait for you to come down."

Her TV was in the living room on the main floor, on the other side of the house, and he could hear her. She could hear him and… Wait, was that…? "Oh my God, you are watching the news, I can hear it."

"Easy. Just breathe."

She did as he had ordered and took a deep calming breath. This was crazy. What other freaky things would she be able to do?

"Please come down, Drew. Let's deal with this together." She received the impression of the wolf perking up its ears, as if she understood what Theo was saying. Or did it sense her desire to go to Theo, the need to feel his arms around her, holding her, loving her.

She dropped onto the pillows. "This scares me, Theo."

"I know, baby. It scared me too."

"Well, at least you had an excuse." Her voice got a bit high and a lot squeaky. "You were in the middle of a war, for God's sake. I'm just a stupid vet. I love animals, I love taking care of them. It's becoming one that scares the ever-loving shit out of me. "

"You are not stupid." She could hear him sigh. *"The situation at the time had nothing to do with it. Joining to a wolf is scary, plain and simple. It's normal for you to feel this way."* The sound of heavy steps caught her attention.

She felt the wolf stir and… Wait! Did it just sit up?

Oh my God. She could feel its excitement rising with her own. Theo and the wolf were coming.

"Theo?"

"Yes."

"Did you really have a fiancée?" she asked, toying with the covers on her bed.

"Of all the things you could ask me about, you ask about Johanna. A woman that has been dead for quite a few years now."

He was close, almost at the top of the stairs. Her wolf stood on all fours, her head cocking to the side. Her wolf... "Oh boy." She groaned to herself.

"I know it doesn't make any sense. I have a lot of questions, and I can't guarantee they will all come out in the order you or I want."

"I guess I'll just have to get used to it."

She sighed. "What was she like? You don't say much about her in your journal."

"Johanna was very prim and proper and came from a wealthy, well-known family. Our engagement was brief — her father called it off when I announced that I had joined up to serve in World War One. He said he wanted a whole man to care for his daughter, not one that might return in pieces. I don't blame him. I was different when I got back."

"Was she pretty?"

"I thought she was at the time. But my perspective changed long ago. My vision of beauty is now lying on her bed scowling at the ceiling." The last sentence came from her bedroom door.

Excitement and desire filled every cell in her body and she could feel the wolf in her mind staring at Theo expectantly, almost willing his wolf to walk closer to them.

She bit the inside of her mouth, keeping her smile at bay. Guess she wasn't the only one in love.

A musky scent suddenly filled her head. It was a sexy masculine smell, layered with lust and love and…coffee and something sweet and minty and… "I smell cookies."

His deep chuckle did make her smile this time.

"Did you eat…?" She paused. She could smell what he had been eating. She covered her forehead trying to wrap her head around the idea. "You ate my chocolate mint cookies."

He stopped at the foot of her bed and crossed his arms. "Sure did." He looked at her seriously. "You read the journal, then?"

She grabbed a pillow and flipped onto her side, hugging it tight. "Twice."

"Then you know what I say is the truth. You will adjust quickly and if you have any problems, I'll be here for you."

The end of the bed dipped and she felt her back heat up before Theo pulled her into his chest. "I promise you will get used to things." Having Theo fit their two bodies together felt like…home.

There was a long sigh in her head that mingled with her own.

"Is Tom related to Jonathan? You didn't say much about him."

"Yes. Jonathan was Tom's great-great-grandfather."

"I thought they might be. The last name kind of gave it away."

He kissed her head. "Smart girl."

She grinned to herself. "What happened to him…? To Jonathan?"

"I don't know. I never saw him leave."

"Oh." She knew it didn't make any sense, but she felt sad for Jonathan.

"I learned from Tom's grandfather that Jonathan's real name was Yuma and that he changed it so he could join the Canadian Expeditionary Force in 1914. He was also the son of Chief Maquinna of the *Nuu-Chah-Nulth* people."

She shifted and looked over her shoulder at him. "Why do I know that name?"

"Chief Maquinna is the very same Chief that welcomed explorer Captain James Cook to the shores of British Columbia in 1759."

She exhaled a slow breath. She had really had no idea how far this wolf-joining thing went until that very moment. She grabbed the pillow and squeezed it against her chest. "That's… Wow."

"Is there anything else you want to ask?" He curled his arms around her middle, wedging his fingers under her waist.

"Not right now. I'm still trying to absorb everything."

He brushed her ear with a kiss. "Okay. Whenever you're ready, I'll be here." He squeezed her tightly and pressed his lips to the skin on her neck. "You know that, right?"

The way he stressed the question made her heart flip. She rolled onto her opposite side and looked at him. The worry lines were back. She cupped his face and kissed him gently. "I know."

Relief filled his sigh and he buried his face in her neck and kissed her pulse. "God, I love you, Drew. I'm sorry for everything that happened. My intention was to take you out to my cabin to keep you safe. I never considered that they would follow us that night in the dark."

"You knew they would follow, though."

"Of course. But the next day. Not many people are comfortable with boating at night and that stretch of water can be tricky during the day with the protruding rocks, let alone at night." He tucked a pink streak of hair behind her ear. "My plan was to tell you about the wolf first and then Linde. I was going to take you to the Reservation the next morning after you'd had time to deal with what I am. I wanted you safe."

"But Linde showed up before you got the chance." She pushed him back so she could look into his face, because she wanted the truth. "What were you going to do once I was safe?"

His eyes flashed a bright silver. "I was going to kill Linde and his hired shooter."

"Hired shooter. But you knew it was Kevin—I mean Ken? Didn't you?"

"No. I didn't. But I should have. He is very good at hiding his scent."

"How could he hide his scent?" She shook her head. "Wait. You can smell people's scents?"

"Yes." He gave her a tender smile. "You will learn to recognize different scents too."

"Oh boy! How lucky am I." She rolled her eyes.

"It's not that bad, Drew."

"I guess you've never sat on the bus during rush hour on a hot July day." She wrinkled her nose. "Some people don't smell all that good." She smiled when he laughed. "I'm sorry. What were you saying about Ken's scent?"

"He used local vegetation to mask his odor. He was probably trained to keep his hunting clothes in a garbage bag filled with dirt and leaves, moss, twigs. He probably used scent-masking soaps and shampoos and deodorants. The Marines trained him very well."

"How do you know all of this?" She took his hand and held it in both of hers.

His look turned serious. "I've been hunted many times. It only made sense to teach myself how to hunt, so I could avoid being hunted."

"Did it work? Teaching yourself all that stuff?" Because if it did she wanted him to teach her everything he knew. Nobody was going to skin her wolf for the fur.

"I think so." He shrugged. "I've made a few mistakes along the way, obviously. I'm constantly learning and so is the wolf. In the end, it's safer to live in areas that are less populated. The northern area from Quebec to BC is fine and the Territories too. But I prefer western BC. I like being in this area, it feels like home."

Home. Would they ever really have a home?

"Theo." She toyed with his fingers. "How is this going to work? You have moved around so much, you're used to it. What if I can't do it? What if I screw things up for you? What if I do the wrong thing or say the wrong thing to the wrong person?" She took a shaky breath. "What if someone tries to hunt you…us, because of me?"

"I will teach you what you need to know to be safe and until then, I don't want you swapping into the wolf without me with you. Okay?"

She nodded. "Okay."

He rolled onto his back, taking her with him. "Let's not worry about that until the time comes."

She rested her head on his chest, felt the strong beats of his heart.

"We have more pressing issues right now."

"You mean Linde and Ken?"

"Yes. I don't know where Ken has gone. I followed his scent to the airport. He took the midnight run to Vancouver and the pilot hasn't returned yet. He's due back in tonight."

"You think he knows where Ken was going?"

"I hope so."

"What are we going to do about Linde?"

"Tom and I have taken care of that."

"What do you mean?" She gripped at his shirt. "Does the BCPP know...? You couldn't have told them... You have to have lied?"

"Of course I lied." He laughed. "They'd think I was nuts if I told them the truth."

"What did you tell them?"

"I told them Linde was interested in you and jealous of our relationship." He rubbed his hand up and down her back. "That he followed us over with the intent of killing me and that while he threatened us at gunpoint, he was attacked by what looked like a couple of stray dogs." He shrugged. "Not really a lie, more of an enhancement of the truth."

She chuckled.

He loved that husky sound. It vibrated through his body, setting his blood on fire.

For all she had learned, and what she had become, Drew was handling things very well. He'd had her join with the wolf without her consent. It had been a desperate act and one he would repeat if required. It was deeply engrained in the wolf to protect his mate and that instinct spilled over into Theo. Drew was his mate, his life, his heart. He would always do whatever was necessary to keep her safe.

He tightened his hold on her. "We will have to lie a lot to protect our life. Do you think you will be able to do that?"

"If I have to protect you, then yes."

A funny weight sat heavy in his chest close to his heart. "Us. We're in this together."

She slid her hand up his chest and curled it around his neck. "Us."

"So, who will I have to lie to about Linde?"

"The boys at the station want you to give a statement about what happened. And the sooner you give it the sooner all this will be over."

"In other words you want me to give it today." She gently played with his ear.

"Yes, please."

"I think I can do that. How should I act? Should I be the angry victim, or cry hysterically the whole time?"

He smiled. "As funny as it is watching Ben and the boys deal with a hysterical female, I would rather you just be yourself."

"That's boring."

He laughed and pressed his lips to her forehead pulling her sweet scent into his lungs.

After a minute of silence, Drew asked, "What about Ken? Did you mention him to the cops?"

"No."

"Why?"

He shouldn't answer her, it might impede the case against Ken.

"Theo. You have to tell them about him. He could just hook up with another freak and start killing for them. And what if the next thing he hunts isn't animals? What if it's people?"

"Believe me, I've thought about that."

"Then you have to tell them."

He shook his head. "Evidence was found in Linde's rental cottage on Ken. If we tell them Ken was there that night, more questions will be asked and you might be put at risk and I will not allow that."

She pushed up and looked at him, a frown puckering her thin eyebrows. "What evidence?"

"I can't tell you."

"Sounds like he'll get away with it." She was clearly outraged by the idea. His mate demanded justice, and she would have it, one way or another. He hoped the justice system didn't fail this time because he didn't want Drew to know what he — the man — was capable of should Ken slip through the cracks.

He kissed the top of her cheek. "Don't worry about him right now. He's gone and he won't be coming back here."

"How do you know...?" She narrowed her eyes at him then gasped. "You're going to hunt him down."

How in the hell?

He got the impression of his wolf chuckling. *"Just Drew smart mate."*

"Too smart. That's not going to bode well for us."

The wolf sent him a mental shrug. *"Mate, perfect match. Balance out dark with light."*

His wolf was right. Drew did balance him out, and in a good way.

She gasped a second time. "I'm right! Holy shit I'm right. I smelled something weird, like a feeling swirling around in the air and then I knew... Or I felt it. Not sure. But I'm right." She poked him in the chest. "Right?"

He sighed her name. "Drew. It's not what you're thinking. I don't want you—"

"When you go after him, I'm going with you," she declared. "And that is not up for discussion."

He jerked her down onto his chest. "We'll talk about it."

"No. I don't want to—"

He stopped her with a kiss. He held her still and ravaged her mouth until she relaxed into him and threaded her fingers into his hair. His tongue met hers and he felt his body twitch and harden and the wolf had nothing to do with it.

He pulled his mouth away when her aroused scent hit him. It was stronger than before, more demanding. It filled his nostrils and caused his head to spin and his cock to thicken. "Drew." He growled, gripping her behind roughly and pulled her against him. He met her heavy stare, watched as her eyes changed from a beautiful amber to a swirling pool of gold. Her desire was heightened to a level that matched his own.

She pushed against his chest and sat up, her core rubbing against his lengthening shaft. "You're right." She licked her lips. "We have more important things to attend to." Her eyes suddenly flashed bright. "Now, Officer Grey, what did you do with those handcuffs?"

Epilogue

The day was hot and dry, not a single cloud dotted the sky. There was no rain, no humidity, no fog, and the only wildlife, besides lizards, was the locals out on a Friday night. Arizona in the summer was his favorite place to be.

Matt slowed his pickup truck to a stop under his carport and climbed out. The temperature even in the shade was easily above a hundred, it was almost suffocating. He loved it.

He grabbed his groceries then kicked the door shut. Just as he rounded the front of his truck, his neighbor's kids ran by the fence.

"Hey, Mr Jackson!" the boys called in unison.

"Hey, boys." He grinned at the twins. "Where you two headed?"

The boys stopped and the eldest, Andy, looked over his shoulder toward his house. When he was satisfied that no one was listening he waved Matt closer.

Matt closed the distance and smirked at the twin faces staring back at him. Strawberry blond hair, blue eyes, freckles and they both wore a hearing aid in the same ear. Twins through and through. "What's going on, boys?"

Mack, the youngest, held up a brown paper bag. "We took some meat out of the fridge for our pet wolves. We're goin' to feed them."

"Oh yah!" Matt nodded toward the bag. "Let's see."

The young boy unraveled the top and held it open for him. A large T-bone steak wrapped in a clear plastic bag. Matt laughed.

"Your mom isn't going to be pleased when she tries to cook your dad his dinner tonight only to find out you gave it to a couple of local dogs."

The boy snatched the bag back. "They're not dogs. They're wolves."

"You sure about that?" He leaned closer. "If they were really wolves they would have eaten you two for a *snack*." He barked out the last word and laughed when they both jumped.

Andy stepped forward and grasped the fence. "They would never hurt us." The look on the kid's face was so serious that Matt actually paused. "The lady said so."

"What lady?"

"The lady with the blonde hair. She looks after the wolves when we're in camp."

Matt straightened and looked toward the back of his property, where the start of a forest began.

"Blonde hair," he said to himself. He was intrigued—he liked blondes. "She must be a wildlife officer. Checking on the Mexican gray wolves in the area."

"She said she was a veterinarian," Mack spoke up. "I want to be a vet when I get older."

His brother elbowed him in the ribs. "You say that 'cause you think she's pretty."

"So." Mack shoved his brother. "You said the pink in her hair was cool."

"Did not." Andy shoved back.

"Enough!" Matt barked out the command. "Andy, what did you say? That she has pink in her hair?"

The boy nodded. Once again, Matt scanned the trees at the edge of his yard. As though waiting for its cue, a large wolf silently crept out of the trees and stood watching them.

"There it is. " Mack pointed. "That's one of our wolves."

The beast standing there was no Mexican gray wolf. It was too big, and the coloring was all wrong. That was a British Colombian gray wolf. He should know, he had shot three. Two were dead, the other... He exhaled slowly. The only one that survived, the female, had ripped Linde's throat out.

Never taking his eyes off the animal, he asked the twins, "What does the other wolf look like?"

"He's really big," Andy answered, using his arms to show the size. "But he's black, not gray like that one."

A black wolf. A gray wolf. And a blonde with pink in her hair.

"Fuck," he whispered. He looked to the twins and barked out an order. "You boys get back into the house now before I call your mother. And stay there. Understand? Those wolves are dangerous."

"But they're not. The gray one licked my knee when I fell on the rocks and the black one likes when we scratch his chin," Andy called out.

"They won't hurt us. They're our friends!" Mack yelled.

"They are not your friends. They are wild animals and you shouldn't have been near them. Now get in that house!"

The boys ran home screaming for their mother.

Matt bolted for the side door, entered the house and locked it behind him. He dropped his groceries on the kitchen table before making his way to his bedroom. He didn't know if this was a coincidence or not but he wasn't taking any chances and the only way to do that was to kill those damn wolves.

He marched through the house, reassuring himself. "There is no way he tracked me here and why would he bring the wolf and Drew with him? It doesn't make sense."

He grabbed his rifle and a box of bullets from his bedroom closet and went into the living room to load the gun.

As he entered the room, he jumped when he saw Theo Grey casually leaning against the far wall.

"Hello, Ken. Or would you rather I call you by your given name?" Grey opened the manila folder he was holding. "Matthew David Jackson."

For the first time in his life, Matt froze, his heart pounding. Grey knew his name. His real name.

"Born December ninth, 1978. To David and Rachel Jackson. You have one older sister and one younger brother." Grey locked his steely eyes on him. "It says here that you were a Staff Sergeant in the United States Marines Corp." He cocked his head to the side and studied him. "And that you joined right out of high school. Your skill on the rifle range was above expert so you were sent to sniper school. After that, you did three tours in Iraq and two in Afghanistan. You released in 2010 and moved back to your hometown of Prescott Valley, Arizona. Which is when, I presume, you began working for Linde."

Rage built swiftly. He clenched his teeth. "How the hell do you know all that?" He tightened his hold on the gun.

"Don't panic. I'm not here to kill you so you can put down the gun. It wouldn't work anyways." Grey's eyes flashed a silvery-white. He crossed his arms. "My wolf took you shooting us personally, as did Drew. She thinks I've come in here to kill you."

"Is she right?" He gripped the gun and thought about how best to use it as a club if Grey attacked.

"There was a time I would have set the wolf free so he could tear you apart, but we both agree you protected Drew from Linde. And after I had time to calm down and think about it, I believe you were acting in her best interest at the entire time. So, after serious consideration, I've decided *not* to kill you." He shook his head. "Which — considering what I've gone through to survive this long with the wolf — is very generous."

"You still didn't answer my question."

Grey closed the folder and held it up. "This is a copy of the dossier found in Red Cedar Cottage where Linde was staying. It has everything we needed to know about you. Your real identity, your fake identities, your family history. I have to admit Linde was more thorough than I gave him credit for."

He exhaled. "Is that all?"

"No. I'm here to give you a heads up."

"Oh yeah?" He shifted slightly onto his right foot, readying himself in case Grey had lied and made a move. If he was lucky he'd get in a solid hit that would give him enough time to get to his truck.

"Mmm, there has been a warrant issued for your arrest. Your ties to Linde might not have been recorded on your end, but they were on his. He even had pictures." He pulled out a photo and held it up. "This one of you getting into Linde's limo is my favorite — very incriminating. Why you would trust a guy like Linde is beyond me."

His heart skipped a beat. *Fuck.*

"The BCPP have shared the information they gathered with Canadian Border Security as well as the Federal Law Enforcement agencies here in the U.S."

Grey placed the photo back in the folder and closed it. "In other words, you're being hunted, but not by me." Grey walked past him and into the kitchen. He opened the door and stopped. "If by some miracle you manage to elude jail time and I get wind of you even remotely close to Drew or I find out you have returned to your old tracking job, I won't be the one waiting for you next time, it'll be the wolf." Grey exited the house after he had issued the threat.

Matt walked to the kitchen window and watched as Grey approached the wolf standing at the edge of the forest. The animal stood and trotted to his side where it proceeded to rub its face and body along his leg like an oversized house cat. Then it darted off into the woods with Grey following.

Matt braced his hands against the windowsill, listening to the police sirens echoing in the distance.

"Fuck."

About the Author

Nancy's addiction for a good trash novel began in her late-teens when her grandmother gave her a bag of Harlequin Romance books. She was hooked and spent the next few years lurking in the dark corners of used bookstores searching for her next fix. Until, one marriage and two kids later, her own ideas had her jumping up at 3 am (much to her husband's annoyance) and typing them into her laptop. Beside her husband and children, Nancy has three passions, rearranging furniture, buying bed linens and, of course, writing. Nancy lives in Eastern Ontario with her family and two over sized lap dogs.

Nancy Adams loves to hear from readers. You can find her contact information, website details and author profile page at http://www.totallybound.com.

Totally Bound Publishing

Home of Erotic Romance